ONE PINK LINE

D1316173

ONE PINK LINE

Dina Silver

amazonpublishing

Text copyright © 2013 Dina Silver

Published by Amazon Publishing
PO Box 400818
Las Vegas, NV 89140

ISBN-13: 9781612183718
ISBN-10: 1612183719
Library of Congress Control Number: 2013902950

TO JEFF AND RYAN

CHAPTER ONE
Sydney

Finals week hit me like a gust of wind, and before I knew it, I was cramming for my last round of college exams and trying to convince my mother to let me move back home after graduation. It was 1991, and she'd just started taking Prozac that year, so there was hope. A couple months earlier, after attending Purdue's spring career day, I sent my résumé to five hotels in the Chicago area, and was offered an entry-level job at the Inter-Continental on Michigan Avenue. I was due to start August 1st of that year, but had to get through finals, graduation, and potentially another summer living at home with that woman.

I knew my Spanish exam would be the hardest because I barely paid any attention in that class, so I dedicated the most studying hours to that particular subject. Thursday night, as the intricacies of foreign grammar loomed heavily on *mi cerebro*, it occurred to me that I hadn't had my period in a while. How that uncertainty popped into my head at that particular moment, I have no idea. My conscience had snuck up behind me, tapped me on the shoulder, and derailed my train of thought.

I remembered the last time I'd had it, though, because I was trapped in an English lit lecture hall with no panty liner, no tampon, and no break for an hour. As soon as the bell rang, I sprinted to the bathroom, only to discover the tampon dispenser hadn't been refilled since the turn of the century. It was a long, slow walk home with a wad of parchment-like toilet paper shifting around in my panties.

I grabbed my day planner and started flipping back through the pages to check the date of that lecture. The topic was "Wicked Women," and it was exactly eight weeks before finals. A small cloud of wicked panic moved in overhead as I realized I might be pregnant.

I grabbed the phone book and dialed the number for Walmart. The woman who answered told me they were open until ten o'clock every evening, which meant I had exactly twenty-five minutes to get there. Unlike my mother's support, my menstrual cycle was always something I could count on, which is why I quickly abandoned my books that night and drove to the nearest (yet not so near someone might see me) superstore. I convinced myself during the fifteen-minute ride that I was not pregnant. It had to be the stress of finals, the end-of-college anticipation, and starting my big-girl job that was causing my ovaries to rebel. However, there was not a chance I would get through exam week without confirmation either way.

The Walmart was just off State Road 52 and noticeably cleaner than the one back home. When I arrived ten minutes before closing, it was nearly empty, with the exception of a few weary people in the checkout lanes. I raced past them toward the sobering and well-lit pharmacy aisles, and managed to find the pregnancy tests ironically right next to the contraceptives. It took me all of four minutes to grab one, pay for it, and make my way out of there with nary a judgmental glance from the sales clerk. I tossed the bag in the passenger seat next to me, and sped home. My phone was ringing as I put the key in the door, but I ignored it and let the answering machine pick up. My instinct was to grab it because I hadn't heard from Ethan in three days, but I needed to stay focused on clearing my mind and getting back to my studies. The caller did not leave a message.

Once the bag was in my hands, I seized the box, dropped the receipt on the floor, and began to read the instructions. Since I hadn't paid any attention to what brand I snatched off the shelf, I needed to know exactly what type of signal would inform me that I wasn't pregnant. It was a First Response test, and after unfolding the origami-like instruction booklet, I learned that my ultimate goal was to see one pink line upon completion. One pink line, one pink line, one pink line…

First: Remove the stick from the foil wrapper and remove the Overcap.
Easy enough.

Second: Hold the test stick by the Thumb-Grip with the Result Window facing away from you.
Done.

Third: Place the Absorbent Tip in your urine stream for exactly 5 seconds.
Damn.

I sat the test stick down on the edge of my pedestal sink and went to grab a Diet Coke and a NoDoz. I drank half the can as fast as I could without inflicting brain freeze, and then waited. I wasn't sure which would be more stressful: waiting to pee or waiting for the results. My phone rang two more times, but I continued to let the machine answer it. The third time it was Jenna, but I couldn't take her call either. Instead, I threw a scrunchie in my hair, took the small white stick in my hand, and sat on the toilet with my sweatpants balled up around my ankles. The box said five seconds exactly, so I began to count as soon as I felt my bladder relax and release.

One-one thousand, two-one thousand, three-one thousand, four-one thousand, five-one thousand.

Fourth: Replace the Overcap, and lay the stick on a flat surface with the Result Window facing up.
Mission complete.

Fifth: Wait three minutes before reading results.

Wait on the toilet? Wait in the kitchen? Where was step six explaining how to maintain composure and process said results?

Five seconds passed.

I stood, pulled my sweatpants up, rolled the top to keep them from slipping, and checked the stick. Nothing.

Common sense whispered to me, "Move away from the stick."

Fifteen seconds passed.

A flash of warm nausea came and went, so I walked to the kitchen for some cold water. Two ice cubes that were fused together slipped out of my hands onto the floor, and I just stood and watched them begin their transformation into a small puddle. I had only one concern.

One minute down.

I walked back to the bathroom and sat on the floor opposite the sink with my toes pushed up against the white porcelain base. The air felt heavy and absent of oxygen. I closed my eyes and breathed slowly through my nose.

Two minutes passed.

By that point I'd convinced myself that looking at the stick prematurely would no doubt be misleading and uninformative. I pictured it like a slot machine, with various pink lines spinning around the tiny results window.

Two and a half minutes passed.

My lungs were contracting, so I walked back to the kitchen, but sadly the air in there wasn't any better, and my socks were wet. I glanced at the clock on the microwave. Three minutes had passed.

I don't recall ever walking back into the bathroom…only sitting on the toilet staring at the stick on the edge of my sink, my shoulders slumped and heavy, keeping me from lifting my neck and properly viewing the window. I leaned forward, grabbed the stick tentatively like a shard of glass, and just as I brought it toward me, two bright pink lines appeared in the results window.

"Holy shit," I said aloud.

I held the little test stick, which now seemed so technologically unadvanced that I could hardly believe something so disposable was capable of delivering such life-altering information. But there they were: two gleaming, fuchsia lines, and neither one was remotely pale in color or incomplete. I placed it back on the sink and buried my head in my hands because, as if seeing those neon stripes staring back at me wasn't bad enough, next came the realization of who the father was.

The slowest three minutes of my life were then followed by the passing of two hours in the blink of an eye. I sat on the floor, catatonic in front of my books until after midnight when I took my phone off the hook and went to bed.

Two Tylenol PMs and a Bud Light were all it took to get me to sleep.

CHAPTER TWO

Almost exactly four years prior to that evening it was June 10th, 1987, and I would soon be celebrating my high school graduation at Taylor's house. Taylor was my best friend, and her parents were throwing her an elaborate backyard pool party for two hundred of her closest classmates—an event she and I had looked forward to for months. In fact, I would've rather been stranded with my mother on a deserted island—where I certainly couldn't do anything right there either—than miss one minute of Taylor's graduation party.

"Sydney!" my mother shouted around four o'clock that afternoon.

I scurried into the kitchen, where she was calling me from, because she hated when my sister or I would answer her scream with a reply scream of our own. "What, Mom?" I said as I pushed my way through the swinging saloon-style doors. I hated those doors. As the shortest member of my immediate family, I was the only one who couldn't see what activity was going on prior to entering the room. Unless said activity required the use of one's feet.

Her head was buried in the fridge. "What time is the party tonight?"

"It starts at nine," I said, and sat down on one of the two wooden stools that flanked our bakers table.

"Are Taylor's parents going to be home?" she asked and emerged with a small tray of lamb chops.

"Yes, the Golds are throwing the graduation party for her. You know that," I said and immediately regretted it.

She placed the tray on the counter and looked at me. "If I'd known that, Sydney, then why on earth would I have just asked you?"

Her question did not require an answer.

My mother was almost never wrong. Hard to believe, yet painfully true. And if perchance the stars failed to align, causing the earth to shift and her to be wrong, it was always best not to point it out to her. She did, however, spend most of her time telling me where I'd gone wrong and reciting a litany of ways to redeem myself.

"All right, well, I don't want you driving anyone else. Just yourself, and be home by midnight, okay?"

"Midnight?!" I asked loudly and tensed up.

"Lower your voice, Sydney, and sit up straight for once."

I wasn't yelling, but I was also not going to agree to be home by midnight. A debate I feared would not end well. "Mom," I began as calmly as I could, and spun to face the sink where she was standing. "I'm not coming home at midnight," I said to her back, gently shaking my head in defiance. "Some kids are even allowed to sleep over in Taylor's backyard, which I may decide to do, so I will definitely not be home by midnight."

Mom had this move where she'd pivot slowly, face me, and then lower her chin before speaking with utter composure. I assumed she procured it from one of the many child-development books that gathered dust under her nightstand over the years. My sister, Kendra, and I used to sneak the books into our room and laugh about the sound advice she regularly failed to follow.

"I'm not going to have this argument with you," she said matter-of-factly. "You can stay out past midnight, but you may not sleep over there. That is out of the question, and I want you home by one o'clock at the latest." She lifted her chin back to center. "It's your high school graduation tomorrow, Sydney, and we have lots of family coming over."

"Graduation is at two o'clock in the afternoon."

"Precisely. And I don't need to be banging on your door at noon trying to wake the dead when I should be cutting fruit."

I lowered my head in defeat.

"You're welcome," she said in a victorious tone and wiped her hands on a pink-and-green plaid dish towel. "So, is Andrew going to be there?" (*Chapter three of child-development book number four clearly states: Be a companion to your child when the opportunity presents itself. Act interested in her friends and hobbies, even when it pains you to do so.*)

Andrew Harrington was a guy I'd lusted over for most of my youth, and one my mother would've loved for me to date. He was a year ahead of me in school and lived three blocks from us in a gorgeous Tudor-style mansion, but we were never more than neighborly friends. He was on the football team and pretty much only dated among his own kind. Cheerleaders mostly. I tried out for the cheerleading squad—at my mother's insistence—my freshman year of high school, but never made it past the first round where you basically stand there and state your name. Mom had made me bring a jean skirt and tank top to wear for tryouts, but I never bothered to change out of my Dr. Martens and flannel shirt. Nor did I bother checking the bulletin board the next day to see if I'd been called back for round two. Because regardless of whether my name was on that list or not, I had no plans to be on the cheerleading team. I was friendly with many of those girls anyway, and perfectly content to reap their social benefits by association. I didn't always dress like a complete stoner, but my appearance was much more of a low-rent, rebellious cheerleader. Dirty-blonde hair, blue eyes, petite figure, but each feature more average than the next. My short stature never helped me stand out in a crowd much either, but all characteristics combined were a nice, nonthreatening complement to my sarcastic personality.

My hair was my biggest nemesis. Temperamental waves around my face; straight, random wispy hairs in the back; and tiny little baby hairs that shingled the top of my forehead. It was a constant battle of mine. After my mother took my sister, Kendra, for a perm one day, I begged her to do the same for me, but she insisted it wouldn't help. So instead I woke up an extra thirty minutes early every morning to dry my hair, laboriously pull it up on both sides of my head, and secure it into a metal barrette in the back. Only it took me at least twelve tries and every last second of that extra half hour before I was remotely satisfied with the results...results that were never quite worthy of Andrew Harrington's attention. He'd come home from college prior to our graduation, so Taylor invited him and some of the older class to her party. Regardless, it was none of my mother's business.

"I really don't know—or care—if he'll be there," I lied.

"Do you want me to find out? I could call Mrs. Harrington..." she offered. Mom was always desperate for a reason to be in Mrs. Harrington's graces, good or bad.

I glared at the back of her neck and interrupted. "Ab-so-lute-ly not."

She waved her hands in mock fear. "Okay, okay." She giggled, trying to be playful. "Just be smart," she warned, before leaving me alone in the kitchen.

Of course I was always eager to see Andrew, whether it was at a party or a premeditated chance encounter in front of his house. But

I certainly wasn't going to let my mom know that. I came to terms with the fact that he wasn't interested in me early on, yet that never made the anticipation of seeing him any less exciting. He had one of those magnetic personalities. Tall, dark, and handsome, yes, but he was a true mover and shaker, even in high school. He could make people feel good about themselves even while poking fun at them, and he could command a room without saying a word. He'd just saunter through a doorway, give a nod, and have everyone's attention.

Growing up in Winnetka, Illinois, there was no shortage of wealthy friends and neighbors, and New Trier High School was notorious for educating the overindulged. My family, however, was a rare exception. We lived in one of the few remaining teardowns that were still fit to be inhabited, nicely tucked away between two sprawling estates on either side. My mother never failed to tell people that our renovations would take place "any day now."

"This is the year!" she'd say, adding one of her signature excuses. "The plans are finally drawn up; we're just waiting on those pesky village permits."

And the money.

My parents bought our home when I was in the fourth grade, with every intention of building their dream house on the lot. Then Dad lost his job and ended up taking another one with a much lower salary. After that, the dream house was put on hold, along with fancy cars, summer camp, Caribbean spring breaks, and my mother's pride.

But despite my lack of designer clothes and an indoor swimming pool, I never felt deprived of material things. My father was kind and generous and did everything possible to give Kendra and me the most he could.

After my mom left the kitchen, I checked the clock and then ran upstairs to get changed for Taylor's party. Her father, Jeremy

Gold, managed one of the largest mutual funds in the country, and the party was being held at their enormous home on Fox Lane. Taylor's house was a popular hangout during our high school years because it had an Olympic-size pool in the backyard with a hot tub at each end, and four air-conditioned cabanas on either side. Not to mention the bowling alley and projection TV in her basement. There was even a fully equipped outdoor fridge that her mom kept stocked with a variety of soft drinks and Good Humor bars.

About three weeks before the party, my dad took me shopping so I'd have something new to wear. Mom had given him explicit directions on what type of dress I should come home with, but all I really wanted was a new pair of Guess jeans: acid-washed with leather swatches on the pockets. He had no problem defying my mother and buying me what I wanted, and she would never argue with me over something that was his decision. I wore a black tank top from The Limited and a pair of enormous beaded chandelier earrings from The Mexican Shop in Evanston to complete the look. The weather that night was warm and humid, and some of the kids were bringing their bathing suits, but I had no intention of sporting the wet look at any point during the evening.

I arrived at Taylor's house just before seven o'clock, nearly two hours before anyone else. The front door was open as usual, so I let myself in as I had for the past ten years, and found Taylor in her room standing over a pile of clothes on her bed. She, too, was wearing acid-washed jeans, rolled tight at the ankle, and a wide-necked, periwinkle-blue sweatshirt hanging off one shoulder.

Taylor, who'd made the cheerleading team every year, was beautiful and would've looked spectacular wearing a pillowcase, but she was obsessed with fashion. And Madonna.

She had long, silky black hair, amber eyes, and—thanks to Dr. Neil Feinberg—the perfect nose. She'd always been tall, and wore heels to further accentuate her legs and height. Guys loved her, and most girls I knew would've killed for the contents of her closet. We'd been best friends since the fifth grade, ever since I defended her against notorious playground bully Rachel Weiss.

Back then, Taylor had glasses, a gap between her front teeth, her original nose, and was a constant target for Rachel's elementary school torment. One day in the gym locker room, I overheard her yelling at Taylor and playing on her many adolescent insecurities. I didn't care much for Rachel, so I told her to shut up. That was really all I did—I told Rachel to shut up and walked away—but Taylor never forgot how I stood up for her, and we've been best friends ever since.

"Andrew's bringing, like, ten guys with him tonight," she informed me with teenage enthusiasm. She and Andrew dated during our junior year when he was a senior, but broke things off when he went away to University of Michigan.

"Anyone we know, or want to know?" I asked.

"Do you remember Bob Cunningham, Bryan Martin, Tim Sullen, Ethan Reynolds, or Gabe Douglas? They were all a year ahead of us."

"I only recognize Gabe's name."

"Don't you know Tim and Ethan?" she asked from her vanity. "They played hockey with Andrew as freshmen."

"No," I said. "Only Gabe."

I shoved her stack of rejected clothing aside, sat down on the bed, and watched her scoop her hair into a low side-ponytail. Then she took her bangs in her left hand and sprayed them with hair spray until they stood at attention.

"Well, I'll introduce you. Tim is gorgeous; I saw him at the club last Friday, and he looks amazing. A little short for me, but not for my Syd." She smiled. Taylor's parents belonged to North Shore

Country Club, and she spent most of her weekend afternoons there ordering Cobb salads and flirting with other wealthy offspring by the pool.

"I can't wait."

"Great jeans by the way. New?"

"But of course," I answered and watched smoke signals rise from her hair as she ran a curling iron through the ends, attempting to smooth out a few unruly strands.

"Tonight is going to be amazing," she said as she stared into the mirror, chin lowered, patting down the top of her bangs. "I hid two packs of smokes and a bottle of gin behind the outdoor cooler. I've got other stuff, too, if you're up for it."

Taylor started doing cocaine when we were sophomores. She was hanging out with some older kids whose parents gave them hoards of money for no particular reason. In those days there wasn't much to do besides hang out at the local McDonald's or at Wilmette Beach. Neither of which required very much funding, but somehow these kids were able to access large amounts of cash with little or no trouble at all. Since many of the popular kids at our school were doing drugs at the time, I never thought much about it. I tried cocaine one night when Taylor's parents were out of town, after drinking three glasses of straight gin from her parents' liquor cabinet, and vomited for an hour afterward. I blamed the drugs and stuck to weed and wine coolers after that.

Sometime around eleven o'clock, when the graduation party was in full swing and about forty of the two hundred guests were in the pool, Taylor grabbed my arm and dragged me into one of the cabanas. I'd been hanging out by the fire pit eating Double Stuf Oreos with our friend Angela, so I dragged Angela and the cookies along with me. When we reached the cabana, we found Angela's twin sister, Debbie, and three guys lying on the couches.

"We're all here!" Taylor exclaimed as we entered. "Syd, Ange, this is Tim, Ethan, and of course you know Mr. Harrington."

Andrew stood and gave me an obligatory hug.

"Hey, Andy," I said, and felt my cheeks turn pink.

"Hey, neighbor. What's up?"

"Not too much. How was freshman year?"

"I managed to keep the freshman fifteen at bay," he said and lifted his white T-shirt to expose an abdomen Michelangelo would've been proud of. My cheeks flushed harder.

"Nicely done," I said, and followed his shirt down like I was peeking under a garage door as he lowered it.

Taylor clapped and spoke up. "We're playing spin the bottle," she informed us and lifted a bottle of vodka in the air. "And you have to chug it, then kiss whoever it lands on. So, everyone sit on the floor. Syd, pull the front curtains."

I looked around at everyone there and saw that Ethan seemed a little put off by his entrapment. His eyes narrowed as I unhooked the cords, pulling the striped fabric loosely over the cabana entrance.

Taylor's hands were flailing. "Boy-girl formation please."

We all sat down, and by sheer luck—and a little shoving—I ended up next to Andrew.

Taylor placed the bottle in the center of the group. "I'll go first."

"No offense, but I'm not kissing any girls," Angela stated and exchanged a look of disgust with her sister.

"Fine." Taylor rolled her eyes. "Boy-girl kisses only."

I'd never been uncomfortable or put off by tasteless behavior. In fact, I would've had no problem kissing any of the girls in the circle, but it certainly wouldn't have been my first choice. My first choice was sitting right next to me.

Taylor spun the bottle, and we watched as it landed on Angela twice before her third try pointed at Tim. I didn't remember Ethan from high school, but apparently he played on the hockey team with Tim and Andrew. Tim was on the shorter side, but very attractive in a preppy, country club sort of way. He had long blond hair that was parted way over to the right side, and which kept falling onto his face until he'd jerk his neck to move it away from his eyes. I found out later that his family moved to Lake Forest his senior year, but he commuted to New Trier to finish up high school. Ethan was much taller and had more of an appropriate build for someone who played ice hockey. Broad shoulders, thick calves, large biceps, and a chipped front tooth. I also noticed he had deep-set eyes and ultra-high cheekbones. He looked like he could turn into a real badass if the opportunity were to present itself.

I focused my attention back on the game just as Debbie was the next to lean in and kiss Tim. It was looking like a banner evening for him at that point. Next it was Andrew's turn. He spun the vodka bottle and it slowly inched its way toward me, then past me, and ultimately landed on Ethan. He spun again. The half-filled jug whirled around and stopped at Taylor. Figured. She leaned in toward him and they kissed in a way that made everyone uncomfortable.

"All right, all right," Tim said, as Taylor retracted her torso and giggled.

"Syd's turn!" she said, clapping.

I crossed my fingers in my head. When the bottle started spinning, I playfully covered my eyes and acted as though I wasn't interested in the outcome. Just as I pulled my hand away from my face, the bottle stopped abruptly at Ethan. We paused for an awkward moment before I was forced to take a swig and lean toward him. I gave him an apologetic look, and then went for it. It was brief, but his lips were soft and he smelled like coconut oil.

"You're up, Tim," Ethan spoke.

Tim's turn landed on Debbie. Then Angela's landed on Debbie, causing Taylor to let out her signature laugh, which sounded like a balloon popping. Her next spin landed on Andy, of course. Then Ethan was next. He lifted his long arm, reached into the center of the group, and spun the bottle with great strength. It went about thirty rotations before ultimately landing on me.

"Well, well, well," Taylor murmured. "I think we may have a love connection."

As if oversize, dentally challenged Ethan didn't already feel self-conscious crammed into cabana four, I could tell that Taylor's comment only enhanced his desire to be anywhere else. He looked at me and I faked like I was spraying Binaca in my mouth. My second brush with coconut oil was equally enjoyable, and this time he placed his hand under my chin...sending Taylor into a tailspin.

"This is awesome!" She applauded. "Deb, you're up."

Everyone proceeded to take his or her turn, and neither Andy's nor Tim's spin landed on me. When it was my turn, I sort of hoped that it would stop at Ethan, mostly to see Taylor's reaction. I gave it a whirl and got my wish. Taylor yelled so loud that someone actually peeked in the cabana from the outside.

"Oh...my...God!" Taylor said. "We are all leaving so the two of you can take care of business." And with that, she yanked Tim's and Debbie's arms and stood up.

"Are you kidding me?" I said and stood up with them, but they never looked back. Andrew even tousled my hair on his way out, making me feel like I was six years old. Everyone started exiting the cabana except Ethan, who just sat there. I didn't want to be rude and make him feel like I didn't want to be left alone with him, but I certainly didn't want to be forced into it by Taylor and her vodka spinner.

"I'll check back in twenty," she said, popping her head back in before disappearing.

I turned to Ethan, who was still seated on the floor with his back pressed against the couch, legs outstretched and crossed at the ankle.

"You don't have to kiss me, but honestly, I was looking for any excuse to end the game," he said.

"Sorry about her. She can be…how do I say this nicely? Affectionately aggressive at times."

"Well put."

I sat back down, cross-legged in front of him. His manner was very laid back and unaffected. He was almost yawning during the game while everyone else attempted to mask their nerves with crude jokes and exaggerated gestures. "So you graduated last year?" I asked.

"Yeah."

"Where are you now?"

"Kansas."

"I had a cousin that went to KU. Are you happy there?"

"I'm happy everywhere," he said simply and smiled. "How about you? Where are you going?"

"Purdue."

He nodded his head and his eyes landed on the bag of Double Stuf Oreos I'd brought with me. I handed him the bag and watched as he tore into them three at a time. "You were in my art history class," he managed to say with his mouth full and dark-chocolate dust flying out.

"I was?"

"Yeah. My senior year. Mrs. Bartholomew," he clarified. "You don't remember."

He was right. I didn't remember him. "I'm ashamed to say that two of my best friends were with me in that class, and we hardly noticed anything but the notes we passed each other."

"No sweat, Syd." He leaned in. "Oreo?"

"I brought them, actually. They're my favorite. Thanks for sharing," I joked.

I took the cookie and was a little surprised at myself. There was a good-looking guy—great body, sweet disposition—and I'd never even given him a second look. Maybe because he was older than I was, and the older boys traditionally ignored me anyway. Or maybe because my friends and I were always drooling over the football and baseball players, and were too dumb to realize that the sport of ice hockey required much more brute force than either of those other two. Regardless, there he was, all large and relaxed, and essentially waiting for a kiss from me.

"Well, third time's a charm. Can we kiss and make up?" My question was as cheesy as it sounded.

"Don't worry about it," he said, and nicely rejected me.

Ethan picked himself up off the floor, slipped his flip-flops back on, and grabbed a stick of gum from his pocket. "Gotta run. Tim wants to go for a swim," he said, and grabbed three more Oreos. "Any interest in a dip?"

I looked at his face, and it appeared as though he honestly wanted me to go with him, but I had sworn that I would not be found within ten feet of the pool.

"Sure," I spat out.

"Great. Are you going in those?" He gestured to my new jeans.

I ran my hand through my hair, which had taken me no less than an hour to fix. A record twenty attempts at perfecting the position of that damn barrette, while poofing just the right amount of hair in the front. "I'll get a suit from Taylor and meet you out there."

He smiled and held the cabana curtain for me, then ducked to exit.

Ethan vanished into the crowd while I located Taylor and Angela behind the outdoor kitchen smoking a cigarette and sniffling.

"There you are! We've been dying!" Taylor said as soon as I approached them.

"First of all, you suck." I began counting with my fingers. "Secondly, how could you ditch me and my Oreos like that?"

"Don't freak out, Syd. It was hysterical, and everyone was looking for a reason to get out of there," she said and tapped her ashes into the base of a rose bush.

"Including me!" I said.

"Gin shot?" Angela asked and held up a bottle.

I cringed. "No thanks. I puked hard on that stuff about two months ago. The smell alone is making my stomach turn." I turned to Taylor. "Can I borrow a suit?"

"I thought you weren't going in."

"Changed my mind."

She rubbed her head. "If you go in, then I have to go in," she said.

"You bought a new bikini. I thought you were planning on it."

"I just wanted the new bikini, but not for tonight."

Angela's facial features crumpled in distortion as she took one last sip of Beefeater. "I'll go with you, Syd. I wore a black bra and panties just in case."

Taylor looked at me. "You know where they are. Bottom drawer, pink dresser."

"Thanks. I'll be back in ten," I said, and took off toward the house.

When I returned, I was wearing Taylor's second-favorite suit, the yellow string bikini with a baby-doll ruffle on the bottoms. I knew if I'd pranced out to the pool deck in her new black one with the beaded fridge, I'd never hear the end of it. I wrapped a pink-and-white-striped bath towel around my waist and began looking for Angela, when a large, dripping-wet silhouette invaded my personal space.

"Thought you'd disappeared," Ethan said with a devilish grin.

"Wipe that look off your face because if you're even thinking of throwing me in, I will kill you."

"Funny," he cocked his head. "I'm not the least bit scared."

And with that, he scooped me up kicking and screaming and ran to the edge of the deep end. Rather than accept my fate—and the fact that I'd planned on going in anyway—I reactively grabbed on to his wide neck and began to plead with him as two other guys in the pool gently suggested I be thrown in topless.

"Please don't turn me into the girl who lost her top at the graduation party. I'll do anything," I said, and begged with my eyes.

"How about that kiss you owe me?"

"Deal."

The next thing I knew, we were both airborne and his mouth was pressed against mine seconds before we were engulfed with water. His lips were soft, his skin was warm, and his arms were thick and protective.

When I came to the surface he was waiting for me.

"Nice intimidation tactic," I said.

"Just stooping to your level."

The party was rocking by the time my initial curfew had come and gone. I said good-bye to my friends close to two in the morning and headed for the Golds' front driveway where my car was parked.

"Sydney," Ethan called after me.

I turned and stopped a few yards away from my car. "The roots of my hair are nearly dry, so keep your distance," I pointed at him.

"Just wanted to say good-bye."

"Thanks," I said and studied his physique. He was wearing only his bathing suit and flip-flops. His hairless chest was muscular and toned, and his stomach was so flat it was almost concave. His swim trunks were struggling to stay on his waist.

"So, what are your plans this summer?"

"Not too much. I'm waitressing part time at the Onwentsia country club in Lake Forest, and just hanging out," I said, my voice filled with hope.

"Sounds nice."

We stood there for a second before I looked at my Swatch: two thirty in the morning.

"I'm so sorry, but my curfew was days ago, and if I don't get home soon, my summer plans will be much different than the ones I've just mentioned."

Ethan ran a hand through his damp hair. "That's cool. Maybe I can call you and we can hang out together sometime."

"I would love that," I said quickly. "Would you like my number?"

He looked down at his outfit. "I don't have a pen."

"We're in the book. Last name is Shephard, on Maple Street."

"Thanks, Syd. I'll find it," he said and took a couple steps closer. I could smell the chlorine on his skin. "I had a great time with you tonight," he said.

I looked up at him. "Me, too."

Ethan bent down and kissed me. It happened so quickly that our heads turned and our lips clicked into place immediately. I felt light-headed as he wrapped one of his large arms around my back and pulled me tightly into his chest.

The evening began with nary a romantic expectation.

Despite that, I fell madly in love.

CHAPTER THREE

During the two weeks I was grounded after Taylor's graduation party, Ethan had called my house and left a message for me at some point, but our date was postponed until my mother and I were on speaking terms again. As soon as she was able to get past my defiance, I was allowed to return Ethan's call... four days late. Since all I cared about during high school was spending time with my friends, cutting me off from them was typically my mother's punishment of choice.

"Hi, Ethan. It's Sydney Shephard," I announced when he answered the phone.

"I was beginning to think you were mad at me for throwing you in the pool," he said.

Hearing his voice made me smile. "I was grounded: forbidden from using the phone, leaving the house after eight o'clock, and making eye contact with my mother."

"Sounds rough."

"It's over," I informed him. "I'm actually heading over to Taylor's in a little bit."

"Do you want to get together later?" he asked.

I had the phone cord wrapped around my index finger. "I would love to. What did you have in mind?"

"I'll pick you up at eight, and we'll decide from there."

I ran downstairs, past the staged family photos we'd sat through over the years, and found Kendra having a bowl of cereal in the kitchen.

"I have a date tonight!"

"With Ethan?" she asked excitedly.

Kendra was my rock. And having her home for the summer made it bearable for me to live under the same roof as my mother. My dad would always make an honest attempt to defend me against my mom's wrath, but he was a naturally soft-spoken man who hated confrontation. Many times after he'd listen to me arguing with my mother and then endure the sound of slamming doors, Dad would come into my room and tell me to ignore her. Which was nearly impossible, but it was his way of trying to clean up the mess without getting his hands dirty. But Kendra was a different story. My mother worshipped her, and if Kendra defended me when I was in trouble, my mom would back off in a heartbeat. When we were young, Mom had Kendra in art classes, dance classes, and skating lessons. I remember being dragged along to all of them. I'd sit there next to my mom and dream about the day I'd be old enough to take the same classes, but that day never came. She never signed me up for anything except Girl Scouts, and only because my next-door neighbor's mom was the troop leader and offered to drive me every week. When I was old enough to ask her why, she'd just say Kendra was better at those things.

I resented my mother for that, but not my sister. My sister was the kindest, most loving, beautiful person I knew. She was smart and accomplished, and she was fiercely protective of me. And even though she wore skinny headbands, pearl earrings, and Bermuda shorts, she never once tried to convince me to be anything other than who I was. She inherited the good height and hair genes, but her beauty was so natural that I couldn't begrudge her for being prettier than me even if I'd wanted to. She simply was born that way.

"Syd, that's wonderful. Where's he taking you?"

"I'm not sure," I said and took the stool opposite her at the table.

"What are you going to wear?"

Despite the time I spent fine-tuning my hair each morning, I never gave my clothes very much thought. If the occasion called for anything more than a T-shirt and jeans, chances were I wasn't going. "Just jeans, I guess."

"Well, help yourself to anything of mine if you want," she said and walked her empty bowl to the sink. "I can't wait to hear about it. I'm so excited for you," she said and squeezed my arm.

"Thanks."

I had to tell my mom about Ethan because he was coming to the house to pick me up. She was sitting at her dressing table, and as soon as I mentioned his last name, her eyes lit up.

"Caroline Reynolds is one of the town's biggest philanthropists," she enlightened me. "In fact, she was chairman of the JDF ball last spring. Have you seen their home? It's the crown jewel of the Holiday Home Tour every winter. What a wonderful family." She whispered the last line to herself. "How did you meet this boy?"

"His name is Ethan. We met at Taylor's graduation party."

She nodded slowly, planning the wedding in her head.

I sat through a five-minute biography of Ethan's mother and her many claims to local fame, until my mother stopped abruptly and looked me over. "Please put some makeup on before you leave, and make sure he comes in and says hello to your father." She took a breath and folded her hands in front of her. "Would you like to discuss how you're feeling about him?"

I stared at her, speechless.

Chapter seven of child-rearing book number three clearly states: Encourage romantic interests with caution and counsel. Allow your child a comfort zone so that she feels she can come to you with sensitive subject matter. Keep conversation light so she doesn't think you're focusing on her private business. Act like you care, even if you don't.

"I know!" she continued excitedly as though Caroline Reynolds had just asked her over for lunch. "Would you like to borrow my long silver earrings? You know, the ones I bought when your father and I were in New Orleans. You're always saying how much you like them every time I have them on."

"No thanks, Mom."

"You sure?"

"I'm sure," I reiterated. Not a special occasion went by when she didn't try to push those damn Cajun sparklers on me. I barely recalled complimenting them once—in an effort to distract her from something else—and I've never lived it down since. For sure, they're the only things she'll be leaving me in her will.

"You know the ones I mean, right? They would look so nice if you wear your hair down."

"I know the ones, Mom, and I'm quite sure. Thank you."

She turned to the mirror and finished applying her mascara. "Well, have fun then, and be smart."

"I always am."

Ethan pulled into the driveway at five minutes to eight o'clock. I begged my dad to greet him at the door so Ethan wouldn't feel awkward, and Dad was happy to oblige.

"G'nite!" I yelled after speeding through the introductions and hurrying Ethan back to the car.

"Be smart…" I heard from behind me.

෨

Ethan suggested we head to Gilson Beach in Wilmette, and all I wanted him to do was kiss me like he had in Taylor's driveway. He was dressed in long khaki shorts, a navy-blue polo shirt, and Paco Rabanne cologne—a smell that sends chills down my spine to this day.

We walked down the long gravel path to the sand, and spent about three minutes deciding on the perfect spot to lay the blanket he'd brought with him.

Ethan kicked off his flip-flops and plopped down on one side, propping his body up on his left elbow. "Any chance you want to skinny-dip?" he asked me.

"Not on the first date."

"You free tomorrow night?" he said with a smirk.

I nodded. "So, why'd you wait so long to call me after Taylor's party?"

"Did I?"

"Just kidding." I backpedaled, thinking I'd just sprayed a mist of desperation in the air.

"No, seriously, were you waiting for me to call?"

Yes, I was waiting for him to call! In fact, since I was grounded at the time, I had really nothing more to do than pray it was him on the line every time I'd hear the phone ring. It was at least a week before Kendra ran into my room with the good news. "No, I was just kidding," I said again.

"No, you weren't."

I could see him looking at me as I straightened out the blanket underneath us. "Just drop it," I mumbled as my cheeks got warm.

The sky was black as ink, with the exception of the moon, and the air was breezy but warm. He tapped the ground next to him. "You could drive a car between us. Care to come closer?"

I gladly inched my way over to him and he placed his hand on my knee.

"I love coming down here at night," Ethan said.

"With all your dates?"

"You're the first—girl I've brought down here, not my first date," he clarified. "That came out wrong." He smiled at me. "I actually wanted to ask you out years ago."

I was stunned. I hadn't even known he existed prior to Taylor's party. "Really?"

"Really. Even though you were too busy to notice a six-foot-two hockey player you had three classes with."

He was right. I'd spent my entire high school career lusting after Andrew Harrington. How many other amazing men had I overlooked? "I'm flattered," I said.

Ethan talked about college and how he was trying to decide on a major by the start of his sophomore year, which was only a couple months away. He asked me about my family, my sister, and my fears about leaving them in the fall. We talked for two hours about our lives, our dreams, our friends, and how weird it was that we never connected with each other before that night.

Ethan sat upright. "I think you're beautiful, Sydney," he said so abruptly and honestly that I almost cried. "Can I kiss you?"

Our eyes met, and his body came over me like a large shadow, forcing me to lie down in the sand and disappear beneath him.

I playfully put a hand over his mouth. "Aren't you going to wait for my answer?"

"Nope."

And with that, we had our first real kiss. His mouth was smooth and open, and not too moist. We lay there in various positions in the sand, kissing and tugging each other's hair for almost an hour. He seemed much larger in that dominating state, and I was straining to get my arms around his chest at times. We were both highly focused, panting and breathing rapidly, but neither he nor I attempted to take it to the next level. There was nothing I remember doing that I enjoyed so much in all my life, and I never wanted it to end.

"You okay? I feel like I'm crushing you," he asked, backing away slightly.

I sat up and shook out my hair. "I'm great."

After another fifteen glorious minutes, he reluctantly inched away, stood up, and offered me his hand. I took it disappointedly because I knew it meant he was taking me home.

"We don't want to get you grounded again, do we?" he said.

"Some things are worth the risk."

Ethan pulled into my driveway and put his car in park. "Can I see you tomorrow?"

"I would love that."

"Good night, Sydney."

"Thank you for tonight, and for not crushing me," I said with a grin.

"My pleasure."

I memorized his face before exiting the car. I'd dated a few guys before that, but none that had given me butterflies the way Ethan did. I could feel them fluttering their way through my body, first at my toes, then at my waist, and finally landing inside my head at the root of my unruly hair. I watched him drive away, and then entered my house through the garage door. It was dark inside, except for the light in the kitchen, which my mom always left on to deter potential thieves.

The next two months were spent with Ethan, kissing in the sand and taking our relationship to the next level.

Ethan was not my first, but he was my first love. I'd had sex once before with a guy named Charlie Fleetwood, behind the public tennis courts near my house, and it was quite a disappointment. In fact, we weren't even naked, just lying with our pants pulled down and grass in our hair. The sex was almost as quick as my entire relationship with Charlie.

But with Ethan it was different, and felt more like what I would have wanted my first time to be like. We were at the beach one night, him lying on his back, me on my side, and we began to kiss. I moved on top of his stomach, leaning over his body, and he lifted my shirt over my head. It was the first time he'd seen me without my top on. He paused and propped himself up on his elbows.

"You look amazing," he said, excitement in his eyes.

"Thank you," I said and blushed.

Ethan stood and removed his own shirt, too. His chest was as smooth and solid as a slab of marble, and his muscles were so naturally thick that they flexed with every little gesture he made. I lay down on my back and he stroked my hair, kissing my neck and bra.

He paused to look at me. "Are you okay?" he asked, which was code for "Will you have sex with me?"

I nodded.

"Are you sure?" he politely confirmed.

I nodded again and pulled him closer to me, my hands shaking, body trembling with indescribable anticipation.

And he did not disappoint.

CHAPTER FOUR
Grace

I've looked down on my mom since I was nine years old.

Not because she was an embarrassment or led her life in a contemptible manner, but because at nine years old, I was a towering five feet six inches to her five feet two. I've always been tall, and people have never ceased to remind me.

"Grace is so tall!" they would say.

"Yes, she is," my mom would add.

"Where does she get her height?" they would ask.

"Her father," Mom would add.

"Well, she got your looks and his height I guess," they would conclude with a wink, while I would just stand there feeling shy and ridiculous. I may have been tall, but deaf I was not.

People were right; I did look like my mom with her almond-shaped blue eyes, sun-kissed blonde hair, and full lips. But physically that's where the similarities ended. She was petite and small-boned, and I had broad shoulders and more of an athletic build. My dad stood just over six-feet tall, not a giant by any means, but larger than most people in our family. He had much darker features though.

My mom used to tell me how my infant and toddler clothing was always two sizes ahead of my age, and how she and I shared T-shirts when I was seven. My rapid vertical development never had much of an effect on me until someone else would comment about it, and the remarks over the years left me with mixed emotions. At first, my self-esteem took a hit. I would get embarrassed and inch closer to my parents, thinking if I stood behind them people would shut up. Honestly, what sort of response did they expect to get from telling me how tall I was?

Then one day I was with my dad at the grocery begging him for Lucky Charms when our neighbor Mrs. Phelan barged in and opened her big mouth.

"She's going to need a king-size bed soon!" she exclaimed, and winked her intrusive eye at my father.

My dad turned and looked at me in confusion, then back at her. "What do you mean?" he asked.

"She's just getting so tall," she said with her smeared cherry-red lips.

My dad looked at me and sensed my discomfort. "Should she be getting smaller?" He posed the question to Mrs. Phelan with the utmost concern for my well-being.

Mrs. Phelan strummed the handle of her cart with her inch-long fingernails and looked away from us both. "I just can't believe… Well, you know, she's just getting to be such a big girl…a lady… you know."

My dad rubbed his head, lifted my arms carefully one at a time, like they were covered in hives, and looked me over in horror. I just giggled and reveled in Mrs. Phelan's own embarrassment.

"Nice to see you both," she said, and waddled off.

From that day forward, I learned how to handle people in almost any given situation. If someone was going to make me feel awkward, they were going to regret it. I credit my mom with my looks, and my dad with my personality.

I've always had a great relationship with my parents. One that was honest and open. They always encouraged my brother, Patch, and me to talk things out with them rather than resort to a shouting match. However, my teen years were the most harrowing on my relationship with my mother. She and I would easily kick talking to the curb and have it out over things like what I was wearing, how much I talked on the phone, and how often I smacked Patch.

Patch is five years younger than me and has always been a peanut. A tiny, skinny little guy who hadn't a care in the world, least of all bumping his head on anything. I remember when he was four years old our pediatrician said he was in the 25th percentile for height, and the 25th percentile for weight. That same day, she said I was in the 100th percentile for height, and the 90th percentile for weight. We looked forward to doctor's appointments back then because it was a tradition that we'd go for Dairy Queen after each visit, regardless of whether it was an annual checkup or vaccination. I remember that particular appointment because I was just beginning to understand what the percentages meant, and it was the last appointment I looked forward to. The nurse asked my mom if I'd gotten my period yet when she was finishing her routine check.

"Oh, no, Grace hasn't even turned ten years old," Mom said.

The nurse reexamined my charts. "Yes, of course, she's just so tall!" she wailed. "I'm always thinking she's so much older."

I gave her an evil look. "Maybe you should check Patch for pubic hair," I suggested.

My mother's jaw dropped, and only Patch got ice cream that day.

Whenever my mother was annoyed with something I'd done, she would ask my dad to have a word with me about my behavior. Oftentimes, he would just saunter into my room and say, "Mom wants me to have a word with you about your behavior." And we would both smile and roll our eyes. I wasn't a bad kid, and he knew it. Once he'd leave the room, I'd go looking for my mom and tell her that I loved her. She would hug me, and we'd move on. She never liked for there to be animosity between us.

There were times when she and I would go shopping and spend hours at the mall. She'd pack sandwiches for both of us, and we would take turns sitting on the floor of various dressing rooms while the other tried on outfits. We had a very straightforward thumbs-up, thumbs-down rating system for things. No gray area, she'd say to me; either I thought she looked fabulous in the clothes, or they should be burned. Unfortunately we could never share anything because I was so much bigger than her.

I received a Christmas gift from my Nana Lynne the same year I turned ten years old. As usual, it came via UPS in an enormous pink box. Patch looked at me and the elegantly wrapped package with envy because there was nothing from Nana Lynne for him. Inside were two shiny, new American Girl dolls surrounded by loads of miniature contemporary fashions and matching accessories. A vacation in the Swiss Alps? They'd be prepared. Horseback riding in Telluride? No sweat. Yachting in Bermuda? These gals had ascots in four colors. The problem was that I'd grown tired of American Girl dolls the year before. But as I unloaded the contents of the box, underneath the patriotic beauties and their travel gear was another smaller box wrapped in red glitter paper. I fished it out and read the card.

With love from your Aunts, it read.

I tore open the paper and inside was a brand new iPod. Apple's newest musical phenom, which had only just been introduced to the public, and there it was, like the Hope Diamond in my hands. My friend Amy's older brother had one, but that was the only one I'd ever seen. I cradled it like it was an American Girl doll and I was five years old.

"Mom!" I shouted from the kitchen.

"In here, Grace," she yelled from the family room.

"You have to come here!"

"On my way," she said, and I could hear her place the remote onto the glass coffee table.

I was holding the iPod high in the air as she walked in the kitchen where the pink and red boxes had exploded in a frenzy of sparkles and tissue.

"What is it?"

I walked over to her and placed it in her hand. "It's an iPod. Can I use your computer?"

She looked at me like I'd just gotten away with something. "This is too much for you. That was very generous of them."

"Mom, can I use your computer?"

"Use your dad's."

"I can't. It has to be a Mac, and I can download a ton of music onto this tiny thing."

My mom handed it back to me. "Okay, sweetie, but please call Nana Lynne and thank her first."

Patch walked in to survey the excitement. "Can I listen, too?"

I ran past him up to my parents' room, closed the door, and spent the next two hours with the instruction booklet and her computer. By the time I emerged, my mom was in the kitchen preparing her broccoli casserole to bring over to Grandma's. Dad hated green beans.

She smiled at me when I sat down at our breakfast table, which looked like a restaurant booth tucked away in an alcove near the back door. She was happy when I was happy. I adjusted my headphones and listened to the ten or so songs I'd downloaded—Christina Aguilera and Britney Spears mostly—and watched as my brother ran in and out of the kitchen showing Mom different drawings of frogs that he'd been working on while she was cooking. From where I was sitting, each frog looked like a misshapen green circle, but she reacted like he worked for Pixar, sending him running with glee back to his waterproof markers to work on his next creation.

"Why doesn't Nana Lynne send anything for Patch?" I asked, and then pulled one of the earphones out of my head and let it dangle on my shoulder.

She answered, but kept to her casserole. "You know why, honey."

"Tell me again."

"She sends him a card on his birthday sometimes," she said, reminding me of his consolation prize.

"Why nothing at Christmas?"

"I don't know. She's not related to Patch, honey," she said quietly. "Just you."

I got a similar answer every time I asked, and each year I hoped for a few more details on the matter...but they never came, and I never pressed the issue. I was only ten years old and not well-versed enough in the art of interrogation. I popped the earphone back into my head and easily fell back into my musical euphoria.

It was a year later, when I was in the fifth grade, that I learned my height and my gifts from Nana Lynne weren't the only things that made me different.

CHAPTER FIVE

wo days before my fifth-grade class was set to study sex education, a note was sent home to our parents. We were instructed not to open the sealed envelope that it was housed in, but since no other notes from school came home in a sealed envelope, I tossed the envelope and read the note on the walk home.

Dear Pleasant View fifth-grade parents:

Next week we begin our studies in human sexuality. As you may have already heard from your child, we will be doing some of the lessons in a unisex group, but most will be taught in segregated boy or girl clusters. With this sensitive subject, there are typically many topics that can be intimidating and confusing to our children. Because of this, we want you to know that we are here for you if you should need any assistance in answering questions at home, or simply need someone to talk to yourself.

We have set up a hotline that will be available to you from the hours of 11:30 a.m.–1:00 p.m. Thank you for your cooperation.

Best regards,

The Pleasant View Staff

"Are they serious?" I asked myself aloud. The infinitesimal group of kids in my grade who didn't know what sex was could be narrowed down to Deborah Zernagen, Miles Hurphman, and Cletus Marberg. And quite honestly, I could've sworn I saw Cletus dry humping his backpack once.

I tossed the note and continued walking. I remember laughing to myself, thinking how smart I already was, and how hilarious it would be to watch my teachers try and teach us things about sex that we already knew. I mean, I was eleven years old, what more was there to know?

Later that week, I sat through two jaw-dropping, cringe-worthy days of lessons on sexual anatomy and intercourse, in which the word *penis* was said seventeen times, *testicles* eleven, *vagina* fifteen, *uterus* ten, and *ovaries* nine.

When day three ended, and our lesson on sexual reproduction was complete, I realized I wasn't laughing or feeling full of myself anymore. No, I was struck with a reality baseball bat, and realized I still had a lot to learn about exactly how I came into this world… and the answers were not at school.

From what I'd just been told, the only way to create a life was for the sperm to enter the egg on the day of conception. How then was I conceived if my parents married when I was two years old?

Prior to having my dad in my life, it was just my mom and me in the old apartment. I don't remember everything that happened to me at that age, but I do have vivid memories of their wedding day. Mom even framed the pink ballerina dress and lavender sash I wore in a Lucite frame that hung in our second-floor hallway. She said that I wouldn't walk down the aisle unless I had a purple ribbon and a ballerina skirt. She also said I refused to drop flower petals and insisted on carrying her bridal bouquet instead.

My memories of that day remain intact, due partly to the seven photo albums we have, and partly because we moved into a house with my dad the very next day. Boxes were hauled in, Grandma was unpacking dishes and making lemonade, and everyone was congratulating me on getting my dad.

"Hi, special girl," he shouted when I entered the room. "Guess what? You can call me Daddy now," he said and threw me in the air, igniting my signature toddler giggles. "You are the most beautiful little princess, you know that?"

"I know that!" I yelled on the descent.

He always called me his beautiful little princess.

Sitting in class at Pleasant View, after learning precisely everything I didn't know about sex, I went numb. My mouth was dry as dirt, my skin was tight, and my stomach felt like someone was stepping on it. I left the classroom without permission that day and ran to the nurse's office.

Nurse Goode greeted me as soon as I crossed the threshold. "Hello, Grace," she said. "What can I help you with?"

I sat on the squeaky vinyl daybed and looked into her eyes. She was a sweet, quiet woman who always had the right answer. She never made anyone feel like they were a burden to her, and whether she knew which students were hypochondriacs or not, she always treated every ailment with kid gloves.

"I don't know who my father is." The words erupted from the pit in my stomach and caught both of us off guard. I had every intention of complaining about a sore throat.

She spun her stool around and faced me before standing up and closing the door. Then she sat back down, smiled caringly, and folded her hands in her lap. "Grace, what's going on?"

"My dad didn't come until I was two." I was talking fast. "And the sperm needs to travel through the cervix into the uterus and plant itself into the egg before fertilization can begin. Only then can a fetus be created, and it's nine to ten months from there." I took her through everything I'd just learned, as though she didn't know. "So how could he have come along two years after I was born?"

I'll never forget the look on Nurse Goode's face. I'd stumped the panel. I'd taken that lovely, unassuming woman who could dispense Neosporin faster than the speed of light, and rendered her speechless. She was frozen, instant-read thermometer in hand, but frozen nonetheless. "Maybe we should call your mom?"

After about twenty minutes and a brief, softly spoken phone conversation with Nurse Goode, my mom arrived at the school. She was wearing her workout clothes and looked like she needed a shower.

"I'll leave you two alone," Nurse Goode said, and patted my mom's back on her way out.

My hands were shaking, and I knew—simply based on the fact that Nurse Goode answered none of my questions and instead called my mom to the school—something wasn't right. I had just literally learned about sperm, ovaries, and fertilization, so my mind was incapable of coming up with any answers on my own. My friends and I had never discussed when their fathers had come into their lives, so I had nothing to compare my situation to. I couldn't help but wonder in that moment whether or not I was alone in my situation…whatever it was.

"Why do I feel scared?" I asked my mom, but kept my gaze securely fixed on the floor. I saw her wipe her eyes in my peripheral vision.

She took a seat on the wheeled nurse's stool. "I'd hoped the school was going to send a note home letting us know when you were scheduled to begin your sex-ed lessons."

I couldn't look at her, but I was desperate to hear what she had to say.

My mom rolled closer to me and took my hand in hers before she spoke. It looked like she was holding an empty glove.

CHAPTER SIX
Sydney

The night before I was supposed to meet Ethan's parents for the first time, I was plagued with horrible menstrual cramps. So in addition to the nerves, I had cramping and bloating. The Reynolds were having their annual summer block party, and Ethan had invited me as his guest. He seemed to have a close relationship with his parents and talked fondly of them. Ethan was Catholic, and although we were only in our late teens, my mother had warned me that all Catholic mothers want their sons to marry nice, full-blooded Catholic girls. She also warned me to be on my best behavior, to thank Mrs. Reynolds for the invitation immediately upon arrival, to introduce myself using my full name (not just my first), and to be sure and give her the gift that my mother sent along. Lastly, she reminded me that I was not Catholic.

"All I'm saying is that my Jewish roommate in college dated a Catholic boy from New York, and their relationship ended soon after she met his mother," Mom informed me an hour before the Reynolds' gala.

"Thanks for the confidence boost, Mom. But we're not Jewish."

Kendra looked at me from across the kitchen table and shook her head.

"But we're also not Catholic," Mom added. "In fact, your grandma Edie was Jewish, and the rest of her family is Protestant. And what, with Uncle George being an atheist…All I'm saying is that you don't have that edge going in."

"Let the girl enjoy the block party for God's sake," Kendra interrupted with food in her mouth.

Mom put her hands up in defense; she didn't make a habit of arguing with Kendra. "I'm just saying I've seen it happen. Anyway, don't forget the wine for Caroline." She gasped, "Only don't call her Caroline!" Her finger waved in front of me. "And be smart." She paused to contain herself. "Do you want to borrow my silver earrings? Or, I know, how about my sandals? You know, the ones with the gold anchors on them?"

"Nope, I'm good," I said, strumming my fingers on the table.

"You sure? You always say how much you love them when I have them on."

"On you, I do."

"What do you mean by that?" she asked defensively.

"She's just fine, Mom," Kendra said to appease her and to keep me from getting into it with my mother. My sister was always trying to train me on how to handle that woman. Kendra was no idiot; she and everyone else saw how my mother would torment me even over the littlest things. Simple questions could turn into arguments in a New York minute.

Mom turned away and left the kitchen. *Chapter ten of child-rearing book number two clearly states: choose your battles.*

I made a gesture like I was ringing someone's neck with my hands, and Kendra just looked at me like I should stop. "Relax and enjoy yourself. Ethan is nuts about you, and who cares what his mother thinks anyway? If she doesn't like you, she must be crazy."

"And we've filled our crazy-mother quota already," I added.

"Why don't you bake her a potato kugel and say it's your grandma Edie's famous Passover recipe," Kendra said with a laugh.

"Oy!" I yelled.

I drove over to Ethan's house around six o'clock. The iron gates at the end of his driveway were open, so I pulled my car up to the valet, grabbed my hostess gift off the passenger seat, and rang the bell. Although we'd been dating for five weeks, it was the first time I'd met his parents. I rang the bell a second time, and just as I was about to walk around back, his father answered the door and proved to be the source of Ethan's height and deep-set eyes.

"You must be Sydney," he greeted me with a baritone voice as their golden retriever, Sparky, galloped up beside him.

I lifted my head and shoulders to meet his gaze. "Hello, Mr. Reynolds. Thank you for having me. You have a beautiful home. I'm Sydney Shep…"

"Ethan is out back with the others," he said and left me at the door. Sparky sniffed my crotch, then chased after him. Meeting the father was a breeze.

I stepped inside their foyer and marveled at the intricate moldings and elegant decor. My house did not have a foyer. In fact, the bottom of our stairwell was so close to the front door, it felt like you were stepping onto an escalator when you walked in. The Reynolds' reception area was covered in black-and-white, square marble floor tiles, and there was a large circular table in the center of the entry that held family photos and a four-foot ceramic vase of hydrangea stems. I walked past it, through the library and out the double glass doors onto their back patio. Ethan was sitting on a cement ledge that surrounded the terrace.

"Hey, you." He stood and walked over to me. "Come with me to the kitchen. My mom said to bring you over as soon as you got here."

Ethan looked amazing. He was wearing a white linen dress shirt with a pair of faded Levi's and no shoes. He kissed my cheek as soon as he reached me.

"I brought her some wine," I held up the bottle. "Well, my mom sent her some wine actually."

In the short time that we'd been dating, we'd had ample conversations about our families, and he knew the challenges I faced living with a woman who wiped her feet on my self-esteem almost daily. I'd told him how she'd always favored Kendra, and how, try as I might, there was nearly nothing I could do to impress my mother. These were things I never shared with anyone, and eighteen-year-old boys weren't necessarily bred to be therapists, but confiding in Ethan always made me feel better.

When he and I walked into his kitchen, Mrs. Caroline Reynolds was standing near the sink, telling the caterers to keep the ice buckets full and the wine chilled. Nothing is worse than lukewarm chardonnay, I heard her pronounce. She instructed them to uncork a few of the bottles—so guests could easily pour their own glasses if they wanted, but they should offer first—to clear the empties immediately, and to be sure to put glass and plastics in the recycling bin. She was a pioneer in that field.

Mrs. Reynolds was tall and rail thin. She wore a Lilly Pulitzer miniskirt and a long-sleeve, white, cable-knit sweater that accentuated her tan. Her blonde hair was pulled into a tight, short ponytail. I immediately pictured her closet filled with Vera Bradley bags and tennis rackets.

"Mom," Ethan called from behind her. "Sydney's here."

She immediately turned around and smiled. "Hello, darling. It's wonderful to finally see you," she said with a smoker's voice as she approached. "Ethan is notorious for giving me very little information, so I hope we can sit together like girls and have a proper chat later?"

"She's not interested," he joked, and I smacked his arm.

"I'd love to. Just tell me when." I handed her the bottle of chardonnay I'd brought, unchilled.

She looked me up and down and all around, so much so that I had to resist the compulsion to spin.

"Why, thank you, Sydney," she said as a caterer hurried over and grabbed the wine from her. "Later, okay? I'll find you in a little bit and we'll talk."

"Let's go." Ethan grabbed my hand. "Good luck finding her," he teased.

About two hours into the party, Mrs. Reynolds approached us. "My turn," she said, holding a wine glass and a cigarette so thin, it looked like the stem of a Tootsie Pop.

"I'm ready." I jumped up and locked elbows with her. She was much taller than me, about five foot eight in flats. I could hear my mother's voice in the back of my head, so I arched my back and stood as straight as I could.

We walked inside through the double glass doors and she guided me to a set of couches, upholstered in a pale-green paisley fabric. The couches were flanked with antique wooden end tables, each with matching table lamps and an assortment of jeweled frames and coasters.

"Please have a seat," she gestured to me, and then waited for me to sit down.

"Your house is beautiful, Mrs. Reynolds."

"How sweet. Thank you."

The Reynolds had three children. Ethan was the youngest, and his older twin sisters were away at UCLA. They stayed in Los Angeles that summer attending summer school and interning on the Paramount Pictures lot, so I hadn't had a chance to meet them. Ethan told me they were working on the set of *Cheers* because his dad was friends with a famous television producer and got them the gig.

"Do you miss having the girls around this summer?" I asked.

"I'm adjusting, but I've been out there twice already," she said with a wink. "We stayed at the Beverly Hilton just last weekend." Her tone indicated I should be impressed.

A moment later, Sparky joined us...much to my displeasure. I have never been comfortable around dogs, and I was even less comfortable around people who assumed I should enjoy their dog's company as much as they did. Sparky began slobbering on my leg, so I discreetly tried to pull away from him.

"Sparkeeeee, nooooo," she said calmly. "He's a lovebug."

Sparky was undeterred and kept licking me, so I tried petting him lightly on the back. It wasn't a very welcoming stroke though; it looked more like I was testing an iron to see if it was hot.

"Ethan tells me you're going to Purdue."

"Yes," I answered, shifting my body away from the dog's nose.

"Do you know anyone else going there?"

"No, I don't."

She questioned me for fifteen minutes about various aspects of my life, and she was much more nonthreatening than I had expected her to be. There was an air about her, for sure, but she reacted to my responses without judgment, and was very easy to talk to. Ethan barged in just as she was inquiring about my mother.

"Sparky, out!" he shouted. "Mom, she hates dogs. Out, Sparky!"

Mrs. Reynolds looked at me like I'd just admitted I had no idea what the Beverly Hilton was.

I let out a nervous laugh and glared at him. "I don't hate dogs, Ethan. I'm just more of a cat person, but I do not *hate* dogs."

"You said you hated dogs," Ethan remarked.

"Well, I don't," I repeated, shaking my head assuredly at Mrs. Reynolds.

"We're leaving anyway," he announced and grabbed my arm. His mom turned her cheek as I stood, and Ethan leaned in and gave her a kiss.

"Nice to finally meet you," I told her.

"See ya, Mom," Ethan said.

"Good-bye, darling."

Ethan dragged me back though the front foyer and out onto his driveway. "Follow me. I have a present for you."

We walked, holding hands, over to his Volkswagen Jetta. He opened the passenger door, reached under the front seat, and pulled out a black velvet box.

"I got you a little something," he said as I took the box from him.

My eyes widened. "E, you didn't have to do that."

"I know."

The lid made a tiny little "pop" sound as I opened the box and uncovered a strand of charcoal-colored freshwater pearls inside. Opening that box took my breath away and made me feel like a princess. Or a queen. Or someone who is used to being handed velvet boxes with jeweled treasures inside. Never before had anyone ever done something so generous and unexpected for me. I cradled the necklace and rolled the individual pearls between my fingers. I looked up at him, my mouth agape.

"I don't know what to say."

"How about 'thank you'?" he said and we both laughed.

"Thank you, Ethan. Thank you so much."

"It's my pleasure, and you deserve it for being so sweet to me all the time."

I unhooked the necklace and Ethan placed it around my neck.

Those pearls were a bond, and I felt protected every time I wore them.

CHAPTER SEVEN

Ethan's parents went to California to visit his sisters two weeks after their block party, and left his grandmother to look after him. Although he was about to start his second year of college, Ethan's mother refused to leave her home and her beloved Sparky in his care. Thankfully, his grandma had a grueling bridge schedule and wasn't around much, so he and I would rent movies, order food, and spend hours rolling around naked in his bed, basement, and backyard. My mother had no idea that his parents were gone, since she was never able to befriend Mrs. Reynolds, so she assumed I was hanging out with Taylor on my days off. And despite her overall lack of confidence in me, she knew I wasn't much of a liar, so she never bothered to corroborate my stories.

Those two weeks were heaven. Every minute I spent with him was pure, stress-free bliss, so much so that I would have a sickly pit in my stomach when the time would come each day for me to go home. My body began to have physical reactions to Ethan: tingling euphoria when we were together, and numb depression when we were apart. My head ached at the thought of going away to college and leaving him. I began to lose sleep, my appetite was nonexistent, and my tolerance for my mother drained lower and lower. The last night of Ethan's parents' vacation, my mom decided that she wanted me to stay home and go through my closet with her so I could start packing my trunk for school.

"Not tonight, Mom," I said, not feeling any urgency to tackle that chore anyway. "We can do it tomorrow."

"We're having dinner with the Carlins tomorrow, so you and I will have to get this done tonight."

My hands began to shake as my body temperature rose. "I have plans tonight."

She turned to face me with a confused look on her face. It was an expression that read, "Am I to understand that you are defying me?" and one I was nauseatingly familiar with. "Then cancel them," she said with no regard for what I'd just said.

I swallowed the lump in my throat and smartly weighed my options before exploding. Option A: start an argument with her, which could result in me being grounded for the night, ultimately ruining my plans for sure, and sending me into a catatonic state. Option B: appease her, and divert her attention so she feels comfortable and confident that she has triumphed over me.

"Mom," I began robotically, "Kendra actually said that she would help me go through everything this weekend." I paused for a second. "And that she was really excited to help." One more beat. "Also, I was wondering if I could borrow those silver earrings of yours. You know, the long ones that you got in New Orleans."

I had her at "Kendra" but her smile ignited when I asked for the earrings. "Oh, all right. Let me get them for you."

My evening alone with Ethan was restored, and there was nothing else I cared about. Literally nothing.

He was standing in his driveway when I pulled up, with a six-pack of beer and a four-pack of Bartles & Jaymes wine coolers. Ethan drank, but he didn't smoke pot, so it'd been a weed-free few months for me. "Hey, you," he said and smiled. "I just got back from Eddie's." He hoisted his stash in the air. Fresh Eddie's was a liquor store in Evanston that was known across the North Shore for selling booze and cigarettes to underage kids.

We took our beverages around to the back patio, sat on the ground, and leaned back against the half wall that circled the Reynolds' terrace.

"When's Grandma coming home?"

"Should be close to nine, so we have at least two hours to ourselves." He took a swig of his Bud Light. His legs were stretched out in front of him and crossed at the ankles. He was wearing a pair of jeans, flip-flops, and a Hawaiian shirt. "I thought maybe we could try and watch *Caddyshack* again." He winked.

He and I both had a mutual love for that movie, and I'd learned that reciting some of my favorite lines from the film worked like an aphrodisiac on him. Only our hormones got the best of us every time we'd lie on the couch, turn out the lights, and put the movie on, so we'd never been able to watch it together in its entirety.

Our last night alone in his parents' house was no different.

We were scheduled to leave for our respective colleges during the last week of August. My parents had planned to take me down to Purdue on that Wednesday, and Ethan was driving himself back to Lawrence, Kansas, on Friday. Mom gifted me an extended curfew—with Kendra's prodding—so I could spend Tuesday night with Ethan. Kendra had seen my mood deteriorate over those last couple weeks and lent a soft, supportive, sisterly shoulder to cry on.

"What if Ethan is the *one*, and us going to different schools destroys our future together?" I asked her through drippy eyes as we sat on the floor of my room, sorting through my clothes one day.

She looked at me with her signature sympathetic smile. "Syd, you are so young, and you're going to meet so many people in the next few years. If you and Ethan are meant to have a future together, it will happen. And if not, you will find the right person at the right time."

Kendra was three years ahead of me and entering her senior year at the University of Illinois. For my whole life, I'd assumed she knew so much more about everything than I did, and I'd imagined that I could never make up that three-year difference. I'd assumed one day when I was eighty-two and she was eighty-five, she'd still be able to teach me things. But truth be told, she'd never been in love like me. I'd seen her date numerous guys over the years, some longer than others, but I'd never seen her emotionally attached to any one of them like I was to Ethan.

"I've found the right person; I want to be with Ethan," I said as drips spun into actual tears.

"Oh, Syd, I know you two love each other, but you're both so young…"

"I'm eighteen, and you're only three years older than me, so stop saying I'm so young," I whined and slumped back against the side of my bed.

She looked like she was trying to find the most sincere words to use. "Okay, well you're younger than me, and when I was heading off to college, I remember really looking forward to meeting new people. I realize I didn't have a boyfriend at the time, but not only will you meet other boys at school, you're going to form new, lifelong best friends."

"I just don't want to leave him. It hurts my heart every time I think about him meeting some other girl at school."

"Well, there's no sense in creating scenarios before they happen. Aren't you planning on seeing him for October break?"

"Yes."

"There you go. That's less than two months away," she said, folding a sweater. "Have you two discussed how you're going to handle the long-distance thing?"

I looked at the pile of clothes, which I cared nothing about, and shook my head. Ethan and I hadn't talked about our future together. Maybe because we were both avoiding the topic.

"Then why don't you ask him?" she suggested.

"I think I will."

Ethan and I planned to spend our last night together at Gilson Beach.

"My mom found a condom." He greeted me with a devilish grin as I got in his car.

"Excuse me?" I choked.

He drove away from my house and headed for the beach, but not before letting out a long sigh.

"Well, let's just say it found her. Apparently your aversion to Sparky last month didn't go unnoticed by his keen canine senses, and he went through the trash in the basement, dragged a condom up to the kitchen, and proudly dropped it at my mother's feet."

"What?!" I shrieked.

As if Ethan's mother didn't already disapprove of my mutt-like religious lineage, she now had to stomach the fact that her son and I were sleeping together—in her marble-laden home no less.

"How could you have left one in the garbage? And what kind of dog digs condoms out of the garbage?!" I asked, appalled.

Ethan was in near hysterics laughing about it. "Mine, I guess."

I slapped his bicep as hard as I could. "This is not funny. I can no longer show my face there. Seriously, do not ever invite me over to your home again because I won't go."

"Ow! Tell me about it," he said. "I woke up to a three-page letter outlining the dangers of premarital sex, stapled to a *Newsweek* article on the rise of teenage pregnancy."

I buried my head in my hands. "Oh my God, I am mortified. Can you say it wasn't yours?" I asked, and quickly looked over at him.

"No, it's done," he said, trying to contain his amusement. "Don't sweat it."

"Easy for you to say," I said, embarrassed beyond words. My mother would have literally collapsed and lost the ability to breathe air into her lungs had she known.

"Sorry." He snorted one last chuckle. "Let's not let it ruin our last night."

We arrived at the beach equipped with four Amstel Lights from his parents' garage fridge, a bag of Cheetos, and two oatmeal chocolate-chip cookies.

"Okay, Miss College Girl," he said, and raised his bottle. "Here's to you and the freshman fifteen. I hope you gain it all in your chest."

"Thanks," I said, embarrassed.

"I'm kidding. Even if you come back with a fat ass, I will still worship it."

I burst into tears.

"Syd, you know I'm teasing."

I nodded.

"Come here, girl," he said and scooped me up onto his lap. "Shhhh, don't get all weepy on me. We're not breaking up, just apart."

Through a parade of sniffles and snot, I made myself speak. "I'm so scared of what's going to happen to us. I don't want to leave you, and I don't want to go." I sounded five years old. "What's going to happen to our relationship?"

He squeezed me tight. "You have nothing to worry about. You're going to have a great time, meet new people, and we're solid, so don't sweat it."

"I'm so tired of hearing that I'll meet new people. I don't want new people; I'm happy with my old people."

He laughed.

"It's not funny," I said in a tone that now sounded like I'd regressed to age three.

Ethan turned my chin toward his face. "You are going to want to meet new people, and whether you like it or not, they are going to want to meet you. Girls and boys." He looked away for a second. "And I don't want you to feel like you can't go out with other people, or feel like our relationship is holding you back in any way."

"You just assured me that we're not breaking up."

"We're not, but I want you to know that you should do whatever you want to do, Syd. You only have one shot at this, and I don't want you to regret anything, especially on my account," he said and rubbed my back.

I was tugging at the ends of my hair, wishing Father Time would freeze and I never had to leave that beach. I had no way of knowing what college would be like for me, but I felt like he was trying to let me down easy and lessen the blow for when he'd want nothing more to do with me in a month. All I wanted was to get through my freshman year with passing grades and see Ethan whenever possible.

"I see you wore the necklace." He gently elevated the strand of charcoal pearls from the skin on my neck.

"I barely take it off."

"I'm happy you like them."

"I love them, and you."

Ethan wiped my tears with the back of his hand and gave me a kiss. "Here, maybe this will make you feel better," he said and handed me another black velvet box, much smaller than the one that housed the pearls.

My jaw opened slowly as I reached for it. "Oh my God, Ethan."

He smiled and urged me to open it. "Go ahead. I know you're going to love it."

"I don't know what to say."

"Just open it, and then 'thank you,' I imagine, would be the appropriate response."

I opened the box and there was a single chocolate-covered Double Stuf Oreo in the center of the box.

Ethan kissed my forehead. "I love you, too, Syd."

I gave him a hug. "Your dog's a piece of shit."

CHAPTER EIGHT
Grace

S itting in the nurse's office, waiting for my mom to formulate her words, my mind wandered to happier, more secure times, like celebrating my mom's birthday the week before. My dad was always finding creative ways to surprise her, and that year he'd decided to get her a cat for her birthday. She loved cats, and I'd begged her for one, but she knew my dad wasn't crazy about them so she'd always told Patch and me that Dad was allergic.

"But you're allergic to cats," I cautioned him when he started to tell me of his plan.

"No, I'm not." He looked at me like I was crazy.

"Mom says you are," I said with smug, childlike expertise.

Patch nodded in agreement.

"She must say that because I don't actually want a cat in the house," he told us. "But I want her to have one."

So the night of Mom's birthday, my aunt came over to stay with us while my parents went out to dinner. Once they'd pulled out of the driveway, my aunt hurried us into the garage.

"Come help me unload everything!" she squealed with excitement. In the back seat of her car was a litter box, a case of cat food, a vented pooper-scooper, two bags of kitty litter, and about a dozen furry toys shaped like mice and miniature potato sacks. In the front seat of her car sat a white cardboard box with holes on the side and a handle on top. It was shifting back and forth on its own when I craned my neck to look at it.

"Where's the kitty?" Patch asked loudly.

"In the cage, sweetie," my aunt told him.

Patch eyed the floor of her car. "Where's the cage?"

"It's in the front seat. I'll get it," she said, and lugged the cardboard cage into the house. "Your mom thinks Daddy is taking her on vacation this weekend, and that I'm staying with you two, so we're going to put the cats in a suitcase and surprise her when she gets home," she said to us.

"Cats?" I asked.

"Yes, there are two kittens in here."

Wow, all she ever wanted was one cat, and my dad, who hates cats, went and bought her two.

"What if she'd rather have the vacation?" I asked.

My aunt shot me a dirty look. "Just please go and get me their largest bag, okay, Grace?"

I ran back up from the basement with an oversize suitcase, the one Patch and I were forced to share anytime we traveled.

"Perfect, Grace. Thank you." She took the bag from me. "We don't have much time to set this all up, play with them, feed them, and then get them zipped into this thing."

I watched her frantically search for bowls to put their food and water in.

"Why are they coming home if she thinks they're going on vacation?" I questioned.

She was examining two bright-blue dishes that Mom used for Patch's Goldfish crackers. "I don't know. Your dad has some story planned."

About an hour later, my aunt's cell phone rang.

"Okay, we're ready," I heard her say, then hang up. "Help me get them in the suitcase. They're almost home!"

We laid a beach towel in the bottom of the bag, and placed the two tabby gray kittens inside. Once they were nestled, my aunt tied a pink ribbon around each of their necks, and they both curled up on the towel with no interest in ever leaving that suitcase. As soon as my parents' car pulled in the driveway, we zipped it up and sat at the bottom of the stairs in the front foyer.

My mom walked in, saw the suitcase, then looked at my dad. "I knew it!" she said, and smacked his arm. She looked back at us, as if to say good-bye or ask if we packed for her, and my aunt slowly unzipped the bag and revealed the two tiny fur balls.

My mom gasped, slapped a hand over her mouth, and began to cry.

Dad leaned over to me and gave me a high five. "Nice work, Gracie."

I slapped his hand, and took the credit he was giving me for pulling it off. It was a great day, and Mom let Patch and me name the cats. Tiger and Gray-Gray.

The only other times I'd seen her cry, up until that point, were once in a huge argument with my dad and once when Patch fell out of a tree. The next time she cried was sitting there in the nurse's office, holding my limp hand.

She took a few deep breaths before making eye contact with me. "Grace, your dad and I love you very much," she started. "And I was hoping he could be here with me today."

"At the nurse's office?"

"No, not at the nurse's office. Here when you learned about how you and he came into my life...our lives."

I studied her face but did not have the maturity to comprehend what she might say. All I remember was being worried and, for the first time in my life, having a sixth sense that something was very wrong. My mother's eyes were glassy.

"I'm scared," I said.

She tilted her head and touched my long hair with her other hand. "What are you scared about?"

"I'm scared that I'm not your daughter."

Her lips pursed into half of a smile. "Of course you're my daughter, and I love you more than anything," she said emphatically. "You know that."

"Then how was I *conceived*, and why are you and Nurse Goode acting so weird?"

"Your dad is not your biological father," she said, but she could tell from my expression that I was going to need a little more clarification. She cleared her throat. "When I was in college, I had *intercourse* with another man—not your dad—and I got pregnant." She formulated a smile and looked at me to make sure I was following along. "And once I realized that I was pregnant, I was so excited and so thrilled to be blessed with a baby."

"Why didn't you have sex with Dad?"

She released my hand. "Your dad and I weren't together at the time, and I hadn't planned on having a baby back then; it just happened. And I thank God that it did because now we have you, and we can't imagine our lives without you." She mustered a smile.

"Oh my God." I was shocked; I couldn't believe what she was saying. "Does Daddy know?"

"Yes, he does."

"Who is my real dad?" I asked, and the words hung in the air like a bad odor. The question made my mother's body recoil, but I repeated it. "Who is my real dad?"

She sniffed and reached for a tissue from atop Nurse Goode's desk. "Your dad who loves you and kisses you every night is your real dad. Your biological father is a man I had a friendship with a long time ago," she said.

"Where is he?"

"He lives out of state, with his family."

His family? Wasn't I his family? Suddenly it was like I was trapped at the bottom of a sewer pipe, and my mom was aboveground trying to shout down to me. I felt alone. Removed. Deceived.

My head fell into my hands. "Why didn't you tell me?" I looked up. My hands were stiff. "How could you not tell me this?" I begged for an answer.

She was weak and defenseless. "I have always planned on telling you, but I didn't just want to drop a bomb. I figured that, once you learned about human sexuality and how babies were made, you'd come to me with questions," she muttered. "This was certainly not where I pictured having the conversation."

She reached for my hand again but I stood and crossed my arms.

"Let's go home, Grace. Daddy is going to meet us there." Her voice was quieter.

"I don't want to see him."

She sighed loudly. "Grace, he loves you, and he wants us to be together."

"What about Patch? Who's his dad?"

"Patch came from Daddy and me."

Of course he did. That lucky little piece of annoying filth. My life began to flash before my eyes.

My freakish height.

My Nana Lynne.

My lack of resemblance to my dad and my brother.

What would my friends think?

How was I to bear this humiliation?

Why hadn't my real father ever called me?

We looked at each other for a moment, my mom and I, both our faces worried and confused.

"I don't want anyone to know," I blurted out.

"Well, you don't have to say anything to anyone if you don't want to, but there are a few people who know in the family already."

I shook my head in disbelief. "Like who?"

"Like your grandparents and aunts and uncles, and everyone who loves you and has been in your life since the day you were born."

I clenched my teeth and it hurt my brain, but the throbbing was a welcome distraction from the topic of discussion.

"Let's go home, Grace, and let Nurse Goode back in her office."

"I'm not going home. It's almost lunch period and I want to stay at school."

Mom looked at me with sad eyes, wishing I would join her with enthusiasm as I would under normal circumstances. "I'd rather not leave you here, sweetie."

"Well, I'm staying," I insisted and grabbed my backpack. I brushed past my mom and she let me by without saying anything further. The nurse was sitting outside writing on a clipboard as I left her in my wake as well. I ran into the nearest bathroom and cried into a brown, kraft paper towel that scratched my face. Trapped and alone.

When I came home from school that day, my dad was not home like Mom had said he would be, so I went straight upstairs and locked myself in my room. Two hours later, there was a knock at my door.

"I'm asleep," I said.

"It's me, Gracie. Can I come in?" my dad asked. His voice, which was normally a source of comfort, was instead embarrassing for me to hear, and felt distant.

I didn't want to see him. I was so angry with both of them for lying to me, but I loved my dad, and deep down I wanted so badly to be consoled.

He knocked again. "Can I come in, please?"

I opened the door and then sat at my desk chair facing the wall, not wanting to look at him.

"Thank you," he said, and sat on my bed behind me. "Your mother told me what happened today, and she's very upset. I don't think I have to tell you how much we both love you, but I'm going to say it anyway because I don't want you to doubt it, or forget it for one second," he said. "You mean everything to us, we love you more than anything, and to see you hurting like this is even more painful for us, if you can believe it." He paused. "I'm sure you must have lots of questions, so I want you to know that I will answer anything you ask. Anything."

He was right about one thing: I had hundreds of questions. But I had no idea where to begin. "Why did everyone lie to me?"

"We didn't lie, Grace. We just hadn't told you everything yet. We had planned on it; we just didn't want to scare you at any point. I'm terribly sorry that it had to unfold this way."

I was twirling a pencil and staring at the fraying stickers on my desktop, while my dad and I sat in silence. All I wanted to do was run over to him and have him wrap me in his strong arms, but my stubborn nature kept me firmly planted on the chair.

"Well, you both were wrong. You should have told me," I said after two dreadfully long minutes.

"Yes, we should have."

"And now I feel stupid, and like I'm not part of this family."

"Well, you are."

"And I'm so mad at you." I started to cry, and the tears came pouring out, soaking my homework. I didn't move to wipe them off my face because I didn't want him to know how upset I was, but he walked over to me and knelt beside my chair. I threw myself on his shoulder and he held me.

"I'm so sorry, Gracie. I love you so much."

I knew he did.

Mom came in my room after he left. "Can we talk?"

There were so many questions spinning around in my head—first and foremost, when could I meet my real father?—but I couldn't muster the energy to talk about it any longer that evening. "Not now," I said.

"Are you sure?"

I went to my closet and grabbed a pair of pajamas from the bottom drawer of my dresser. "I'm sure."

Mom placed a glass of ice water on the nightstand next to my bed. Then she walked over to me, leaned up, and kissed my cheek. "I love you, sweetie. Good night." She squeezed my elbow and started to leave the room.

"Mom," I said.

She turned around at the doorway. "Yeah?"

"I want to talk to my dad—my real dad—and I want you to call him tomorrow."

CHAPTER NINE
Sydney

My college roommate was a girl named Louise Anderson. And like most people who went to Purdue, she was from a small town in Indiana, and was floored when I told her my high school graduating class had 1,200 people in it. Hers had 220.

Louise was a nice, simple girl. She had long blonde hair and wore glasses with no makeup. Very Jan Brady, the later years. She attended services at the campus church every Sunday and Wednesday morning, Bible study on Saturdays, and in her spare time, she read Christian novels. We had pretty much nothing in common, other than we both had boyfriends we'd left behind in search of higher education. Louise had dated her boyfriend, Mark, since the sixth grade. He grew up on a dairy farm, and was set to take over his family's business one day. She told me all about it in great detail, but all I wondered was if they'd had sex or not, and how offended she'd be if I asked.

We hung out and ate meals together that first week because neither of us knew anyone else. But by week two, I was eager to find some other girls who were interested in sneaking liquor or weed into the dorm.

One of the first girls I met was Jenna Fielding. She was in a room across the hall and two doors down from Louise and me. Jenna was also from Chicago, but not the suburbs like me. She'd grown up in the city and attended private schools her whole life. She'd wanted to go to NYU, but her parents were both Purdue alumni, and said they wouldn't pay for her to go anywhere else. I think I initially gravitated to her because she reminded me of Taylor. She was really pretty, had similar dark features, and after only one week of being on campus, she had loads of friends. Her roommate was a basic carbon copy of Louise, so we begged them to do a roomie swap with us, but since it was against the rules they both declined.

I talked to Ethan all the time in the beginning. We had scheduled times each day so that we wouldn't miss each other's call, and if we did miss one, we had backup call times. Sometimes when I hadn't heard from him, my stomach would cramp up, and I couldn't relax until I heard the sound of his voice. Jenna would make fun of me, and did her best to understand our relationship, but mostly she'd try and encourage me to go out and meet other guys.

"Sigma Chi is having a toga party on Saturday—underwear optional—with thirty kegs," she informed me. "And you and I are going."

I smiled. "I see. Underwear is optional, but my attendance is not."

"Correct."

Most of our weekends consisted of much the same conversations. And unlike high school, weekends in college started on Thursday night. She and I, and some other girls we'd befriended at the dorm, would flirt our way into frat parties and drink for free until one of us puked or passed out. Then I'd crawl into bed and call Ethan in the wee hours of the night, either waking him or not reaching him at all. If I did reach him, we'd talk on the phone for hours, and oftentimes I'd fall asleep with the receiver on my pillow—behavior that would earn me two days of the silent treatment from Louise.

By early October, Ethan and I had begun to talk of nothing but our fall break, and despite a few flirtatious evenings with drunken fraternity boys, I was really looking forward to seeing him back at home.

One morning, Jenna rushed into my room. "You're not going to believe this!" she screamed.

"What's up?"

"My parents are taking me to New York for October break, and they said I could bring a friend." She looked at me, waiting for my equally enthusiastic reaction, but I didn't have one. "I'm inviting you, you moron!"

I made a weird face that was part excited, part apologetic. "You know I'm going home to see Ethan," I said, trying hard not to be a buzzkill. "He would be so pissed at me if I went to New York instead."

She was vibrating with energy as she sat down on the edge of my bed and started talking really fast. "Listen, you've never been to New York, right?" she asked and I nodded. "Okay, so Ethan would not want you to miss out on an all-expense-paid weekend there, would he?"

I acted as though I was considering what he'd want. "No, I'm pretty sure he could give a shit about me going to New York over break. He and I have been obsessing about seeing each other for the past two weeks...and my sister is going to be home, too," I said. "I'm sorry. Trust me, it sounds amazing, but there's no way I can change my plans."

Jenna must have known there was no way I'd go with her. She probably knew it before she asked, but thought she'd give it a try anyway.

"I understand," she said as she rolled her eyes. "We're staying at the Plaza..." She dangled one last carrot.

"You suck. That's awesome, but I can't."

She jumped off my bed and buzzed toward the door. "I gotta pack!"

Louise weighed in quietly from her desk. "You made the right decision."

The last day of classes, Jenna flew to LaGuardia, and I put my name on a carpool board and got dropped off at the Carson Pirie Scott just off the expressway at Edens Plaza in Wilmette. My sister was there waiting for me with a bag of fried chicken from Little Red Hen in Glencoe. My favorite.

Seeing her face almost made me cry. "Hi, Ken," I said as we hugged. "I missed you…and fried chicken," I said and inhaled the aroma seeping out of the greasy brown paper bag in her backseat. When Kendra turned sixteen, my parents bought her a red, convertible Volkswagen Cabriolet. When I turned sixteen, I was allowed to invite three friends to dinner at Ron of Japan, where they cook the shrimp at your table.

"Hello, gorgeous. You look tired."

"Do I look tired or gorgeous?"

She drove me home, and we endured an afternoon with my parents, then dinner at the mall. My mother was actually quite tolerable that first night, and made only two negative comments in regard to my appearance. The first was that my oversize hooded sweatshirt wasn't appropriate attire for dining out, and the second was that I needed a haircut. Both equally mild on a scale of one to offensive.

Kendra was in her senior year at the University of Illinois, and that weekend wasn't an official school break for her, but she'd come home to be there for me.

"So how much time do I have with you?" she asked.

"Ethan's not getting in until noon tomorrow."

"Good, we can go for breakfast together!"

I rubbed my belly; everything in college revolved around food, and the free soft-serve machine in the school cafeteria wasn't helping my waistline. "Can't we just go for coffee or something?"

"No, we cannot. You love that Walker Brothers Pancake House. We'll go there for apple pancake fritters or whatever."

"Fine." It really wasn't hard to convince me.

After breakfast the next morning, Ethan called and said he was having lunch with his mom, and he'd come over once they were through. I couldn't wait.

My being home from college didn't seem to make an impression on my mother's schedule at all, which turned out nicely for me. She had two tennis matches on Saturday, and a friend's birthday lunch on Sunday that she "really would hate to cancel." I begged her to keep her plans, assuring her that I wanted to spend time with Ethan and Kendra.

"Do you want to borrow my silver earrings?" Mom asked.

"No thanks, Mom."

"Are you sure? Here, why don't you take them back to school with you?" She handed them to me. "You love them."

Finally, I realized there was only one way to make her stop asking, so I took the earrings. "Thank you. I do love these."

She smiled. "I can tell you're excited to see him."

"I really missed him, Mom."

"Well then, I'm happy for you, sweetie. Have fun, and be smart, okay?"

"Always am," I assured her.

I watched the end of my driveway for fifteen minutes from the window in my bedroom, and began to pant like a dog as I saw the front end of Ethan's car come around the edge of our trees. I ran downstairs as he put the car in park, flung the door open, and attacked him.

"Oh—my—God, you smell so friggin' good," I spoke, my voice muffled, buried in his shirt.

He kissed my head and squeezed me really tight. "I missed you, Syd," he said.

Ethan was wearing jeans, a long-sleeve, white cotton, waffle-knit shirt, and a baseball hat turned backward. He looked as big and wonderful as ever.

"Where are we headed?" I asked.

Ethan gestured to the blankets in his backseat. "To the beach of course."

We spent hours catching up under Ethan's childhood comforter on the cold sand at Gilson Beach. His body was like a radiator, and I warmed every last appendage of mine on it. The air was about sixty-five degrees, and we lay like a burrito, talking, kissing, and nuzzling each other until the sun began to set.

CHAPTER TEN

Jenna and I pledged the same sorority, Kappa Kappa Gamma, and were inseparable for the remainder of our freshman year. My mom got a new car that winter, so I was allowed to take her old Chevy Blazer back to campus during second semester. When summer came, Jenna and I drove back home together, and I dropped her at her parents' penthouse apartment at 1040 Lake Shore Drive. She spent two of those summer months between our freshman and sophomore year in Aspen, and I spent the summer at Camp Ethan.

I had convinced my dad that the pressures of college were so much harder than I'd expected, and my appreciation for an employment-free summer break would manifest itself in the form of housework and as an errand girl. I promised him that he and my mother could have me at their beck and call, if only I didn't have to serve Cobb salads at the Onwentsia country club anymore. He acquiesced and helped me convince my mother. Kendra opted for summer school at the University of Illinois, and so did her new boyfriend.

Camp Ethan consisted of hanging out by his parents' pool, having one of his sisters make sandwiches for us, and spending evenings at the beach with all of our high school friends. On the days when Camp Ethan was closed, I would settle for the equally enjoyable Camp Taylor.

"Don't you ever wish you had your freedom at school?" she asked me one afternoon, as we sat inside cabana four.

"What are you getting at?"

"Well, I mean, are you really going to cut yourself off from college guys completely for the next three years? You know I love Ethan, but you are really missing out…and so is he."

"Thanks."

"My concern is more for you, of course," she said and shifted her body so that she was facing me. "Did I tell you that I made out with three guys in one night? It was a stupid Pimp 'n' Ho theme, but ho was it fun! I just can't imagine not having the freedom to let loose and experiment."

"And be a ho?"

She laughed. "Trust me, you are going to want to be able to live a little. We will never have another chance to behave like this in all of our adult life."

I admired Taylor, I really did, and there was almost nothing she did without schoolgirl enthusiasm, but she and I were different when it came to dating. She had her pick of the litter, and I was typically left with her pick's friend.

"I love Ethan, and he loves me, and the fact that we met each other right before college does have its complications, but it keeps us close," I told her.

"You know I'm not saying you should break up. I just wish you could experience the fun and the men. That sounds stupid, but you know what I mean," she said, then inched closer to me. "Do you think he's been loyal to you?" she sniffed.

Of course I thought he'd been loyal to me. Why wouldn't he have been? But her putting the question out there made me concerned. "Yes, I do."

She sensed my insecurity. "No, I'm sure he has; don't take that the wrong way. I just wondered if you two ever talked about being allowed to date other people, or whatever."

"We haven't, but we probably should, I guess…I don't know. So far we're having a great summer, and that's all I care to concern myself with," I said and rested my head back down on the chaise.

When August rolled around and camp was over, Ethan and I continued what would be our annual ritual of parting ways: him leaning against his car, me buried deep within his arms sobbing, and the clock ticking well into the night.

We never did have a discussion about dating other people. It was just understood. Ethan and I were in love, and why would anyone who's in love with someone want to date anyone else?

CHAPTER ELEVEN

Three years of college passed almost as quickly as people had told me they would. Every adult I've ever known has always bored me with tales of years flying by and what seemed like empty threats of my youth slipping away from me. But by the time I was about to enter my senior year at Purdue, I felt like I truly understood what they meant. Time had indeed flown by like a Learjet, and I was a new woman—one who was educated, mature, used to living without rules, and nervous about giving up my credit card with its two-hundred-dollar limit, which my dad paid for each month. My relationship with Ethan over the years had stayed strong on the friendship-end, but not so solid when it came to romance. We'd had our struggles over jealousy, distance, and apathy, but we remained committed to repairing our emotional wounds and making it work.

Ethan graduated college in June of 1990 and was set to move to Boston to start a job as an IT manager. His parents took him and his sisters to Italy for a graduation gift, so I didn't get to see him until late July. I remember not being very upset about it at the time. Instead, I spent my days working at the country club, only that time I was answering phones and working in the member relations department, fielding complaints from disgruntled members about flat Diet Coke, pool towels with frayed edges, and how they had to wait over forty-five seconds for the valet. All were met with gasps and profuse apologies from me. It was grueling work, but since it fell within my hospitality major, I was awarded two college credits for all my genuflecting. And once I realized that I should treat my mother like one of the club members, we began to get along swimmingly.

My job at Onwentsia didn't leave me much time for Ethan or my friends however, so he'd pick me up after work most nights, and we'd go to the beach or hang out at his house for a few hours. The week before I was due to go back to school, he took me out for dinner and pinned me down for a heart-to-heart.

"Syd," he started over a potato skins appetizer at Timbers restaurant. "I was thinking maybe we should have a talk, about us."

I placed my menu on the table and looked him in the eyes. "What about us?"

"About our relationship," he said. "You're going into your senior year, and I'm moving to Boston. I mean, don't you think we should talk about where we stand and how we plan on staying together or seeing each other?" He studied my face, "Do you ever give any thought to our future?"

I knew my answer should have been "of course I do, all the time," but I couldn't honestly say that to him. "Yes, I've given it some thought," I assured him. "But we've been apart for the past few years and made it work, so I really didn't think this was going to be much different."

"Well, it is different, Syd. I'm done with school, I'm moving out of state to a job where I don't get summers off." He made a flippant gesture with his hand. "I'll be lucky to come home for the weekend over Christmas." His tone was authoritative and made me feel very naive. "I love you, Sydney, and I want us to be faithful to each other, and I know it will be hard, but I need to know that you are committed to this relationship."

I wondered if he threw the word "faithful" in as some sort of a test. Ethan and I had done our best over the years to remain true to one another, but we'd both gone to college dances with other people, hung out with members of the opposite sex, and both of us were very social beings. He had lots of female friends, and I had lots of male friends, some of whom I was extremely close with. It was college for God's sake, and we gave each other the freedom to enjoy it without feeling chained down to a long-distance relationship. Apparently once he graduated, he wanted that to change.

I took a deep breath. "I love you, too, but I'm not ready to give up my social life during my senior year."

"I'm not asking you to tear apart your busy calendar," he said sarcastically. "I'm just asking that we make more of a commitment to each other, that's all."

"I don't know…" I looked away. "I'm not ready to make that promise, and quite honestly, I'm not even sure what it entails. And I think things are fine the way they are. You're making me feel very pressured."

He shifted uncomfortably in his chair. "Sydney, I'm not trying to pressure you. I'm trying to tell you how much I love you, and that I want to focus my attention on us and our relationship as best I can…and for you and I to be more serious about what we have."

His eyes were wide and his right hand was in a fist on the table. Ethan had changed; he was much more settled with himself and his playful spirit had all but vanished. He sat tall in his chair, like one of those adults who spewed their infinite wisdom about how quickly time flies, and how we shouldn't take things for granted. I still loved him very much, but I was not ready to do what he was asking.

"Well, maybe you'll feel differently once you move to Boston, and you won't want to be tied down to some girl back home."

His expression turned to frustration. "Why are you trying to turn this around on me?"

"I don't know," I said quietly and fumbled with my fork. "It's just that, I'm not feeling what you're feeling right now. I love you, but I don't want to have to work at taking this relationship to the next level. I just want to have fun this year and not worry about things between us."

He nodded, more in defeat than in agreement.

"I'm sorry, Ethan. I didn't bring this up; you did. We have a great relationship, and we've made it work, so why go there?"

He waited a moment before answering. "Because I think I want more than you do."

I folded my hands in my lap. "I don't know what you mean by that. I just want to get through senior year and find a job and make a life for myself."

"With me or without me?" he asked.

"With you," I snapped.

He looked hard at my face, trying to determine whether or not I believed what I was saying. When I glanced back at his questioning expression, I felt like getting up from that table and walking away, but I didn't. I'd made sacrifices for him over the years and he knew it. I'd never let myself get emotionally involved with anyone else because I cared about Ethan and his feelings…and our relationship. But I was going to be a senior in college, and I had little patience for him making me feel guilty about enjoying it.

Given our distance and growth as human beings over the years, we'd naturally drifted apart, but we still had made a conscious effort to hold on to what we had, as much as we could. I never loved anyone like I loved Ethan, and in the back of my mind I knew one day we'd be together forever. I assumed he felt the same way.

Saying good-bye to him that summer before my final year of college was bittersweet. It was sad to see his car packed up, not knowing when we'd be together again, yet I was really looking forward to getting back to school and seeing Jenna and all my friends. When Ethan pulled out of my driveway, on his way to Boston, he did his best to hide the tears in his eyes. But I saw them.

CHAPTER TWELVE

FLUSHING!"
Jenna and I lived in the Kappa Kappa Gamma sorority house for our sophomore and junior years and shared three bathrooms with eighty other girls. Anytime you were in one of the five toilet stalls, and someone else was in one of the four shower stalls, you had to announce that you were flushing the toilet so they could prepare themselves for the surge of intensely hot water that would hit them as a result. That was only one of the many reasons we decided to get our own apartments by the time we were seniors. Sharing six telephones with eighty girls was another.

She found a place near the student union, and mine was just a block off campus. I never, not for one minute, feared living alone, and welcomed the peace and solitude after two years in the sorority. My dad had taken me to Kmart before I left home that August, and we filled my car with new bedding, new towels, cleaning supplies, throw pillows, nonperishable foods, a tool set, lightbulbs, a shower curtain, an answering machine, an alarm clock, and a twenty-piece kit that had glassware, stemware, and plate service for four. That day at Kmart was one of the most fun afternoons with my dad that I've ever had. My mother had attempted to take me, but the trip turned into a screaming match over buying an extra garbage can. She insisted that one in the kitchen would suffice, and I insisted that there be one in the bathroom as well. I left with nothing more than a dustpan, and begged my father to take me without her.

My campus apartment was very generic. Not dilapidated or icky, just really, really generic, almost asylum-like. It was a furnished one bedroom, one bathroom, with a living area that had a kitchenette against one wall, a couch against the other, and a faux-wood coffee table in front of it. Each of the three rooms was perfectly square in shape and had white walls the color of a T-shirt that had been washed too many times. The landlord had cleaned the beige carpeting prior to my moving in, but that was it. I was allowed to hang things on the walls but forbidden to paint. And the metallic vertical blinds would have made any hospice proud. The string that was once used for opening and closing the blinds was so frayed that some student before me had threaded a shoelace through instead. But despite the lack of personality, it was mine alone, and I was thrilled to display my new coordinating toothbrush holder, soap dish, and water glass trio.

The first night back at school, two days before classes began, Jenna threw a party at her apartment for some of our best friends: Amy Bornheimer, Alexa Giannoules, Andrea Ingrilli, and three of our closest guy friends, Kevin Hansen, his roommate Rocco D'Ancona, and their fraternity brother Tim Miller. The eight of us had become family over the years, and I couldn't imagine not having them in my postcollege life. I couldn't imagine much of anything in my post-college life for that matter. But our close-knit group of friends had been through so much together: road trips, tailgating, spring break in Cancun, sorority dances, all-nighters during finals, family crises, and parents' weekends with more family crises. Especially when my mother would visit. One time all my close friends and their parents reserved the back room at the nicest restaurant near campus.

There was a huge group of us—probably thirty people including some random siblings, parents, and friends—and the first thing my mother did was ask for separate checks.

I nudged my father and whispered in his ear. "Everyone just planned on splitting up the bill when we're done."

He turned to my mother. "That's not necessary," he said to her. "We'll just divide it up at the end."

The waiter looked at my mother for her blessing. He didn't get it.

"I'd rather have our own check. I'm not very hungry, and you're not drinking, so I'd prefer not to split up a large bill."

At this point, conversations around the table came to a standstill, and all eyes were on my parents and the waiter as they attempted to work things out. My body temperature reached boiling, and Jenna squeezed my knee to help me relax.

My father looked at the waiter. "One check for the table will be fine."

Mom had a puss on her face for the rest of the evening and didn't say a word to anyone. She also ate nothing but breadsticks.

Rocco and Kevin were roommates and fraternity brothers, and the two people whom Jenna and I had known the longest. We met them our second week of freshman year as they were trying to get into an off-campus party with no luck. Just as we walked up, they were trudging away, defeated. Jenna took pity on them and we all went back to our dorm, listened to music, ate microwave pizza, and got acquainted. Rocco grew up in New York and came from a large Jewish-Italian family, which was easy to determine once he opened his mouth and spoke. He was physically strong, but a teddy bear at heart—always telling everyone he loved them—and was crazy close with his "Ma." He'd talk to her for hours on the phone and would call her for advice whenever one of us was ill. Almost every remedy she gave him included ginger ale.

He was attractive in a dark European way but had the manners of a mama's boy. Once I fell asleep studying with him late at night, and woke next to him shaving with an electric razor as his tiny hair fragments fell into the cracks of my calculator. He had no shame, and I loved him like a brother. Kevin was yin to his yang. He was from Los Angeles, had more of a handsome surfer appeal, and preferred a much more low-key existence. While Rocco would be at the head of a conga line, Kevin and his six-foot-five frame would be glued to a chair somewhere, with his long legs outstretched, always enjoying his surroundings from the sidelines. But where Rocco loved everybody, Kevin had only a few close-knit friends that he was fiercely loyal to—and fiercely protective of. Friends such as Jenna and me. Anytime we needed anything—a ride, a meal, a plumber, a shoulder to cry on—he would take care of it. He was simply one of those people who would drop absolutely everything to help a friend, and over the years I'd gone out of my way to always make sure he was happy because he deserved it.

"A toast: to senior year, fabulous friends, and lots of beer!" Jenna christened the evening that first night back.

"Hear, hear!" I shouted.

We spent the next eight months doing much of the same thing.

By springtime, schoolwork kicked into survival mode. We were all doing whatever it took to pass and graduate on time, without giving up an ounce of our social life. Most of my classes were scheduled in the morning, from eight thirty to twelve thirty, so by one o'clock I was free. On the days I felt disciplined, I would head straight to the student lounge, do my homework, and meet up with my friends for dinner. Kevin and Rocco were great cooks and hosted Elvis Hour two nights a week at their place. Guests were in charge of bringing alcohol, appetizers, or desserts, and they would serve up everything from pan-seared steaks to classic spaghetti carbonara to enchiladas, along with endless tunes from the King of Rock and Roll. The pasta dishes were always my favorite, and one night when only Jenna and I were able to make it, Rocco broke out a bottle of black-truffle oil that his mom sent him and drizzled it all over the noodles. I have never been the same.

"Rocco," I swooned.

"Yes."

"I'm going to need a bottle of that truffle oil."

Jenna looked at the tiny two-ounce bottle on the table in front of us. "You can buy this anywhere," she said.

Rocco looked at her, offended. "No, Jen, you can't."

"I've seen it before," she said.

He lifted the bottle and held it obnoxiously close to her face. "You ain't seen nothing but truffle-infused olive oil *before*, a commoner's substitute. This is all truffle, baby."

She pushed his arm away.

"Don't drop the bottle!" I gasped.

"Don't you worry, Syd," he said as he set it back down, "I'll have Ma send you one." He leaned back in his chair and unbuttoned his jeans. "So, which one of you broads wants to be my date to the Beta formal?" He directed his question to the both of us, but we all knew he wanted Jenna as his date. Rocco had a not-so-subtle crush on her over the years, but she'd made it perfectly clear to him that he was nothing more than a friend. He accepted her refusal to date him, but that didn't stop his liquid nerves from trying time and time again to make out with her.

The Beta house was having their end-of-the-year dance at a hotel in Indianapolis. Jenna and I assumed that one of the guys would ask us to go, since they had no legitimate dates to invite.

"Well, with that chivalrous invitation, how could I say no?" Jenna said in acceptance. "I get shotgun on the drive down."

Kevin looked at me and winked. "Guess that leaves you and me, sister."

"I would love to," I said. "But what about Alexa? You know she's going to blow a gasket if she doesn't get asked by someone."

Rocco belched. "I talked with Tim's housemate Barney. He said he'd take Alexa and double-up with Tim and Andrea," he said as Kevin began to clear the table to "Blue Suede Shoes."

"Great," Jenna clapped. "We have to make sure we get rooms on the same floor, and maybe we can drive down early and spend the day at the indoor pool."

"Can I book a massage for you as well?" Rocco asked sarcastically.

"If you want to make up for the pathetic invite, you can," she told him.

He leaned back, balancing his chair on only two of its four legs. "The dance is in two weeks. If you want to change your mind and catch *Casablanca* at the student union instead, let me know and I'll go stag."

"You're a shit." She slapped him.

Jenna and I did the dishes, and then set up the make-your-own-sundae bar we brought. After we were through, the four of us went to Harry's bar to meet up with the rest of our friends who skipped dinner on account of studies but always made time for Harry's. Three Long Island iced teas later, I was back in my bed, belly full and head spinning. There were three messages from Ethan on my answering machine.

CHAPTER THIRTEEN
Grace

I want to speak with my father tomorrow," I repeated. "Do you know how to reach him?"

Mom glanced at the clock on my nightstand. "I'm not so sure that's a good idea."

"Why not?"

She forcefully gathered some of my clothes off the floor and shoved them in the laundry hamper. "It's just not that easy," she snapped at me, which was not something she did very often. It was clear I'd hit a nerve, but at that age, I struggled to appreciate her sensitivity to the subject.

"Good night, Grace. We can talk more about this later, okay, honey?" she said, regaining her composure.

"Okay, Mom."

She closed the door behind her, and I grew more anxious to understand why she reacted the way she did. My confidence slid off the bed that night as I grew more and more insecure about who I was. My whole world seemed like one huge embarrassment, and all I could picture were people pointing and whispering. Especially people in my own family who'd been privy to my source of shame for years.

"Mom." I approached her in the kitchen the next morning as she was wiping Patch's hands clean.

"Morning, honey," she said to me, and then kneeled in front of Patch. "Go get your book bag and your gym shoes, okay?" she told him.

He scurried away and she began to rinse his cereal bowl. I could feel her wishing me away.

"Mom, I really want to call my dad."

She dropped the bowl in the sink and it sounded like it broke, but didn't. She placed her hands on the edge of the sink. "He's not your dad."

"Why are you getting so mad?" I asked sincerely.

"Because it's very complicated, and this man has never been in your life, and you cannot just call him up out of the blue."

I felt a surge of adolescent defiance when I realized that I wasn't going to get what I wanted. "Well, it wouldn't be out of the blue if you'd told me the truth!"

She gestured to the kitchen island for me to have a seat. "I know this is hard for you, and I knew that once this day came, it would be the hardest thing we would have to face as a family," she said softly.

I could tell that she didn't want this to turn into a fight. She hated arguments and did not respond well to me yelling at her.

Then it hit me. Maybe he didn't even know I existed. I mean, she'd already kept this information from me, the one person she apparently loved more than anything, so maybe my father was also in the dark.

I was breathing heavily, and my face was scrunched in anger, but I lowered my voice. "Does he even know about me?"

She tilted her head toward the ceiling and left it there as she answered. "Yes, Grace, he does know about you." A slow trickle of air escaped her nostrils and she turned to face me. "Which is precisely why this is going to be so difficult for you...and me."

"Why for you?"

"Because it kills me to see you struggling with this, and quite honestly, I have no idea whether he'll be willing to talk to you or not."

Her words slapped me across the face and left a stinging burn.

"What do you mean? I'm his daughter; why wouldn't he want to talk to me?" I asked, thinking she was delusional and selfish. How could she have said that to me?

Patch walked back in the kitchen and handed her his gym shoes. She stood up, placed him on the island, and began to lace him up.

I pushed my stool away from the granite countertop and it screeched loudly against the wood floor. "I want to call him, and he wants to talk to me!" I screamed at her like a frustrated basketball coach, and both she and Patch jumped out of their skins. I grabbed my backpack and headed to the bus stop in tears.

As I approached the corner where two of my neighbors were waiting for the bus, I decided to walk to school instead. The fact that I was going to miss the first bell and be late for classes had literally no effect on me whatsoever. And heck, since I was going to be late, why not skip school altogether?

After about an hour and a half, my mom found me at the park. Her eyes were puffy and red, and she approached me as if she were trying to catch a stray cat.

"You had me worried sick, honey."

I let my feet dangle in the sand beneath my swing.

"Grace, I take full responsibility for everything, okay? I'm not angry with you, and it's completely my fault that you are sitting here." She came closer and crouched down in front of me. "I was completely naive and in denial about the effect all of this would have on you, and if you will give me another chance, I would like to sit you down and explain everything." She reached for my hand and I let her take it. "Please give me the chance to make this right."

I nodded.

CHAPTER FOURTEEN
Sydney

I could hear Ethan leaving a message as I stepped out of the shower. I grabbed my robe and ran into the kitchen.

"Hello," I said breathlessly, and hit the stop button on the answering machine.

"Hey, you, I was just leaving a message."

"Sorry about that. I was in the shower and heard you. How are you?"

Ethan had been getting tired of not being able to reach me. I wasn't home very often during that last semester, and he was always complaining that every time he called he had to talk to the machine.

"I'm good. What are you up to?" he asked.

I was about twenty minutes away from being picked up by Kevin for the Beta formal in Indy, but I hadn't told Ethan about any of it. He knew I spent a lot of time with Kevin, Rocco, and my other guy friends, but an out-of-town overnighter might have pushed him over the edge of his tolerance wall.

"Just getting ready to go out." Enough said. "How's work?"

"It's work."

"Have you finished training your intern?" I asked. Ethan was given an intern for the spring, and he had been bringing him up to speed.

"Yeah, he was here every afternoon for two weeks, and then he starts full time in June. It'll be nice having someone to boss around.

Anyway, *Caddyshack* is on WGN tonight. Maybe we can watch it together on the phone? We might even get through the whole thing."

I glanced at the clock; Kevin was due to be at my apartment in ten minutes. "You're going to be annoyed with me, but Jenna is going to be here any minute, and I'm dripping wet."

"Sounds hot."

"Pretty chilly actually," I said.

He let out a sigh of frustration. If he only knew…"All right, Syd, have fun, and be careful. I love you."

"Love you, too."

"Call me later, okay?"

"Okay," I said, and my knees buckled from the guilt. I lied to Ethan and I wouldn't call him later. Kevin and I were just friends, but Ethan would never tolerate me spending the night with him in a hotel room, and I didn't have the energy to argue about it. This was one of my last collegiate hurrahs, and I simply had no desire to create unnecessary drama. I knew I would have to spend Sunday afternoon on the phone with Ethan backpedaling and apologizing.

We said our good-byes, then I hung up the phone and shook my head. I was annoyed, but I wasn't going to let Ethan bring me down this weekend. He was always making me feel bad about enjoying myself. Not this time. I removed the charcoal pearl necklace I'd just put on, grabbed my bag, and headed for the door.

"I thought you called shotgun," I said to Jenna as I peeked inside Kevin's car. She was already in the backseat with Rocco when they picked me up for the dance.

"My date is riding back here with me." Rocco answered for her and threw his arm around the back of her neck.

Jenna grimaced and shook it off her shoulders.

The drive to Indianapolis was about an hour, during which we stopped at McDonald's for Jenna and me, Hardee's for Rocco, Steak 'n Shake for Kevin, and Dairy Queen for the group. The lingering scent of fried grease was barely tolerable.

After arriving at the hotel and checking in, Jenna and I went straight to our rooms while the guys went straight to the bar.

When we reached the fourth floor, our rooms were at opposite ends of the hall, so we parted and agreed to meet back at the elevators in fifteen minutes. I put my tote bag on the bed and hung my dress in the closet in hopes of removing the wrinkles inflicted from Kevin's trunk. I fished my LeSportsac makeup case out of my backpack, reapplied some eyeliner, and brushed the Quarter Pounder off my tongue in less than five minutes. Then I thought of Ethan. Staring at the two queen-size beds meant for Kevin and me made me think of Ethan. I tugged on the roots of my hair. All I wanted was guilt-free fun, but instead I felt like a naughty toddler. I would get mad at Ethan for making me feel bad, and then I would feel like a complete shithead for blaming him.

I left the room and waited for Jenna in the hallway.

"Sorry, my curling iron took forever to warm up," she said, walking briskly toward me and zipping her purse.

"I'm feeling bad about Ethan."

She gave me a knowing eye roll. "Why, what'd he say?"

"Nothing. He called me this morning, but he doesn't know where I am."

"So no worries then, my pretty," she said and repeatedly tapped the elevator button.

"How does he always seem to know when I'm out doing something I shouldn't be doing?" I asked.

"What shouldn't you be doing, Syd?" She dabbed her lower lip, then tucked her lip gloss into her front pocket. "He's miles away, and what does he expect?"

"He doesn't expect anything...except that maybe I'm not road-tripping with frat boys all over Indiana."

Jenna waved me off like it was no big deal. Which I guess it wasn't to me either, since I never bothered to mention it to Ethan or ask his opinion...or permission. But she was right. Why should I feel guilty about being out with someone and enjoying myself? How dare he make me feel like I was going behind his back and misbehaving? I was not going to let Ethan ruin my evening.

We met up with our dates at the bar, where a huge crowd of people who were attending the dance had congregated. Jenna took off looking for Rocco, and I sat down on a stool Kevin had saved for me.

When it came right down to it, Kevin and I were mostly drinking buddies, but we actually had a pretty good time together even when we were sober. I discovered how handy he was one day at my apartment while we were studying for a Spanish exam, when two of my bookshelves abruptly fell off the wall behind my couch. He grabbed a toolbox from his trunk and had them back up in less than ten minutes. And the time my refrigerator was making a buzzing sound for two days, he pulled the whole thing away from its nook, smacked it around a little, and silence was restored. He grew up in Los Angeles and came from money, but never flaunted it. He drove a Honda Accord and shared an apartment with Rocco, even though his parents had offered to rent him one of the brand-new condos near the student union. His family never came to visit, but they were always sending him airline tickets to meet them in various parts of the world.

"Hey, short stuff," he said as I sat down. "What's your poison?"

· "I'll have what you're having."

"Two more Bud Lights, and two shots of Jäger," he shouted to the bartender.

"Jäger already!" I gasped. "I don't even have my dress on yet."

Kevin took a swig of his beer. "You can hold your own, Syd. I have faith in you."

Soon after that, things began to get interesting, and mildly confusing.

There were more drinks and more shots.

There was Jenna and me holding hands and dashing upstairs to throw our dresses on.

There was dancing and a questionable amount of disco music.

There was Jenna screaming obscenities at Scott Makin, a guy who broke her heart junior year.

Then there was Scott Makin screaming obscenities at Jenna.

Then Rocco yelling at Jenna.

Then Kevin and me on the floor of the ladies' room consoling Jenna with more shots.

Then Kevin pressing me up against the ladies' room wall and kissing my neck while Jenna went to pee.

Then there was me enjoying Kevin kissing my neck.

More dancing, little food, Kevin and me making out in all corners of the ballroom, and still more shots.

I woke up at three o'clock in the morning lying naked next to Kevin in one of our two hotel beds. My head was on fire. It was burning with such intense heat that I winced with pain when I tried to open my eyes. After a few minutes, queasiness coursed through my abdomen leaving a moist, cold sweat in its wake. I sat up slowly, praying I would be able to find the toilet without my vision, but I felt my throat retract and before I knew it, I'd filled the garbage can that Kevin had the foresight to place on the floor next to the bed.

My skin was pulsating and my body gently shook as I lowered it back onto the mattress. I couldn't even shift my arm to reach for the covers. Kevin was sound asleep.

My dress lay two inches from the soiled garbage can, looking much more like crumpled newspaper than anything wearable.

Caddyshack was playing on the TV.

Eight weeks later…

CHAPTER FIFTEEN

I woke up on the floor of my apartment in a fetal position, and then ran to the bathroom. I'm not sure if the puking was a result of the pregnancy, the beers, or the realization that I was carrying Kevin's child. Once I peeled myself away from the arctic base of the toilet bowl, the first thing I did was throw the white test stick in the trash along with the First Response box, the receipt, and the Walmart bag. Then I returned Jenna's call from the night before. It was just about eleven o'clock in the morning.

"What's up, Syd?"

"Just about to hit the español again. Sorry, I had my phone off the hook last night so I could study." My voice was fatigued.

"No worries. I called to see if you wanted to come over and watch *Days* with me; the big wedding is next week."

Jenna and I, like most of our sorority sisters, were addicted to *Days of Our Lives* and had been wildly anticipating the nuptials between Jack and Jennifer.

"You know something's bound to go wrong," she added.

"I think Andrea is going to record it so we can all get together and watch it at night," I told her.

"Well, it starts in ten minutes. Can you get your fat butt over here or not?" she asked.

As soon as she said fat, I began to think about my condition. I knew she was joking around, but had I already begun to gain weight? Had my physique changed noticeably since the Beta formal eight weeks ago?

"Hello?" she snapped when I didn't answer immediately.

"Sorry, I can't be there by eleven."

She made a disappointed *tsk* sound. "So, what's the plan for later? Are we going to Joe's for fifty-cent shots?"

"Sure. I have a couple hours left of Spanish though, then I have to rewrite two pages of my social sciences paper, and then I'm good."

Jenna let out a huge yawn. "Oh my, I better have a Diet Coke transfusion before we hit it later. I'll come get you around nine o'clock."

"What about dinner?" I asked.

"It's dollar-baskets of ranch cheese fries, too, so don't you worry."

"Much better. See you at nine." I said nothing to her about my news and went into full-on sweep-it-under-the-rug mode.

My books were exactly as I'd left them the night before, yet everything had changed. I struggled to remember what exactly triggered the whole turn of events the previous evening. How, while sitting amid my Spanish textbooks on the floor of my apartment, did it occur to me that I hadn't had my period? One minute I'm in the throes of studying for finals, and the next minute I'm the March Hare on a covert mission in search of a pregnancy test. But, as shocking as the results were, I really had more important things on my plate right then. Finals were the following week, and there was no need to add "college flunkie" *and* "knocked-up co-ed" to my list of attributes.

Jenna arrived just before nine o'clock and greeted me with a sub sandwich from Jimmy John's and a bag of chips. "Thought we might need a little pick-me-up," she said.

I grinned. "Doritos. My fave."

"Only the best for you." She tossed the food on my kitchen table.

Jenna was decked out in black satin shorts and a white tank top with an unbuttoned black vest over it. She also had on three-inch, black strappy sandals, and an oversize black-patent tote bag.

"Who are you hoping to run into?" I asked.

"No one special. Just want to go out with a bang on one of our last nights around here."

"Did you hear back from Scott Makin?"

"Maybe." She smiled. Scott had called her after she stalked and berated him in Indianapolis at the Beta formal, and he was apparently attracted to psychotic behavior because he asked her out again.

"Okay, shorty shorts." I grabbed a handful of Doritos and cracked open a Diet Coke. "Excuse me while I do my best to find an outfit that won't divert attention from yours. Shouldn't be too hard."

I went to my closet and decided on a green-and-white striped cotton sundress. With my hair in a ponytail, Jenna and I would make a nice good girl/bad girl combo. I slipped on a pair of laceless white Keds and went to the bathroom to grab a rubber band for my hair. When I walked in, Jenna was standing at the sink holding the First Response box.

"What is this?" Her face was pale.

"Why are you going through my garbage?"

"Answer my question first," she responded quickly. "Syd, are you pregnant?"

She was staring at me in disbelief, waiting for an answer, and I felt like I was going to be sick. "I think I am," I admitted.

"You think you are? What did the test say?"

"It said that I am."

She put the box down on the sink and sat on the edge of the tub. "When did you find out?"

There was a short pause. "Yesterday."

"Oh my God, why didn't you tell me?" She threw her arms up. "When were you going to say something?"

"I don't know." I grabbed the box and tossed it back in the garbage.

"Is it Ethan's?" she asked skeptically, but she knew I hadn't been with him for months.

"It's Kevin's."

She ran her hands through her long dark hair, and then placed them over her mouth. "Oh my God," she said slowly.

"Tell me about it."

"Sydney, come here." She stood up, grabbed my arm, and led me out of the bathroom and onto the couch. "Are you okay? Why are you acting so calm about this? How could you not have told me?"

All I really wanted to do was get to Joe's, start drinking, and get my mind on anything else but the image of those stupid pink lines staring back at me from that shoddy pregnancy test. "I don't know, Jen. I'm stressed out about finals, and I just don't feel like obsessing about it."

"You're in major denial." She was much more panicked than I was. "I will go with you to Planned Parenthood first thing in the morning, and we'll see what you need to do, okay?"

"Fine," I said, hoping she would just shut up about it and move on.

"When did you miss your period?"

"I don't know. It's been a few weeks."

She shook her head. "Like how many?"

"Like seven or eight, I think."

"Eight weeks!" She was now shouting. "You realize you don't have much time…"

"Jenna, please stop!" I interrupted her panic attack. "I don't want to talk about it right now. I don't even want to think about it. So could we please get on with our night as planned?"

She smiled at me like I was pathetic and clueless. I knew she was trying to help and that I could count on her for anything, but all I wanted at that moment was to be free of concern.

"I'm not going to debate the issue, Syd, but are you sure? This is major."

"I'm sure."

She rolled her eyes, got off the couch, and grabbed her bag. "Okay then, let's hit it."

"Thank you."

"Just promise me that when you're ready, you will come to me, and you won't try to handle this on your own," she demanded.

"I promise."

We arrived at Joe's, which was predictably overcrowded due to kids finishing finals and wrapping up the school year. Jenna spotted two girls from her film studies class, and they let us share their booth.

"Why don't I get us some drinks?" I offered before sitting down.

"Great, whatever shots you want, and I'll have a Bud Light, too," she said.

"Anyone else?" I asked the table.

"We're good," Jenna's classmate said without looking up.

I squeezed my way to the bar, through rock concert–like conditions, and waved down my buddy Jeff who'd bartended there for years and had been through almost six fake IDs with me. He knew just about every senior and junior by full name, and if you were underage, all he cared was that your ID card looked remotely like you, or even slightly resembled someone who could pass for a relative of yours. If you met those criteria, he was happy to take your money and serve you the drink of your choice.

"Jeff!" I yelled and waved.

He pointed at me, indicating I was on his radar. Then I watched as he filled a circular bar tray with little plastic shot cups, then took a pitcher of pink medicinal looking liquid and filled each cup, before carefully handing the tray to a waitress.

"Hey, Syd," he said and wiped his hands on a towel tucked into his jeans. "Whadaya need?"

"Two Bud Lights and two tequila shots," I said loudly.

"Shots are on me."

"Thanks, Jeff. How come they're always on you when it's fifty-cent shot night?"

"Don't be a smart-ass or I'll make you drink the pink stuff."

As I waited patiently for our drinks, I heard a familiar voice from behind me. "Is this one giving you trouble, Jeffrey, my good man?"

I turned around just as Kevin finished his sentence and lifted me off my feet. "What's up, sugar?"

"Hey, Kev," I said and wriggled free.

"I'll have what she's having," he shouted to Jeff, then looked back at me. "You here with Jenna?"

"Yeah, why?"

"Rocco's looking for her," he said with a smile.

Jeff handed me my drinks, and I turned to walk away.

"Where are you ladies sitting?" Kevin asked.

"We're, uh, over there under the television with some people from Jenna's film group. I mean film class," I muttered.

"Okay, we'll be over in a minute."

"Great," I said and headed back to our table.

I squeezed a little more aggressively back through the crowd and made my way over to our table. "Kevin and Rocco are here," I said to Jenna—a statement that on any other day would've been entirely uneventful, borderline dull, even. But things had drastically changed within the course of twenty-four hours, and from then on, Kevin's name would forever be associated with a mass of nervous tension.

"Where are they? Do you want to go?" she asked, grabbing her beer and craning her neck over the wood partition.

"No, I don't want to go. I'm fine. It's a little awkward, but only for me, so don't worry about it," I told her. "And obviously, don't say a word about anything!"

"I need my shot. I don't know how you're handling yourself like this, but I'm freaking out," she whispered and downed her tequila shot.

I lifted mine off the table, but the smell made me nauseous, so I just drank my beer instead.

"They're coming over. Rock just waved at me."

"It's fine," I said.

"Hey, guys!" Jenna stood and hugged them, then introduced her film friends.

After about an hour or so, her friends cleared out, and Rocco and Kevin joined us in the booth for jalapeño poppers and cheese fries with ranch dressing. The four of us sat and talked and laughed and teased each other like we had for years, except that every time I looked at Kevin, all I could see were those two pink lines. Seeing him sitting across from me in that crowded booth, so clueless and naive, made me claustrophobic. I glanced over at Jenna, and she was hysterical over some story that Kevin was telling us about a guy named Mitch in their fraternity house who lit his farts with a match.

"I'm going to head out." I stood abruptly and threw my purse strap across my chest.

Jenna composed herself. "You okay?"

"Yeah, it's just that I should be studying, and this has been a long enough break."

"Come on, Syd. I'll drive you back," Kevin offered.

"That's all right. Seriously, I'm fine."

"You sure?" he looked at me like he was genuinely concerned, which he always was.

Kevin and I had been friends for a long time, and he always did right by me. Taking me to dances, driving me home when I was too drunk to find my car, stealing bags of cereal from his fraternity house for me, and hanging out for nearly four years. We were close, and he was one of the people whom I'd met in college that I knew would always be a part of my life. Even more so than high school, college was a place where I developed lifelong friends, like Kendra had said I would. People that knew the real me, and people that I knew would support me in any given situation, regardless of how many years passed between conversations or visits. These were friends who'd spent the critical developmental years of young adulthood with me, and we'd cherish each other forever. Friends who'd shared proud times and unmentionable times together and would never judge each other for anything. Take Mitch from the Beta house, for example. He might be the head of a Fortune 500 company one day, but he'd never live down the fact that he sat in a room with Kevin and Rocco and lit his farts for a crowd of onlookers. And for that, they'll never take him seriously, no matter how much he accomplishes.

"I'm sure. Thanks, Kev," I said and squeezed past Jenna to get out of the booth.

"Why don't I join you?" she asked and stood.

"Totally your call. I seriously have to get to bed at a decent hour, so don't let me drag you down." I glanced at the clock behind the bar, and it was just after midnight.

"I've had my share. Let's hit it," she said and kissed the boys good-bye.

We walked the seven blocks to my apartment building, and all Jenna wanted to talk about was my maternal situation.

"How are you?"

"I'm fine."

"I think you're going through some crazy denial, state-of-shock thing," she diagnosed. "In fact, I'm sure of it."

"You may be right." I was in no mood to argue.

"Was it weird seeing Kevin?"

"It was," I answered honestly. "I don't know what the hell I'm doing. I really have to admit…I just don't want to think about it. I know that sounds so stupid, but the second I saw those two pink lines, it was like my brain started desperately searching for something else to focus on."

"Oh, honey."

"I mean, how am I supposed to get through finals?" We stopped to let a car pass, and then crossed the street to the front of my building.

"I don't know, but I think we should go to the student hospital first thing in the morning and you should get a proper blood test, or whatever," she suggested. "I know Amanda Rosen has been there like sixteen times."

"You're right," I nodded. "Will you come with me?"

"Wouldn't miss it. I'll pick you up at ten o'clock with a sausage biscuit and a supersize Diet Coke."

Jenna was on time, bearing greasy food and artificially sweetened soda, and it was exactly what the doctor ordered. We waltzed into the student hospital just after ten thirty, and were asked to take a seat. We often joked about the slutty girls who went there for the free pregnancy tests, which made me wonder if every single person within ten feet of the building knew exactly why I was there. I myself knew of almost no other reason to go to the student hospital. It wasn't long before a nurse called me into the room, took my blood, and asked me to sit back in the waiting area again.

"How'd it go?" Jenna asked.

"It went pretty quickly."

"How long does it take to find out?"

"Few minutes, I guess," I said, and we waited, but I knew I was pregnant. I went to the student hospital because it truly did seem like the right thing to do, but my instinct didn't need the blood test. I knew.

Sure enough, about fifteen minutes later the nurse called me back in and told me what I'd expected her to say. She then proceeded to hand me a pamphlet from Planned Parenthood and asked if I had any questions. I did not. None she could answer anyway.

Jenna took me back to my apartment and dropped me off because she had a calculus study group at noon.

"Are you going to be all right?" she asked before I got out of her car.

"Yeah."

"I'll be over as soon as I'm done, okay?"

"Thanks, Jen."

"Don't worry, Syd. We'll take care of this together."

I gave her a nod and watched her drive off.

Although I knew what the nurse was going to tell me, there had still been a tiny glimmer of hope. I thought there might be the teeniest chance that the technologically embarrassing First Response stick could've been wrong. I mean, pee on a stick! Come on, seriously?! But a blood test would tell me for sure, and that nurse very well could've entered the room, closed the door behind her, and said, "It's negative!"

But she didn't, and so I was left to cry it out on the curb where Jenna left me.

CHAPTER SIXTEEN

My denial hit full swing after my trip to the student hospital, and I spent the next few days focusing on finals and getting drunk with my senior class. Self-pity and morning sickness were going to have to get in line.

Once my last exam was complete, I figured it was time to face the music and take control of my affairs, so I decided to call my sister. She was working at an advertising agency in Chicago and just recently moved into her own condo. I couldn't quite bring myself to call Taylor, and the last person on earth I could imagine confiding in was my mother. But I needed to talk with someone about it other than Jenna because I desperately needed to dissect the Ethan angle.

Kendra picked up on the first ring. "What's up, doll?"

"Do you have a sec?"

"Of course. Are you okay?"

As soon as she asked me that I started to shake and cry like a little girl who'd just dropped her Popsicle in the sand.

"Sydney, what's the matter?"

I answered her, my voice cracking. "I'm pregnant."

She gasped. "Oh my God," she whispered. "Oh, Syd, shhhh, it's okay, it's going to be okay. Did you tell Ethan?"

I paused and shuddered. "It's not his."

She wasn't as quick to reassure me. "Whose is it?"

"It's this guy named Kevin. He's just a friend, and we went to a dance together…about eight weeks ago."

Kendra was a very rational, organized person. "Listen to me. Try and relax, and just don't get upset, okay? No one died, no one has cancer, and we will handle this." She took a breath. "I can't leave today, but I will come see you tomorrow and we'll figure this out."

"Okay, thanks."

"Everything will be okay, Syd. Just take it easy."

"I will."

As promised, Kendra drove down to West Lafayette and made it there by noon the next day. We met for lunch at a Hardee's, and I hugged her for two whole minutes before we sat down at a table in the back of the restaurant.

"I located the Planned Parenthood on campus, and made an appointment for us at one thirty."

Everyone was dying to get me into Planned Parenthood. "What are they going to say?" I asked and emptied a sugar packet into my iced tea.

"They're going to try and determine exactly how far along you are, and let you know your options. No one has to find out about this, and I will be there for you one hundred percent." She looked at me questioningly. "I assume you want to have an abortion?"

I wasn't sure what I wanted, but I knew that's what both she and Jenna assumed I was going to do. And quite honestly, if it were me sitting across the table from a pregnant Kendra, I'm sure I would assume the same thing about her. But much to my own surprise, I was leaning toward keeping the baby.

Kendra read my mind. "You're not seriously considering having a baby, are you?" Her expression was severe.

"I really don't know yet," I said and stirred the ice cubes in my drink.

She sat back in her chair and folded her arms across her chest. "Syd, do you have any idea what you're saying? Any idea how this will change your life? You're starting your job in a few months."

I felt myself getting emotional again, damn hormones. "Please don't look at me like that. I have been thinking about this every waking hour, and I always go back to the same conclusion. I think I want to have this baby."

She was delicately shaking her head and trying to get me to maintain eye contact with her. "I just don't think you can make a decision like that with so little knowledge of what is required of you. How will you support it? How will you pay for day care? When will you tell your new employer? The list goes on and on!"

"I know, I know, but I don't want an abortion. I'm scared of having an abortion, and for some strange reason, I'm not scared to have this baby. And you really shouldn't be yelling at a pregnant lady," I said in an attempt to lighten the mood.

She smiled for the first time, but she wasn't going down that easy. We spent the next couple hours talking it out at my apartment, and missed my Planned Parenthood appointment.

"When are you going to tell Mom?" she asked me.

Kendra never really understood the tyrant that was my mother because my mother treated her differently. My sister was well aware of the struggles I'd had with our mom over the years, but she consistently forgot about them and would often act like there was no tension between Mom and me.

"I don't know, never," I mumbled, and joined her at my kitchen table.

"If you plan on keeping this baby, you are going to have to tell Mom and Dad as soon as possible."

I moaned and placed my head on the table. "She's going to kill me," I thought aloud, but I was honestly more nervous to tell Ethan than anyone.

"She's not going to kill you, but you must tell her...immediately," Kendra warned.

It was a Saturday night and I was almost nine weeks pregnant.

"I think you should call her now, right now, with me here to support you," she declared and started to dial the phone for me.

"Stop!" I hit the button to hang up. "Are you insane? I can't just call her up and tell her, 'Hey, Mom, yeah, finals are going well. Been studying really hard to make you proud and, oh, yes, one more thing...' She'll drive down here and smother me like a flame of shame."

Kendra was not amused. "When you called me and told me about what's going on with you, all I cared about was making sure you were okay, and that's all Mom and Dad are going to care about as well," she said. "I have to drive back tonight, and I'm not leaving here until you tell them because I want to be here for you when you make that call."

Kendra dialed the phone and then handed it to me. It rang forever before my mother answered.

"Hello," she said, hurried.

"Mom, it's Syd. Do you have a sec?" I cleared my throat.

"Actually, Syd, we have the Carlins and the Friedmans coming for dinner tonight, and I'm in a mad dash to set the table, heat the gravy, and press my blouse. I'll have to give you a call in the morning."

I stared at Kendra, who was looking at me with anticipation. "I really need to talk now," I told her.

She sighed, and I could hear pots and pans banging around my childhood kitchen. "Are you hurt?"

"No, I'm fine."

"Syd, I'm in such a panic. Your father bought a turkey that was a full seven pounds heavier than the one I asked for, and this just isn't the best time for a chat."

I covered the mouthpiece, whispered to Kendra, "She's busy," and shrugged.

"Good Lord." Kendra grabbed the phone. "Mom, it's Kendra. Sydney *really* needs to tell you something."

"What are you doing there?" I heard my mom's voice elevate as she asked, and Kendra handed the phone back to me.

"I'm pregnant," I blurted out and covered my face as though she could see me.

"What? Who said that?!" Mom choked.

"Me, Syd. I'm back on the phone, and I'm the one who is pregnant."

The background clatter and conversation came to a screeching, rubber-burning, pavement-scarring halt.

"Are you there, Mom?"

"I'm here, I…I said I can't talk now. We are going to have to discuss this in the morning." Her words were shaky, and I felt terrible.

"I'm so sorry, Mom," I began to cry. "I wasn't smart."

She sighed. "We'll talk about this tomorrow, okay?"

"I love you, Mom."

Click.

Kendra was dumbfounded. "What the fuck?"

"I told you she was busy," I said and slammed the receiver down.

Kendra snatched the phone from its base and began to redial. She was fuming.

"DON'T!" I hollered and stopped her in her tracks. "Do not call her back. This is my deal. I told her, and she said we'll talk tomorrow."

෴

Kendra had to leave that night, so she wasn't around when my mom called me back at nine o'clock the next morning. The phone woke me up, and I'd spent hours the night before trying to imagine how the conversation with my mother would pan out. I went to bed assuming nothing good would come of it.

"Hi, Sydney," she sighed quietly like she had the night before. "Well, that was an interesting dinner party, what with me crying in the bathroom every thirty minutes." She paused. "I had to convince Lynette Carlin I had pink eye."

I sat up in bed, spoke for fifteen uninterrupted minutes, and brought her up to speed on my situation. Sometimes when I confided in her, which was rare, and made her feel like she was useful, she would soften up a little and take pity on me. I told her about Kevin and the dance, and what admittedly poor choices had led me to where I was. I even told her up-front that my intention was to keep the baby.

"Sydney, I just don't even know what to say," she said after taking a long breath.

Say I'm an idiot. Say you're not surprised. Say that Kendra would've never let this happen. Say you're mortified, I thought to myself.

She continued. "Do you have any idea…let me rephrase that." She paused. "You have *no* idea what you are getting yourself into. You're graduating from college and about to embark on a new career in an entry-level position. How do you think you'll be able to support yourself and a child while working full time?"

It was a fair question, and not one I was prepared to answer.

"I think you are going to have to give this some more thought," Mom concluded as I was taking a sip of water.

"I've given it a lot of thought," I said defensively and placed the glass back on the plastic milk crate next to my bed. "And I just feel like it's the right thing to do."

She made a sound that resembled a laugh, although I'm certain nothing was funny. "Just so you know, your father and I are not able to financially care for a child of yours, Sydney. I hope you aren't thinking that you'll move home and have us raise the baby," she stated, and got that out on the table.

"I'm not, Mom, I swear. I understand that this is my deal, my problem, and I would not make this choice if it meant putting you and Dad in a situation like that."

"Have you honestly weighed your other options? What are your plans then?"

"I don't know exactly what I'm going to do yet, but I've thought of almost nothing else," I responded quickly. "I'm going to try and work it out."

"*Trying* isn't going to cut it, my dear. I mean it, Sydney. You are making a life-altering decision by choosing to have a baby, out of wedlock, with nowhere to live and a salary barely fit to support one person."

I took a deep breath. "I know."

The conversation with my mother was difficult, but not nearly as harrowing as I thought it was going to be. I was able to lie in bed with the phone resting on my shoulder so her voice was slightly more distant than normal. Never once did I assume she'd rush to my aid and assure me that everything would be just fine...that she would be there for me, and celebrate my decision. So, I kept my expectations low and just tried to get through the phone call with as much strength and humility as I could. It was only when she asked if I'd told Ethan that I started to lose my shit.

"I haven't." My voice quivered and my lips pursed.

"Are you going to?"

"I don't have much of a choice, do I?"

She made a breathy sound that was drenched in disappointment, but her response was gentler than I had expected. "Ethan is one of the kindest people I know, but more importantly, he loves you, Syd. And my guess is that his only concern will be for your well-being."

"I doubt it." I closed my eyes and sank back into the mattress.

"Don't underestimate him, or his feelings for you. I've spent almost four years watching the two of you together, and that boy loves you maybe more than you realize."

I was inconsolable. How could I have done this to him? "I'm going to lose him." I started to bawl and soak the pillowcase.

"Shhhh, shhhh. Now you need to calm down. You're not going to lose him."

Her answers were comforting. I had been expecting "Well, you should have thought of that before you slept around," or something like "Of course you're going to lose him, what would he want with someone else's baby?" But instead, she had done something I hadn't—given Ethan the benefit of the doubt.

"You don't know that," I said and wiped my face with the edge of the sheet.

"I know that he is a man of integrity, and that he will respect your decision, whatever it is."

The pace at which I was speaking started to pick up. "I'm paralyzed with fear, literally. I cannot dial his number. We haven't spoken in weeks. I just keep avoiding his calls and blaming everything on school, finals, graduation, et cetera. He must already think something is wrong with me." I rubbed my temples, trying to prevent the headache that was brewing. "And I haven't told Kevin yet either." The thought made me shudder.

"Well, you've got two very tough phone calls to make," she said simply. "I don't know Kevin, but something tells me you may get a better reaction from Ethan. You're going to have to prepare yourself for the worst with both of them, and hopefully you'll be pleasantly surprised."

I took a moment to think about what she'd just said. "I understand, but Kevin and I have been close friends for a long time and he deserves to know." I said the words, but I honestly would've rather kept the whole ordeal to myself than have to break the news to Kevin that I was carrying his child.

"That was very generous of your sister to drive down and be there for you," she noted.

I nodded. "Yes, it was."

"I think you should call those boys sooner than later, Sydney, and let me know how it goes, okay?"

"Okay, Mom."

"We have a lot more to discuss, but your father and I are meeting some friends at North Shore. Daddy was invited to play golf with Dr. Richards and his sons," she said with pride, like she'd moved on from the previous, tiresome topic.

I had one more question though, one that I wasn't sure I wanted the answer to. "Did you tell Dad?"

She inhaled, then slowly released her lungs. "I did, last night after everyone left. It was obvious to him there was something wrong with me."

"Does he want to talk to me?"

"No, Syd, not now. He's very upset...and he's not quite ready to speak to you."

"What does that mean?" I sat back up in bed.

"It means exactly what I said. He's taken this very hard, and he is not ready to address it with you. I haven't told him of your intentions yet, since you've just told them to me yourself."

"Oh God."

"It's okay. I will handle him, and I'm sure he'll come around soon and support whatever you decide."

She'll handle him? He was the one who handled her for me. My dad was a source of rationality and confidence, and I needed him. It hadn't even occurred to me that he'd turn his back on me. I was numb.

"Okay" was all I could say.

"Good-bye, honey, and you better take extra-good care of yourself. You know you're not supposed to drink any alcohol, right?"

My jaw dropped.

CHAPTER SEVENTEEN

I spoke to Ethan on the day I confessed everything to my mother, but it wasn't until a week later that I was able to find the courage to tell him about the pregnancy. I had only a day or two left at Purdue and needed to talk with him before I officially packed up and left school.

I sat soldier-like in the center of my couch, with my back straight and my feet planted firmly on the floor in front of the coffee table. I dialed his number and he answered sounding very sleepy; it was early on a Saturday morning. "Hey, you," he said.

"Hi, what's going on?"

He released a tribal yawn. "Not too much. Long time no talk. You getting ready to get out of there?"

"Yeah, it's been pretty crazy around here," I said, trying to formulate a way to segue into a more serious conversation, but I decided to just cut to the chase. "E, I need to talk to you about something."

"Shoot," he said, unconcerned.

"Well…" I said with a sigh.

"Is everything okay, Syd?"

Damn useless tear ducts began to empty, and, slowly, tears trailed down my cheeks like raindrops on a car window. "Not really. I mean, I'm okay, it's just that I need to tell you something," I said bluntly, knees shaking.

He didn't say anything, so I continued. "There's really no easy way to put this, so here it goes...I'm pregnant."

He still didn't say anything.

"E?" I checked the connection.

"I heard you."

My posture hadn't changed, I was too afraid to relax even one muscle. "Do you hate me?" I asked.

More silence.

I figured he wouldn't initially have much to say. When confronted with a dilemma of any degree, Ethan was always a man of few words, choosing to ponder rather than speak. "I'm so sorry Ethan. I went to a fraternity formal with a friend a couple months ago..." I started rambling.

"Stop," he said.

We sat there for a few minutes on the phone, me sniffling like a baby on my end, and him sighing and grunting quietly on his.

"Whose is it?" he finally asked.

"My friend Kevin's."

"Are you two together now?"

"Right now?" I asked.

"No, are you together, are you dating him?"

"No."

"What are you going to do about the pregnancy?"

Before calling Ethan, I debated whether it was going to be more difficult to tell him I was pregnant, or to tell him that I was keeping the baby. I never was able to determine which would be harder until I'd said them both aloud. "I've decided to have the baby."

"You're having the baby?" His tone made me feel stupid. "And then what, giving it up for adoption?"

I cleared my throat and scooted to the edge of the couch. "No, I'm keeping the baby. I've decided to keep it."

More silence.

"Wow. Well, I guess things have been pretty crazy for you," he said.

I was trying to prepare the perfect thing to say, but my brain could no longer handle the intricacies of all my declarations. "Ethan, throughout this entire ordeal, telling you has been the hardest thing I've had to do. Deciding to keep the baby wasn't nearly as hard as it was to make this phone call. I have been dreading telling you; please don't hate me."

"Why have you been dreading telling me?" he scoffed.

"Why do you think?"

"You tell me, Syd." His voice was hard and less tired.

"I just...I never meant to hurt you, or put this wedge between us, but there's no going back now. And I just don't want to lose you...and our friendship."

"Our friendship?" he said mockingly. "That's a joke."

"I mean it, Ethan."

He made a noise that sounded like he was blowing into a Breathalyzer. "Jesus, Syd, you've dropped a real bomb here, and I'm not really sure what you expect me to say. This is going to take some time to process," he said. "Sorry, I really just...don't know how you could have done this."

I stretched the sleeve of my shirt over my hand and wiped my face. "I understand," I said wearily. "I'm so sorry. Just please don't be mad at me forever."

"What do you want me to do?" He posed the question sternly.

What I truly wanted was for him to come see me, wrap me in his long arms, and tell me everything was going to be okay. Because he was the only person who could make me believe it. But there I was, ambushing him on a Saturday morning, telling him I'd not only slept with someone behind his back, but I was pregnant and keeping this other man's child. What could I reasonably expect from him? What would I do if the tables were turned? Maybe I would find a tiny shred of maturity in my broken heart to forgive him. But it wouldn't be easy, and it wouldn't be quick.

"I know this is going to sound selfish of me, and given the circumstances, I'm not sure I would've even stayed on the phone with you this long if it were you in an equally ugly situation. But having to sacrifice you to have this baby will destroy me, so I hope that in time you can find a way to forgive me."

His lungs must have been nearly empty from all the laborious sighs. "We're always going to be friends. I just don't know about any more than that right now. This is a big deal, Syd, and you are going to have one hell of a year ahead of you."

"I know."

He left me hanging on in silence for about ten seconds. "I really need to go, so, thanks for the call," he said, flippant. "Take care of yourself."

"I will, Ethan. I'm really…"

"Bye, Syd." *Click.*

I lay down on my couch and cried for about twenty minutes with no break. The combination of guilt, missing him, and overactive hormones had gotten to me. Once I was able to calm down, I was grateful for his kindness. I feared the worst, yet Ethan showed his true colors once again. He could have hurled a number of despicable words at me, but he didn't. He was quiet and respectful, and I deserved none of it. He hadn't even tried to talk me out of keeping the baby. In fact, simply talking to Ethan and hearing the distance in his voice was the only time I questioned my decision.

My next confession wasn't going to be as easy. Jenna and I had plans to meet up with Kevin, Rocco, and a bunch of other people for our final night on campus. We'd scheduled a pub crawl with a biscuits-and-gravy chaser at this restaurant that was a Purdue institution, and which served the most sought-after biscuits and gravy in the state of Indiana. It was called Triple XXX, also known as Tri-Chi, and they basically gave you a huge platter of sausage gravy, with two tiny, little buttermilk biscuits buried underneath it.

By the time we'd hit our last pub on the schedule, everyone besides me was hammered. I hadn't had any time alone with Kevin, and I didn't want to break the news to him when he was three sheets to the wind, so I decided to see if he'd talk with me in the morning. I managed to interrupt a conversation he was having with two other guys and pulled him aside while we were waiting for our table.

"So, are you headed out tomorrow?" I asked, and noticed Jenna staring me down. She knew I'd been trying to find a way to get him alone and drop yet one more grenade in someone's lap. She and I tried to come up with a better way to break the news to him, but he'd been impossible to pin down until then.

"Yeah, I haven't packed much yet, but I'm hoping to hit the road after lunch. How about you?"

"I'm leaving tomorrow. Headed to my sister's place in the city."

"Sounds good. We'll have to hook up when I'm there for training next month."

Kevin's father had gotten him an entry-level position with Arthur Andersen, a management-consulting firm located in Chicago, although he'd eventually be transferred to an office in Los Angeles. He had to go through two months of training to learn how to advise other companies on their failures. I couldn't help but wonder why those other companies didn't just do the two months of training with Arthur Andersen themselves.

A waitress signaled that our table was ready.

"Hey, do you think we can get together tomorrow, before you leave?" I asked Kevin, trailing behind him.

"What for?" he trudged ahead.

"Maybe a quick lunch, or coffee or something."

He shook his head. "Don't think so, Syd. Like I said, I've got a ton of packing, and I need to be on the road by one at the latest."

"Maybe you could just stop by my place then, on your way out of town?"

"Doubt it, squirt."

I tugged at the back of his navy-blue T-shirt. "Can you just come by tomorrow? I want to talk to you about something," I said as seriously as I could without letting anyone else in the group hear what I was saying.

He turned only his head around, looked down at me, gave me a perplexed look, and then studied my face. "Call me in the morning," he said and took a seat at the other end of the table.

Jenna made her way over to me. "Did you just tell him?" she asked as we both pulled out rickety wooden chairs from the table and sat down next to each other.

"No, I asked if he'd come by my place in the morning, before he leaves town."

"And what'd he say?"

"He said to call him in the morning."

"Oh my," Jenna said, shaking her head. "One more plate, extra sausage!" she leaned back and shouted to the fry cook.

CHAPTER EIGHTEEN

My nerves were in high gear the next morning, so I kept on the pair of sweats that I'd slept in and just threw a cardigan over my white tank top. I'd spent a week trying to find the most civil way to break the news to Kevin, but there was really only one way to say what I had to say. It was a tough thing to sugarcoat.

I called him that morning, like he had asked, and wiped the perspiration off my forehead when I heard a knock at the door two hours later. When I opened it, he was standing there, hands in his pockets, dark circles under his eyes, and not looking nearly as friendly as he did joking with his buddies over a plate of sausage gravy the night before.

"What's up?" he asked gruffly.

"Come on in." I gestured and stepped back from the doorway.

"I've only got, like, ten minutes," he said looking around. "What's up?"

He seemed very uncomfortable, and it felt like a rain cloud entered the room with him; you could almost see the fog. His edginess surprised me; I'd expected him to be cold and aloof *after* hearing the news, but not before.

"Can I get you something to drink?"

"No thanks," he said and sat on the edge of my coffee table.

I looked at him as he checked his watch. He was not going to make it easy for me.

"Well," I started, and had a seat at my dinette set, a few feet away. "I just wanted to talk to you before you left." He was still looking down. "I have to tell you something." I swallowed.

"What is it?"

I cupped my hands together, and then unsuccessfully tried to make eye contact with him. "I'm pregnant."

He let the words dangle before he spoke. "I thought that's what you were going to say."

He never looked directly at me, and I was quickly schooled in the meaning of painful silence.

I rubbed my hands on my thighs to wipe off the perspiration. "I'm sorry to lay this on you right before you leave, but I thought you should know."

He shook his head slowly. "What are you doing about it?"

"I'm going to keep it," I answered and kept my gaze focused on him.

He laughed. "Don't I have any say?" He stood up. "Assuming it's even mine."

"It's yours."

He started to walk behind the couch toward the door. "So great, you've got your little mind all made up, huh? That's it? 'Hey, Kev, I'm having your baby without your consent…just *thought you should know*.'" He whispered mockingly.

I had no response.

He shook his head with greater force and continued. "So, you're saying this is my kid. Then we both made the same mistake, right? Why the fuck don't I get to choose then? Who died and made you in charge of my life? You've got some nerve, Syd."

I had no response.

He began questioning me again, and finally looked at my face. "What do you want from me?"

His eyes were unrecognizable, and his expression filled with rage and disgust.

"I don't want anything from you, Kevin," I pleaded, as if someone was pointing a gun at me. "We're friends, we've been friends for a long time and I thought you might want to know," I said softly.

"Well, guess what, Syd? I don't want to know." His tone grew crueler. "I don't want to know you or your kid, okay?" He paused. "So leave me the fuck out of it!"

I watched him snatch his keys off the coffee table and head for the door. I wanted to scream after him. I wanted to clamp on to his bicep, spin him around, and look into his eyes. "It's me, Sydney!" I wanted to shout. "I'm your friend, Kevin. I never meant to hurt you with this, you must know that!"

Instead I said nothing as he shook his head and stormed out.

CHAPTER NINETEEN
Grace

A little over three years had passed since I learned the identity of my real father, but I had yet to see or speak to him. And although my desire to do those things hadn't lessened, the desperation had faded. As I grew older, my few attempts at reaching out to him through my mother became more futile and discouraging.

My mom first told me about him when I was ten or eleven years old, after I threatened to run away if she didn't fess up. She'd described him as a friend, a guy who was among a close-knit group of college pals.

"What did he look like?" I asked with eager ears.

"He was very tall and handsome, and had a lot of dark wavy hair," she told me.

I pictured him like Hugh Jackman, and Mom smiled when I told her that.

"What was he like?"

She said his name was Kevin, and that he was strong, helpful, funny, but with a dry sense of humor, and he was always one of her favorite people during her college years. But that had all apparently changed when she told him about me.

"What happened?"

She didn't give me very many details, other than he was unhappy with the news and chose to end their friendship.

"Why?" I asked, feeling guilty for ruining her relationship with him.

She shrugged. "I really don't know, sweetie. He was young and didn't want to deal with having a child, I guess."

"What did he say?"

Mom adjusted her posture on the park bench where we sat and looked away from me. I was old enough to know there were things she didn't want to talk about, but I couldn't tame my curiosity.

"He said that I would have to raise you by myself, which I had intended to do anyway. He wanted me to understand that he wasn't able to take part in raising a child together."

"He didn't want to marry you?"

She shook her head. "No, honey, we weren't dating at the time." She looked away again and batted her eyes before turning back to me. "I know this is hard to understand because it's obviously not the best idea to have sex with someone you're not in a loving relationship with…but sometimes things happen that are out of your control, and this was one of them."

I scratched my head. "It was an accident."

"You were not an accident, but I had not planned on being pregnant and unmarried at such a young age."

"So, I *was* an accident."

Mom's head dropped back slightly, and then she sat straight and her neck made a cracking sound before she smiled at me. "No, you weren't an accident. You were absolutely meant to be in my life. It was just the means in which you came to me that were unexpected."

It sounded reasonable, but accidental nonetheless.

"Do I have any sisters?"

She grinned knowingly; I had always wanted a baby sister. "I don't know much about Kevin's life today, but I do know that he is married, and has two daughters."

My heart beat faster at the thought of him and his family. I wanted so badly to go to their house and spend time with them. I wondered if I looked like him and his daughters, and what his wife was like. I wondered if she would be nice to me, or if she even knew I existed. But instead I was asked to be content with the information my mom had given me because, apparently, Kevin had asked to have no contact with me whatsoever.

I looked down at my lap that day at the park, embarrassed. "But that was a long time ago," I said to my mom. "Maybe he wants to see me now, and doesn't know where to find me," I suggested, my voice filled with hope.

"Let's head home." She stood and grabbed my hand but gave no response to my theory, leaving me to assume he knew exactly how to find me—he just didn't want to.

Right before I was about to start my freshman year of high school, I met a girl who had a similar, screwed-up situation like mine. She'd moved in two blocks from us and was transferring to my school starting in the fall. Her name was Chloe.

Chloe was gorgeous, and all I could picture when we first met was her walking through the halls in slow motion with the wind in her hair as every prepubescent male within a stone's throw turned to stare at her. She had long wavy brown hair down to the small of her back, and almond-shaped eyes the color of smoky quartz. Her teeth were straight and pearly white, and you could see almost every single one of them when she smiled. I asked her if anyone ever told her she looked like Julia Roberts, and she said yes.

We met one day as she was jogging past my house, and I was outside shooting hoops in the driveway. She had a very confident air about her, and approached me almost immediately.

"Excuse me," she said.

"Yes?" I let the ball bounce away from me as I walked toward the end of the driveway.

She extended a long, toned arm. "I'm Chloe, just moved in over on Queens Lane, and I heard you might be the same grade as me."

"Incoming freshman?" I asked as we shook hands.

"Yup, good to meet you. Your name is…?"

"I'm sorry, it's Grace. Nice to meet you, too." We stood almost eye-to-eye, which was a refreshing change. Most girls my age were still at least five to six inches shorter than me, causing me to slouch like an ogre and walk the halls with slumped shoulders. But on Chloe, the height was much more graceful and swan-like, and she wore it like a crown. "Where are you from?" I asked.

"My mom and I moved up from Miami, to be closer to relatives."

"Just you and your mom?"

"Yeah, my dad left when I was young," she said casually.

Her honesty and misfortune made me instantly attracted to her. I knew at that moment we'd be friends.

"I'm sorry to hear that. How old were you?"

"It's fine." She walked toward the ball and bounced it gently until it got higher off the ground. "I was two. Hardly have any memory of him."

"Do you ever talk to him?"

"Nope."

She seemed so cavalier about the whole thing. There was no indication she harbored any anger or bitterness. No signs that her mother had lied to her as a young girl, or that her entire existence was the result of a drunken mistake. Her mom was probably straightforward with her from day one and let Chloe digest the news of her father's absence over the years on her own terms. I envied her disposition.

"What about you?" she started. "Your folks still together?"

"Yes, but my dad is not my real dad." The involuntary, full disclosure shocked me, and I looked away as soon as I said it, feeling shy. I usually avoided discussing my familial situation with kids my own age, but I felt comfortable with Chloe.

"Are you adopted?" she asked and bounced the ball to me.

I took a shot and made it. "I'm adopted by my dad, but my mom is my real mom. She had sex with some dude in college and had me. Then she married my dad when I was two."

"Your adopted dad?"

"Correct."

We both laughed. "You're almost as messed up as I am," she said and slapped me on the shoulder.

"I was thinking the same thing," I smiled.

We shot hoops for about an hour before she checked her cell phone, flipped it closed, and told me she had to go.

"I'll see ya around, Grace." She waved and jogged away.

CHAPTER TWENTY
Sydney

I left Purdue for good with a packed car, and drove the two-hour drive to downtown Chicago. My plan was to stay with Kendra for two months (since my mom declined to offer me my old room), and then get my own place before I was scheduled to start my new job, at which point I would be a little over four months pregnant.

Kendra lived in a renovated building that was a converted chocolate factory, and I was thrilled to see that the lobby had bowls of complimentary candies at all times. I wiped the sweat off my brow, hit the number three button on the elevator, and she was there waiting for me.

"Hi, roomie!" she said excitedly. "Let me help you with those." Kendra grabbed one of the two oversize duffels I was dragging.

"Thanks, this one's a beast," I said and followed her down the hall to the apartment.

"I was thinking we could go for pizza tonight," she suggested, and pulled my bag over by her balcony doors once we entered the apartment.

"Sounds great." I threw myself down on her new, pullout futon, and landed with a thud. "This couch is terribly uncomfortable."

"It's cute though, right?"

"Yeah, it's pretty cute," I agreed, then yawned.

"If you don't want pizza, we can go somewhere else, or I can order in if you're too tired." She was in full hostess mode, wanting me to meet her enthusiasm and rally for a girls' dinner, but all I really wanted to do was find a way to get comfortable on her wooden couch.

"Pizza's fine," I said and rested my heels on her glass-top coffee table.

Kendra grabbed me a bottle of water from her fridge. "I have a blow-up mattress for you in the bedroom, but if you'd be more comfortable sleeping out here and having some space to yourself, just let me know."

"Thanks, Kendra." I smiled at her. I really did appreciate all she was doing, and I could tell she was overcompensating for my parents. It'd been a couple weeks since I broke the news to them, and my father still refused to take my call. Kendra had threatened not to speak to either of them unless they gave me their support, but that hadn't worked, and I begged her not to make them suffer even more for my mistakes. It killed me that I'd brought so much pain on my father. After everything he'd done for me. He was speechless where I was concerned, and I got it.

"Have you talked to Dad lately?" I asked.

"About you?" she asked with a reserved smile, cocking her head.

"Yes, about me."

Kendra took a spot next to me and briefly looked down before answering. "We didn't really talk about your situation. Just that you were going to be staying with me." She patted my leg. "He did give me some extra money for us to go out to dinner and buy groceries."

I smiled at the consolation prize. "I've shamed the family."

She burst out laughing, bent her knees, and put her feet up on the couch. "You haven't shamed the family."

"I've shamed Dad." I nodded, imagining him bravely facing his friends on the golf course after their wives had passed along the gossip about the "Shephard girl."

Kendra held her gentle grin. "No, you haven't. He's worried about you and he loves you. He just doesn't know how to deal, but he will."

"He won't even take my calls."

She nodded. "He will."

We unpacked my things and put some clothes away in the drawers she'd cleared out for me. The rest of my stuff was jammed into a storage cage in the basement of her building. Once we were done, we ordered a pepperoni pizza and a tomato-gorgonzola salad from O'Fame in Lincoln Park. Once Kendra ate all the tomatoes, I was free to dip my pizza slices in the leftover gorgonzola.

"I told Kevin today," I said and wiped the grease from my chin. We were sitting on her floor with our backs resting against the futon.

Her eyes popped, and then she silenced the television with the remote. "Oh my God, today?"

"Yup." My lips curled.

Her gaze was fixed on me. "And?"

"And let's just say you should hold off on buying him a World's Best Dad mug," I said and took a swig of my water. I'd cried enough on the car ride back to Chicago, and convinced myself that Kevin's reaction was for the best. How could I count on someone who behaved so violently under pressure? I wanted nothing from him, and only wished I'd been able to convey that more clearly in my conversation with him. As a glimpse of the Sears Tower came into view, and I crossed over the Gary, Indiana, border, I vowed never to shed a tear over Kevin Hansen again.

"I want to know everything," Kendra demanded, then sat up and grabbed another square slice of pizza.

I nervously played with my napkin, and then tossed it on the coffee table. "He wants nothing to do with me, or the baby."

"What do you mean?" she mumbled with food in her mouth.

"Which part?"

She kicked her feet like a child. "What was his reaction exactly?"

"Exactly what I said, although I spared you the profanities." I paused to reflect on his comments to me. "He wants nothing to do with either of us, and I'd be surprised if I ever see or hear from him again."

She was dumbfounded by this news. Apparently she thought he would've been happy to be a father only months after graduating college, and that maybe she could start planning the bachelorette party.

"What a piece of shit," she murmured. "How could he say that to you?"

"He was pretty pissed off and just didn't want to be bothered," I told her. "The weirdest thing was that he said he knew I was going to tell him that I was pregnant," I said, and started picking balls of gorgonzola out of the tin salad container with my hands and popping them in my mouth.

"When did he know?"

"Last night when we were with our friends, I asked him to come over to talk before he left town, and he said he suspected that I was going to tell him that."

"So basically, his asshole behavior was entirely premeditated."

"That's one way of looking at it."

She shook her head in that "you poor thing" sort of way that I loathed. "I'm so sorry, Syd. I can't imagine that makes your situation any easier."

"Please don't say it like that."

"Sorry," she said and shrugged.

All the practice I was getting by confessing to people about my pregnancy didn't make it any easier. I don't know what I expected from Kevin, but his fury-laden rejection made me feel even more isolated. Even though it was my choice to go it alone, I'd expected to at least have his respect, and assumed he would treat me with a shred of decency. Jenna was even more shocked than Kendra was because she knew Kevin very well and knew the depth of our friendship. There weren't too many things that put Jenna at a loss for words, but his reaction to the news and the way he'd treated me was one of them.

"You must be joking," Jenna had said when I called her later that night. Jenna had moved to New York after graduation and was working at her father's law firm. She held a degree in journalism but was unable to find a job in magazine publishing, so instead she was typing letters and answering phones.

"I'm not making up one word of it."

"I don't believe you."

"I almost don't believe it myself," I told her.

"What did you say back to him?"

"Nothing, I said nothing. I told him I thought he should know, and then he just went off on me. I honestly didn't know he had it in him. I've never seen him get angry about anything."

"I'm calling him," she stated.

"Don't you dare! And don't you dare say anything to Rocco or anyone. Please, Jenna."

"Fine, I won't," she assured me. "I'm so sorry, Syd. What a complete dick. Are you devastated?"

"You know what, Jen? I had it out in the car, but once I was able to digest everything, I was just really disgusted and confused, but not sad."

And that was the truth. Kevin's behavior was so revolting to me that all it did was make me more confident in my decision. His cruelty gave me new strength, and even though I felt he owed me an apology, I knew I would never hear from him again.

CHAPTER TWENTY-ONE

I located an apartment in Old Town, after only four weeks with Kendra, and just three days before I was set to start my job at the InterContinental hotel in their client services department. I used some money that my grandmother had given me as a graduation gift for the security deposit and emptied my savings account of $380 to buy a few necessities. Kendra gave me an old phone, an alarm clock, an end table (which I used as a coffee table), her blow-up mattress, and a floor lamp. I had wall hangings from my school apartment and milk crates for some of my sweaters and books, and I was going to try and go as long as I could without a dresser. It was a small one-bedroom apartment, much smaller than the place I had at school, and barely affordable at $550 a month on my annual starting salary of $28,000.

My first day of work, I was greeted by my supervisor, Midge Larsen. Midge was very tall—at least six feet—and built like a man. Large hands, large feet, large face—basically one of the most physically overbearing women I have ever encountered. And she started almost every sentence with my name.

"Sydney, I'm Midge."

"Sydney, you'll be training on the phones with Trevor and Keri."

"Sydney, your desk is over there."

"Sydney, your blacks don't match."

"My what?" I asked.

Midge grabbed a small section of my sleeve and elevated it like a puppeteer. "Your top is about four shades lighter than your slacks. Please see that they are the same shade of black from now on, otherwise one looks gray, or worse…navy."

She released my arm and left me scanning myself.

"She's very particular about that," Keri leaned over and said to me, referencing our required dark uniform.

"Gotcha," I said. "I guess in this light…" My voice trailed off as I pondered my shirt.

"Don't let her get to you. She runs a tight ship and no one is immune to her neurosis."

I took a chair next to Keri at a square table with four phones, four computers, and four seats that would be my desk for the next year. "How long have you been here?"

"A little over two weeks. Just graduated from Indiana."

"Purdue."

"Uh-oh, we're bitter rivals from day one," she joked. Keri's family was from Naperville, a suburb west of the city, and she was still living at home and commuting downtown every morning. Her plan was to save some money over the winter and then move to the city with her best friend from high school. Keri was short like me, and loved to snack. Everyday she'd bring in a variety of Tupperware containers with things like celery and peanut butter, Wheat Thins with cheddar cheese slices, pretzels, peanut brittle, and—my favorite—minibagels with walnut cream cheese.

My other coworker, Trevor, had been working under Midge's tutelage closer to three weeks and was an Indiana graduate as well. Apparently their job-placement seminars went over well in that state. The three of us sat together each day at that square desk/table and answered calls and faxes all day long. Thankfully the three of us got along great and shared an aversion to Midge's management skills. We determined early on that as long as things around the office went smoothly and we did as we were told, Midge would stay out of our hair.

"Sydney, can you return these messages regarding the bakers' convention?" Midge asked me through the intercom system.

"Sure, Midge," I said, and then realized I didn't have the messages or know what bakers' convention she was referring to. I turned on the intercom system again to get more information from her. "Where are the messages?"

There was a long silence, in which Trevor, Keri, and I exchanged looks of "Did she hear that?" After about a minute, Midge responded. "Sydney, only I am allowed to use the intercom."

I hadn't told Midge or my coworkers about the pregnancy since I hadn't gained much weight and could easily hide my belly with large tops and stretch pants. I was pretty slim before, so at that time I just looked like someone who ate too many platters of biscuits and gravy in college. My sister advised me to wait as long as possible so that they couldn't fire me, but then Jenna said it was against the law for them to fire a pregnant lady anyway.

Soon after I started my job, I found a new gynecologist who informed me that baby and I were progressing nicely, and that my official due date was January 22nd. He also said that he'd be able to reveal the baby's sex on my twenty-week appointment if I was interested in finding out. I was.

I left my doctor's office that day with a huge smile on my face and immediately thought of Ethan. I'd wanted to call him so badly and tell him everything. He and I had kept in touch, talking twice a week, mostly short conversations when it was on Kendra's long-distance dime. I was always thrilled to hear from him.

"Hello," I answered my phone on the third night alone in my new apartment.

"Hey, Syd, how are the new digs?" Ethan asked.

I smiled when I heard his voice. "Quite palatial."

"And how are you feeling?"

"I'm good, you know. Hanging in there, and I feel good," I said and sat on the edge of my blow-up bed, filing a chipped thumbnail and balancing the phone on my right shoulder.

"Glad to hear it," he said. "I talked to my parents yesterday, and my mom said to send her love to you...and the baby."

My heart sank a little. His parents were two people I'd admired and slightly feared for many years. Two people who seemingly had everything together, down to matching coasters and lampshades. Ethan's mother's approval was something I'd tried hard to obtain. Humiliation set in as soon as he confirmed their knowledge of my *situation*. "I'm sure that went over well," I replied somberly.

"You don't give my mom enough credit, Syd. She was actually very proud of you, very happy for you, and really worried about how you're going to support yourself and the baby."

I stopped filing and held the phone in my hand. "Really?"

"Yes, she was very sincere in sending her blessings."

"Please tell her thank you." I arched my back and heard a crack.

She must've been thrilled to know that Ethan and I weren't dating anymore. I could only imagine what his parents actually said to him. Things like "You really dodged a bullet, Son" came to mind. Would she have been sincere in her blessings had I been carrying Ethan's child?

"I'm coming home in two months for my sisters' birthday, and I'd love to see you," he said.

I slumped my shoulders forward, looked down at my bloated stomach and chipped nails, and tried to imagine what I might look like in two months when I'd be six months pregnant. "I really don't want you to see me this way."

He breathed a short snicker of air out his nose. "Are you joking?"

I was shaking my head. "I'm really not. I mean, I would obviously like to see you, but I'd thought about it before you even asked, and I decided I don't want you to see me pregnant."

I imagined him shaking his head at me as well. "It doesn't make it go away, Syd."

"I'm not trying to make it go away. I just don't want *you* to see me."

He didn't say anything else about it. I knew he understood, and there must've been a small part of him that wasn't eager to see me pregnant with someone else's baby either, because he didn't press the issue.

"Fine. If your hormones change your mind, let me know."

A few days before the ultrasound that would reveal my baby's sex, I decided it was time to inform Midge about my pre-existing condition. Kendra and I spent two days thinking of the best possible way to relay the news. Part excitement, part straightforwardness, and part sympathetic smile.

I waited until after she'd had her morning coffee and demi baguette with honey butter before knocking on her door.

"Yes?" I heard from deep within.

"It's Sydney. Do you have a sec?" She didn't answer immediately, so I peeked in through the open door crack. She was staring right at me the moment I got my head all the way through and glanced over to her. "Hey, Midge, do you have a sec?" I repeated.

I took her silence as an invitation to bring the rest of my body in the room.

I closed the door behind me and sat down. She never took her eyes off me. Nothing like a good, honest creep factor to make a situation go from nerve-racking to worse.

"I just wanted to chat with you about something," I chirped.

She leaned back in her chair, gaze focused, and crossed her arms over her abdomen. Her eyebrows rose, an indication that I should proceed.

"Well..." I laughed nervously, and looked upward for a moment. "I'm pregnant." I resorted to blurting it out, my favorite method of disclosure.

Midge was still, then took her reading glasses off her head and tossed them onto her desk. "Sydney, you're pregnant?"

"Yes, twenty weeks," I said proudly, trying to elicit that joyous, congratulatory reaction that most pregnant women expect.

"I thought you were single." She went straight for the judgmental blow.

"I am single."

"So you've obviously known about this for some time."

"Yes, well..." I shifted and smoothed my black stretch pants as if I was wearing a ball gown. "I was told I shouldn't say anything to anyone until I was safely through the first trimester," I said, nodding.

"That was eight weeks ago, according to what you've just told me."

"That is correct..." I began to explain.

"What can I say? I have no idea what your personal life entails, nor do I care to. I'm sure you've researched the laws and know that we cannot let you go, and must provide your same job opportunity to you once your nonpaid maternity leave is over."

I nodded again.

"So, just like I expect everyone else to keep their personal business to themselves, you are no exception. And as you must also know, you have no sick, personal, or vacation days until after twelve months of consecutive employment. Which means any appointments you require in your condition must be done on your own time." She paused to convey her annoyance with me. "Sydney, do you understand?"

"Yes, Midge, thank you."

I stood frozen for a moment, then watched her eyes shift to my stomach.

"Close the door on your way out."

As soon as I'd shut the door behind me, Keri was waving me to come toward her.

"What's going on?" she asked.

Commence blurting. "I'm pregnant," I said with a smile.

All eyes on belly.

Her jaw dropped before looking at my face. "You're kidding!"

"Nope," I said and sat down next to her in my chair.

"Oh my God, Syd. Wow!"

"Yeah, I get that a lot."

"And here I thought we wore the same size!" she said, disappointed. "Whose is it?"

I dreaded that question. Not because I wished I was with Kevin, or wished I was married at that point in my life, but because no one knew how to respond without making me feel like I was doing something regretful. Like they felt sorry for what I was going through. Like they couldn't help but pity me.

"A guy I went to college with. We're not dating. Never were. He's waaaay out of the picture." I made a hand gesture like an airplane taking off. "I'll get into the gory details another time if it's okay?"

"Of course. Wow, I just can't believe it." She briefly placed her hand over her mouth. "Are you keeping it?"

"I am," I said with a smile. "Can I count on you for babysitting?"

"That's why you weren't drinking the other night at the bar. Trevor thought you were lying about the antibiotics."

I turned on my computer screen. "Why'd he think that?"

"I don't know. Maybe because who ever really lets antibiotics stand in the way of a cocktail?" She laughed. "He's going to be so bummed."

I turned to face her. "Why is he going to be bummed?"

"Because he thinks you're cute...has a little crush on Mama." She burst out laughing.

"You're hilarious."

Keri placed a hand on my knee. Her perfectly French-manicured nails caused me to curl my hands into fists. Primping had taken a backseat during those months.

"So, are you excited?" she asked.

No one had posed that question to me before, and her inquiry made me smile and light up. Just because I chose to have a baby at age twenty-two, out of wedlock, and with no place to live, never meant I didn't want the same over-the-top kindness that is bestowed upon every other pregnant woman. The kind where people offer you their seat on the bus, or cock their head and grin as you walk past, or carry your groceries to the car. I longed for the obligatory compassion and excitement that was given to every lady with a baby.

"I am kind of excited," I told her. "A little scared and a lot nervous, too, but ever since the day I decided to keep it, I made a promise to myself that I wouldn't look back with any regret."

"Well, that's great. I'm happy for you." She patted my lap and then unwrapped a granola bar that was on the table in front of her, offering me half. "And no, I will not babysit, but I will take you out anytime you can get a sitter."

"I will hold you to that."

Keri scooted her chair closer to mine and leaned in with a whisper. "What in God's name did Midge say?"

I rolled my eyes. "She reminded me of my rights, and basically said to act like it wasn't happening."

"Bitch," she said, mouth full of granola.

"Honestly, I'm sure she's less than pleased with the whole thing, and I don't really blame her. It was a little deceptive on my part and she knows that I know that."

"She'll get over it. In fact she's probably forgotten about it already." She wiped her chin and we both laughed.

"Do you know what you're having?" Keri asked and sat straight.

"I'm going to find out this week, actually."

"That's exciting. Any preference?"

"Not really," I said and began to check our call log on my computer.

"Well, I hope to have a boy one day," she announced. "And I'd like him to play on an NFL team, preferably the Bears, and be a quarterback...oh, and blond. A blond-haired, blue-eyed, Chicago Bears quarterback," she said with complete confidence.

"I see." I nodded as if it were possible. "What if he's a blond Major League Baseball player?"

"Unacceptable," she said and shrugged.

CHAPTER TWENTY-TWO

Two days later I was given the news that there would be no professional football players in my future; I was having a girl. I phoned Kendra from a pay phone in the lobby as soon as I left my doctor's appointment.

"It's a girl!" I was beaming. It was real. She was real. Inside of me was a little girl. One who would need guidance and love and self-esteem. A girl who would stand at my ankles and look up at me with reverence and admiration and expect that I would and could protect her from anything in the whole world. A delicate little lady who would one day ask me about life and death, and sex and love, and all of the scary things I had had to learn on my own. A little, sweet angel that would never have to question my love and support for her. A precious, innocent heart that was mine to care for and nurture. My little girl.

My heart was pounding fast as reality set in. I was months away from having a daughter and still struggling at how to be one myself.

"Oh, Sydney, that's wonderful," Kendra said. "Well, we certainly know a lot about girls around here. I'm just tickled to hear that, tickled pink!"

As hard as it was for me to believe when I think back, my dad and I still hadn't seen each other or spoken since my college graduation, and there I was almost five months pregnant with his granddaughter.

"Will you let Dad know?"

"Of course I will if you'd like, but maybe you'd like to tell him yourself?"

"You can tell him."

Three days later I arrived home from work and there was a giant package in the lobby of my building addressed to me. I lugged the cardboard box upstairs and opened it on my bed. Inside was a note from my father:

Congratulations on your little girl. She is lucky to have such a wonderful mother. Mom and I can't wait to meet her and see you.

—Dad

I tore through the tissue with tears in my eyes and unearthed a pink quilt, pink teddy bear, pink bunny, and tiny, pink hooded towel. It was my dad's way of making peace and finally acknowledging my baby—and his grandchild. I called him up immediately after opening it and we talked for over an hour.

Against everyone's better judgment, I called Kevin with the news. I left a message on his answering machine that I was having a girl, but never heard back from him.

The next week Kendra and I went home to our parents' house for dinner, where my mom had made an embarrassing array of pink foods. Grapefruit salad, strawberry smoothies, pasta with cream sauce, and pink-frosted doughnuts for dessert. It had only been a few days, and already I hated the color.

Over the next few weeks, I began shopping for maternity clothes, started doing almost everything at a snail's pace, and bought a book of baby names. I wanted to come up with a temporary nickname, something to refer to her as while she was still in utero and while I contemplated the top one hundred girls' names over the last few decades. One day my favorite barista at the new

Starbucks on Michigan Avenue commented on my bun in the oven and made reference to my affinity for their cinnamon scones. He declared I must be carrying a cinnamon bun! Hence her working title was born. Until the day she and I would meet in person, I would refer to her as Cinnamon. A moniker I shared only with immediate family.

When the weekend came for Ethan to be in town for his sisters' birthday, he called again and asked if I'd changed my mind about getting together. I said no. It had been months since we'd seen each other, and I was desperate to spend time with him, but I couldn't bring myself to let him see me all puffed up and pregnant.

"I'm going to be in town for five days. It's ridiculous for us to not get together at least once," he said, shuffling papers in the background.

"I know where you're coming from, and my mom thinks I'm being crazy, too, but I just can't have you see me this way."

"Sydney, please, what do you think is going to happen?"

"I don't know. I'm just not comfortable with it. I guess I would feel embarrassed. I can't explain it. I would love to see you…but I just can't."

He paused and released a long breath into the phone. "There's something I need to tell you," he said.

"You're pregnant," I joked, and laughed at myself as I stood at my sink rinsing dishes and setting them in the drying rack.

"No, Syd, but I've been seeing someone…casually. She's a friend of my cousin's."

I didn't say anything right away. Not because I had any right to feel slighted or angry, simply because I was stunned. I admittedly took Ethan for granted, and easily assumed that one day there might be a chance for us to rekindle our relationship. I was naive, and to hear that he was with someone else was like a slap across the back of the head. It stung.

"Syd?"

"Sorry, you caught me off guard." I stood holding my plate from last night's dinner, covered with dried spaghetti sauce.

"I was hoping to see you, and talk with you in person. I didn't want you to hear it from anyone else. It's not serious, but I thought you should know," he said, using the same words I'd said to Kevin. "She's a friend of Andrew's also, and I thought Taylor might say something to you."

"She hasn't said anything," I said to ease his mind. "Who is she?"

"Her name is Robin, and she's from Wisconsin where my cousin Emma lives, but she—Robin that is—recently moved to Boston."

"How convenient," I said, and immediately regretted it. He did not deserve one ounce of pettiness. Not from me.

"Anyway, it's not serious…" He sensed my discomfort and started to backpedal.

I politely interjected. "It's okay, Ethan. It must be a little bit serious if you're telling me about her, and you wanted to tell me in person."

He cleared his throat. "I just thought you should know. We've been hanging out and I wanted to be honest with you."

I really didn't know what to say. He had every right to date other people, and certainly if I had the right to bear another man's child, it wasn't my place to tell Ethan how to live his life. When he'd said those words to me, I felt like I was standing at the edge of a dock, watching a boat sail away with Ethan and our relationship. I was sad, and it took everything I had not to be selfish and tell him how much I still loved him.

"Thank you for telling me, E," I said.

"Don't get all weird on me, okay?"

"I won't, I promise. I'm happy for you. I am just struggling with how to react and what to say," I said honestly. "I must admit that I'm sort of glad you didn't tell me this in person." I took a breath. "She's one lucky girl."

He snickered. "All right, well, I'll call you anyway when I get in. Please try and think about changing your mind, okay? It would be great to see you."

"Okay," I said, but I had absolutely no intention of letting him see me this way. I loved Ethan, and I always would, and having to face him looking the way I did would have been too much for me to handle. Especially since he was in a relationship with someone else. I pictured him looking at my belly and instantly relating it to me having sex with someone else, all the while thinking that it made this Robin chick look like even more of a prize. Maybe that wouldn't have been the case, but I couldn't take the chance, and I didn't have the self-confidence to look him in the eyes after he looked at my stomach. And I had no intention of making Robin and her flat stomach more desirable than she already was.

I was numb when I hung up the phone. My mind went back to that day when Ethan had all but begged me to stay loyal to him and committed to our relationship. Where would we be now had I not been so self-involved?

CHAPTER TWENTY-THREE
Grace

Chloe!" I yelled as she closed her locker. "I'm going to L.A.!" Nana Lynne had sent me an airline ticket for my seventeenth birthday. She'd been promising to have me out west for years and finally came through during my junior year of high school.

"That's awesome!" Chloe raised her palm for a high five. "When?"

I leaned back against the wall of lockers and tossed my backpack on the ground. "Probably over spring break in April," I said and unwrapped my breakfast, a strawberry-frosted Pop-Tart.

"I'm so excited for you! Are you nervous?"

"I am a little nervous, but really excited. I've been dying to go to California."

"Will you see your dad?" she asked.

I broke the Pop-Tart in half and handed it to her. "I doubt it," I said, but she and I both knew that I wished I would.

I was very insecure where my father was concerned, and although I longed to meet him, I rarely mustered the courage to ask about him. As long as he wanted nothing to do with me, I felt it wasn't my place to force the issue. And no one ever encouraged me to do so, least of all my mother. But even though I was going to Los Angeles under the guise of visiting my aunts and my Nana Lynne, I had hoped to meet my father, Kevin Hansen.

My bag was packed a week before I was set to leave on April 16th. Mom had taken me to Target for a new bikini, matching flip-flops, and a sundress. She talked with my aunt Sharon toward the end of March, and they arranged for her to pick me up at the airport. Four days before my flight, I received an e-mail from her.

Hi, Grace,

We've had some drama around here this week. My mom slipped on her kitchen floor last Monday and broke her hip. She's been in the hospital for a few days, and just found out that she's going to need surgery on Saturday. I am so sorry to be the bearer of bad news, but it looks like we're going to have to reschedule your trip. We were really looking forward to having you here.

—Sharon

I was devastated. I instantly forwarded the e-mail to Chloe, and she texted me back within seconds: *NOOOOOOOO!*

I replied with a lone sad-face icon, and threw my phone on the floor next to my carry-on bag.

Chloe was the only person who had any idea what I was feeling. We'd talk for hours about our elusive father figures and about how we coped with the guilt surrounding our desire to be with them. She couldn't discuss her longing to see him with her mother because her mother hated him and forbade Chloe from mentioning his name. And I wasn't comfortable talking about Kevin with my parents because I didn't want to hurt my dad's feelings. But when my mother found out about Lynne's surgery and my canceled trip, I truly believe she understood the depth of my disappointment.

No person who has a decent relationship with both their parents could quite comprehend the disconnect that people like Chloe and myself lived with. We'd imagine what our real fathers might be like, but grasping those images was like trying to hold water in a strainer. The task is frustrating, and ultimately the strainer winds up empty.

CHAPTER TWENTY-FOUR
Sydney

E than came and went without seeing me, and I was sorry that I missed an opportunity to be with him, but felt good about my decision. He told me he'd be home for the holidays as well, but if I hadn't let him see me at six months, I certainly wasn't going to let him see me at nine months.

One person I was looking forward to seeing was Taylor. She was surprised, yet supportive, when I told her the news about the baby, and we'd planned to get together when she was in town for Christmas. Taylor had moved to Manhattan and worked for a huge event-planning company. She was a public relations assistant and helped arrange press junkets and book signings for celebrities. She was always traveling and sending me photos of her looking gorgeous standing next to someone fabulous. I still have the photo of her and John Grisham standing in front of the Empire State Building. We both had a huge crush on him.

It was a far cry from working for Midge, but I was thrilled for Taylor. She was planning on being in town for five days, so she and Kendra planned a baby shower for me during that time, three days before Christmas. I didn't register anywhere, so I got lots of random pink outfits and animals, and since none of my friends had (or were even thinking about having) kids, the only gifts that served any real purpose were from my mom and Taylor's mom, Mrs. Gold. My mom bought me an oval-shaped bucket that she said was a bathtub, and filled it with baby shampoo, washcloths, and a grooming kit. Mrs. Gold outdid everyone and handed me a page from a catalog with a picture of a crib and changing table from Lazar's in Lincolnwood, worth hundreds of dollars, and priceless to a single mother who would have no paycheck for three months.

My mom asked if I wanted gifts for myself or for the baby that Christmas (indicating I could not have both), and I quickly responded that I would rather have baby gifts than any more tentlike, black maternity tops for me. She promised that once I was back in shape, she would take me shopping for new clothes. I'm still waiting.

New Year's Eve, my parents took pity on me, canceled their dinner reservations at the club, and invited me to sleep over. And as much as I hated moving off of my couch unless absolutely necessary, I was relieved to have something to do. I'm sure everyone thought if I had to spend the holiday alone with my two-ton tummy, I was sure to cry my eyes out over a bucket of Baskin-Robbins mint chocolate chip. So my dad bought some nonalcoholic sparkling cider, and the three of us stayed up and watched the ball drop in Times Square. Sleep was nearly impossible for me at that time, due to the fact that I could never find a comfortable position and, just when I did, I would have to get up and pee. Besides that, it was a really nice evening, and my relationship with my mother began to turn a corner.

She would call and ask if I needed anything. She drove downtown to my apartment every once in a while and would clean up the apartment for me while I was at work. And every now and then she'd even leave fresh groceries in the fridge and homemade cookies on the counter.

Two weeks after the first of the year, around January 15th, I asked Midge if I could begin my maternity leave.

"Sydney, it looks as though you have yet to give birth," she said in her perpetually annoyed tone. Her distaste for me had grown with my stomach.

"Correct you are, Midge, but my due date is coming up, and it's getting increasingly hard to get here every day and then manage my responsibilities on zero to three hours of sleep a night." She loathed excuses, but I just didn't care that day.

As soon as I indicated that my work was suffering, she gave me permission and waved me off. Keri and Trevor took me to lunch and gave me a little present from both of them…something pink, I can't remember exactly what it was.

I spent the next two days napping during the daylight hours and watching TV at night. After Kendra finished work on January 18th, she dragged me off the couch and took me to Walgreens to buy diapers and wipes and other necessities I had neglected to get up until that point.

"Scented, unscented, aloe, or chlorine-free?" she asked me, and we exchanged clueless looks.

"Aloe sounds nice," I said.

"I agree." She shoved five packs of aloe-scented wipes into the cart. "I'm meeting my friend Jane for a drink at seven, so I have to move this along," she told me. "Sorry, don't mean to rush you. Do you have anything to eat at home, or do you want to pick up a sandwich on our way back?"

Just as she asked me, I felt an unusual amount of moisture in my underwear. I set my tote bag down on the linoleum floor and I spread my legs, looking down at my crotch.

"What are you doing?" she whispered embarrassingly and scanned the aisle for other patrons.

I stood upright and touched between my legs; my stretch pants were wet. "It felt like some pee leaked out."

"Eww." She quivered.

"It feels like more is coming. I think I should call my doctor," I said and walked toward her like I'd just gotten off the back of a horse.

"Do you think your water broke? There's no puddle."

"I don't know, but it feels really wet and it soaked through my underwear."

"Oh Lord," she said with a tinge of fear. "Need a wipe?"

CHAPTER TWENTY-FIVE

Despite the fact that I'd sprung a leak, I was feeling strong and was still functioning as a seminormal, asymmetrical person by the time Kendra and I arrived at the hospital. My doctor wasn't expected to be there until the baby was eating solid foods, but the on-call nurses were more than welcoming and ready for my arrival. A woman named Peyton, whom I followed into an examination room, instructed me to undress and put on the green sheet she was holding, along with a diaper-like contraption to help with the constant flow of liquid that began in Walgreens. Kendra placed my overnight bag on the floor and sat down on the vinyl guest chair in the corner of the room. As soon as I had donned the green sheet, Peyton came back in the room and hooked me up to no less than three monitors in no less than ten seconds.

"We're just going to keep an eye on things for a few minutes before getting you upstairs to labor and delivery," she informed us.

"So I'm staying?"

She smiled at me. "Yes, we're admitting you."

Kendra smiled back at her. "She's in denial and would like an extra week if that could be arranged," Kendra joked.

"I'll see what I can do," Peyton told me. "Is there anything I can get you in the meantime? Water? Ice?"

"Are those my only choices?"

"I'm afraid so."

"Water please."

"I'll be right back with some." She jiggled something on monitor number three before heading out and quietly closing the door behind her.

Kendra's chair cushion whistled as she stood up. "Well, it's finally happening. She's on her way, sister. Ain't no turning back," she said and brushed some hairs out of my face. "I'm going to call Mom and let her know it's official, okay?" She looked at me for permission. "You're obviously not going anywhere in that outfit, so hold tight. I'll be back in five." She squeezed my hand and left the room.

I folded my hands over my belly and let the rhythmic beeping noises from the monitors occupy my focus. Even though I was only days away from my due date, and basically pissing myself at Walgreens, Kendra was right. I was in denial. It'd been a pretty easy ride up until then. No morning sickness, no stretch marks. Just a few sleepless nights and killer leg cramps, but most of the horrible things people warned me about (cankles, acne, spotting) never happened. It was a long, hard haul for nearly forty weeks though. And while I had absolutely no clue as to how much my life would change, I was eager to meet my daughter.

Lindsay Carlin, a neighborhood girl who used to babysit Kendra and me when we were little, had warned me about a couple things. And keeping my baby-name choices to myself was one of them.

"Sydney!" she had exclaimed when I bumped into her coming out of my daughter's future pediatrician's office. "Look at you."

"Look at us," I responded, gesturing to her double stroller.

"Wow, the little girl I used to babysit for is having a baby." She exposed a toothy grin any orthodontist would be proud of. "Congratulations!"

"Thanks, Lindsay." I said with a smile. "And I'm guessing these two gorgeous, bald men are yours."

"They are. This is Braden and Jameson," she said and bent forward. "Can you wave hi to Sydney?"

Braden looked at his animal cracker, and Jameson buried his face in the side of the stroller.

"How old are they?" I asked.

"Just had their one-year checkup today. Will this be your pediatrician?"

"I think so. I'm meeting with Dr. Weinstein today to see if he's a good fit."

"Well, I happen to love all of the physicians in the practice here. Just don't be put off by their frankness. They're not hand-holders; they've been doing this for a long time. Very seasoned, very 'been there, seen that,' but they're great doctors."

"Good to know."

"So, do you know what you're having?"

"A girl."

She put her hand to her heart. "Oh, Sydney, that's wonderful. A little girl. I'm so happy for you."

"Thank you. I don't have a name yet," I said. Past conversations with nearly every person I encountered led me to assume that'd be her next question.

She waved her hands in the air as if being attacked by bees, then covered her ears like I was going to reveal the ending of a great book. "Oh, no, I never ask if people have names picked out. It's a horrible question! And trust me, don't reveal your choices to anyone," she warned in a deep and frightening tone. "As soon as I had names picked out for the twins, my mother-in-law told me how horrible they were. I cried for two days, my husband got in a fight with her, and then my own mother admitted she wasn't fond of the names I'd picked out either."

"Did you change their names?"

"I sure did." She stood upright like a soldier. "Because they had tainted them for me, ruined my beautiful choices. And in addition to being bloated and exhausted, I was bitter and angry at the two people who were most likely to relieve me so I could sleep," she said and laughed.

"Well, they're healthy and gorgeous, and you look amazing, and I love their names."

"You look wonderful yourself, and your boobs look great in that V-neck," she said. "I'm jealous!"

"Thanks." I looked down, admiring my temporarily voluptuous figure.

"Which reminds me of one more thing." She waved her index finger in the air. "Do not breast-feed either."

"Oh, okay. Why not?"

"Because, seriously, my cleavage is a thing of the past. A distant memory, gone with my flat stomach and good metabolism. All these woman harping about the glory of breast-feeding and how it helps you lose weight." She pointed to her chest. "The only weight you will lose is in your boobs. See, mine are an empty shell of their former glorious selves."

"Good to know." I nodded, dizzy.

"Good luck with everything, Syd, and I guess I'll be seeing you around here during flu season," she said and gave me an extra-tight squeeze. As she strolled away, it occurred to me that she never asked about my nonexistent husband.

About five minutes after Kendra walked out of my hospital room, she came back in and informed me that she'd called our mom with the news. I was dying to talk with her myself. There are times in life that, no matter the circumstances, a girl needs her mom.

"She's on her way," Kendra told me. "Of course she had to be all the way up in Lake Forest at an early dinner, and she wants to stop at home and change her outfit before heading downtown. But she'll be here as soon as she can. Is there anything I can bring you?"

"Cheese fries?" My voice cracked as I tried to muster up a joke.

Kendra knew me all too well and sensed my nervousness. "Don't get upset, Syd, everything is going to be fine."

I closed my eyes and wiped a tear from my cheek. "Okay."

"I mean it. Now don't you worry about a thing. You're in good hands, and this is a wonderful, joyous day. I love you, and everything is good, okay?" She placed her hand on my leg. "You all right?"

"Just nervous."

"Well, I can't say I blame you, but they seriously look like they know what they're doing around here, so try and relax and think about meeting little Cinnamon."

I'd spent so many days and nights imagining what my daughter might look like, and what kind of person she would be, that it was hard to grasp that I was only a few hours from finding out. Maybe not what kind of person she would be, but certainly what she would look like.

More importantly, I'd worried about what kind of mother I would be, and really, what kind of life I could provide for her. It was no secret that providing for Cinnamon was everyone's biggest concern, including mine. My mom and I had talked the subject to death, and usually the conversation would end where it started—with me having no real grasp of the situation whatsoever.

My father, against my mother's wishes, had generously agreed to help me financially while I was on unpaid maternity leave, but that's pretty much all I had mapped out at that point. Whether you're married or not, young or old, until you've experienced having a child, there isn't a person in the world who can properly prepare you for it. That didn't stop people from trying, of course, but no one could answer my questions except for me...or Cinnamon.

Would we be more like friends than mother-daughter?

Would she think I was annoying?

What insecurities would she have?

Would she hate me for not being married?

There was no going back now because she was on her way whether I was ready or not. A corner of my bedroom and every square inch of my life had been cleared out to accommodate my daughter and all her needs. And my mother repeatedly told me that no matter what age she is, I would never stop worrying about her.

"She could be forty years old, married with kids, and you'll still be worried about her life, her bills, her husband's job, your grand-kid's fever," she'd tell me. "One day you'll understand why I pester you about everything."

So at that moment, lying there in my wanna-be-sage, green caftan, I did try and relax. I rubbed my stomach, sipped my water, and concentrated on the task at hand because in addition to turning my life upside down, I had to first conquer my fear of childbirth—an ominous event that, try as some did, no one could accurately describe, especially the pain and effect that it has on the body. The problem was that everybody is different, and everyone has her own opinion and story to tell. Never for one second did I consider not taking any and all painkillers that would be available to me. I let my doctor know early on that he could go ahead and mark all my charts in thick, red pen: SHE WANTS THE DRUGS.

After about an hour in the examination room—and about three diaper changes—Peyton and another nurse took me up to Labor and Delivery while Kendra followed with my bag and my glass of water. The room was about four times larger than the one I'd just left, and with even more monitors. They immediately hooked me up and I watched as a ticker tape quickly began printing out Cinnamon's stats.

"Everything looks good so far. You're only about two centimeters dilated though, so it could be a while." Peyton addressed both my sister and me.

I glanced at the clock on the wall across from my hospital bed, and it was seven thirty in the evening. "How long do you think?"

"It's hard to say," she said, looking at the ticker tape. "We never know when our guest of honor will appear."

"Dr. Pearl?" I asked hopefully, and saw Kendra roll her eyes.

"No," Peyton said with a smile. "Your baby."

"Gotcha."

She let the ticker tape fall gently against the wall of monitors and grabbed a clipboard before saying she'd be back to check on me soon. Kendra sat on the edge of the bed and rested one hand on the thin sheet covering my legs.

"That must be the receipt for all this special attention, spilling out of that machine," she joked. "Mom should be here in about forty minutes."

"Thanks, Kendra. You know there is no way I could've done any of this without you."

"Stop it, and don't you dare make me cry." She squeezed my hand. "I wouldn't miss this for the world."

"I mean it. Thank you."

"You're welcome. Now how about some television?" she said and flipped through the channels until she landed on *Wheel of Fortune*.

My mom arrived, out of breath and wearing an enormous grin. "My little grandbaby isn't here yet, is she?" she asked as she flew into the room.

My mother had taken on two personalities since I'd become pregnant. The first consisted of her putting on a proud, brave face for friends and neighbors, where she'd delight in the thought of becoming a grandmother in her late forties. The second personality was a version of her prepregnancy self, in which she was more knowledgeable, more prone to lectures, and more of an expert than before. Personality number two had told me on more than one occasion that I would need her more than ever, and I should heed every bit of advice she offered to me. She'd raised two daughters and knew all there was to know about childrearing. She had yet to lend me any of the books on her nightstand. Thankfully personality number one arrived at the hospital that day.

"She's still cooking in there," I said.

Mom placed a brown grocery bag on the floor and put her keys on the table next to me. "Well, Kendra told me the nurse said it might be a bit longer, so I picked up some magazines and a few sandwiches for us."

Kendra dashed over to the bag. "Sydney is fasting, so I will have hers."

Mom looked at me. "Oh, honey, I'm sorry. You're not allowed to eat anything?"

"It's okay. I'm not remotely hungry."

At about nine o'clock the pain started to get really bad. I guess it had been building slowly, but the worst of it came over me very quickly. I went from chatting with my family to being unable to open my eyes, move my legs, or speak. The nurses had said to let them know when my pain was at a ten, and I couldn't conceive of it getting any worse than it was at that moment. It felt like there was a car parked on my lower back...or on my butt, I wasn't exactly sure. Either way, the car was blowing blazing-hot exhaust fumes through my lower torso and preventing me from doing just about anything. It wasn't a pain that I would've normally cried from had I been injured. It was more of a paralyzing, pressure-filled heat in an unexpected location. A few women had likened the pain to horrible menstrual cramps, so I had assumed I would be doubled over, clutching my side. Instead I was lying on my side, clutching the hand rails, wishing this person would move their damn car! I whacked my mom's arm as she tried to rub my forehead, and thankfully she was unfazed by the assault.

"Just try and breathe, sweetie," she said calmly. "The nurse is on her way."

"I can't move. I can't move any part of my lower body." I strained to get those few words out and began sweating profusely.

"I know, honey. Just hang in there."

Peyton came in, walked around to the side of the bed to where my forehead was pressed against the metal railing, and gave me a questioning look.

"Ten!" I said with wide agonized eyes.

"I'll get the epidural," she informed me, and I heard Kendra thank her on my behalf.

Dr. Pearl finally arrived with the anesthesiologist, and I grumbled some crack about how smart he was to have kept his distance until then.

One good thing about getting an epidural, besides the obvious, is that because my labor pains were so bad, I hardly felt the large needle being sunk into my spinal cord. Within what seemed like seconds, the car drove off my butt, the fumes withdrew, and my entire body enjoyed instant relief. It was like walking into a steam room and inhaling warm, jasmine-scented air, causing my limbs to relax and move freely again.

Mom and Kendra were cowering in the corner as a result of my earlier disposition. "How's it going over there?" Kendra called over to me, waving a white hand towel from the bathroom.

"It's safe. I'm a new woman." I smiled and they hustled over to the bed. "Seriously, how could anyone go that alone? How could you not have an epidural?" I asked them anxiously. "Any woman that tells me she chose to have natural childbirth is considered nuts in my book."

"I had both of you naturally," Mom announced proudly.

Kendra and I nodded to each other.

"Well, I'm just glad to have you back," Kendra said. "Water?" She handed me a tall Styrofoam cup with crushed ice and a straw.

The next few hours consisted of the three of us trying to sleep among the beeping monitors, and the nurses turning me around like a rotisserie chicken to keep Cinnamon's heart rate from dropping.

Some time around two o'clock in the morning, Dr. Pearl came in and declared that he was not happy with her fluctuating heart rate, and they needed to get her out as soon as possible.

"Great. Isn't that why we're here?" I asked wearily.

"Yes, but you haven't progressed much and I can't wait any longer for you to dilate. We need to get her out now," he said, as nurses scurried around the room behind him, tapping monitors and folding sheets.

My mom dragged herself off the recliner and over to my hospital bed. "Dr. Pearl, is everything okay?"

"I'm worried about the baby's heart rate. It's dropped below where we like to see it one too many times, so we're prepping for a C-section."

"A C-section?!" Mom and I said in unison.

"Yes, I'm afraid we need to get the baby out right away. Don't be concerned, everything will be fine, but you can only have one person accompany you in there," he said to me. "The nurse will provide that person with scrubs, and I will meet you in surgery." And with that he was gone.

Peyton approached us and took note of our shocked expressions. Kendra was snoring on the daybed. "This happens all the time, so just take a minute and try not to worry like Dr. Pearl said. I will get a set of scrubs, and I'm sorry to rush you, but we do need to get you out of here in the next few minutes," she said and left the room.

I gazed into my mother's eyes like a shocked, frightened six-year-old girl about to get a flu shot. *I didn't want that flu shot. Nobody mentioned I was getting a flu shot today. It was supposed to be a routine checkup with a lollipop chaser. Why did the doctor just say I need to get a flu shot?! Why, Mommy?*

My eyes begged my mother for some immediate comforting. "A C-section? Mom, I don't want a C-section!"

She held my hand and came through for me. "I'm sorry, my dear, but it doesn't look like you have a choice," she said, our fingers entwined nervously. "You are in the very best care and all that matters is getting our little girl out safely, and if Dr. Pearl thinks this is the best and only way to do that, then we can't disagree."

"I don't know anything about a C-section. I didn't read up on them at all. I didn't study the effects, or the pain, or the aftereffects. I have no idea what I'm getting into." I slapped my forehead and the move tugged on my IV cord.

Kendra staggered over to us as my mom continued talking.

"You will have a quick lesson I guess, and like I said, the baby's safety is everyone's first and only concern at this point," Mom said with authority.

"What's up?" Kendra asked.

"She's having a C-section," Mom whispered as if I might freak out having it repeated to me.

Peyton entered the room with one pair of scrubs. "Who's coming with us?"

I began to sob.

"Only one of us can be with her during the surgery," my mom informed Kendra.

Kendra exchanged glances with everyone in the room. I'm sure she would have liked to ask me what my preference was, but just as Kendra did on most occasions, she took control and made the right decision for the group. "Don't even think twice about it, Mom. Go ahead. I wouldn't dream of battling you for this honor," Kendra said, and my mom glowed with delight. "Besides, if I see even one drop of her blood or bodily fluids, I'll vomit."

My mom looked like she was dressed up as a surgeon for Halloween when she followed my bed down the hall as it was wheeled into surgery. I was so drugged up and loopy by then that all I can remember concentrating on was keeping my own vomit at bay, and spitting into the shallow little tray my mom held next to my face. Besides that, I felt nothing. I knew that I was naked from the waist down, and that my legs were spread and strapped to the table, but I felt none of it. Modesty has never been much of an issue since that day.

"Is that her?" I heard my mom ask someone, and then she turned to me. "I think she's out. Oh, Sydney, I think I saw her!" She was giggling and crying.

"Where is she?" I said amid my acid trip.

"I don't know yet." She craned her neck, then called out to the staff, "Is she okay?"

I never heard an answer, but my mom eventually came back to my face. "She's fine. They had to clean her lungs out. She'd apparently inhaled something she shouldn't have."

"Misbehaving already," I mumbled.

My mom was bobbing up and down next to the bed, her priorities forever shifted. She was desperate to be with the baby.

Dr. Pearl walked over with a large pink burrito in his arms and handed it to me. I reached up to grab it and immediately started to throw up. Peyton grabbed the tray and Mom grabbed the baby from Dr. Pearl.

"Can I see her?" I asked once the coast was clear.

"She's beautiful, Sydney. Just perfect," my mom squealed.

And she was.

Her head was perfectly round and covered in a fuzzy layer of caramel-colored hair. Her eyes were closed, but her cheeks were pink and smooth, and she was as quiet as a mouse.

"Do you want to hold her?"

"Okay," I said, trying to keep my eyes open.

My mom tucked her in between my arm and my right side because I was in no condition to be cradling a baby, so she rode there in silence as the nurses pushed my bed out of surgery. I saw my mom give Dr. Pearl a giant bear hug and wipe her eyes as she thanked him over and over.

It was 7:00 a.m. by the time Cinnamon and I were cleaned up, vaccinated, footprinted, and checked into a new hospital room. Kendra had gone home to change and told my mom she'd be back at the hospital by eight o'clock with scones and coffee for everyone.

I was wearing a new green sheet and my hands were so swollen they looked like a pair of blown-up rubber gloves. "I'm the jolly green giant," I said to my mom, but she was oblivious to me, spinning around the room holding the baby and feeding her a tiny bottle of formula.

"Okay, my dear," she sang, addressing me but smiling at her pink bundle. "It's about time we name this little angel, so what's it going to be? I refuse to refer to her as a spice for one moment longer."

I looked up at my daughter, tightly swaddled and secure, and thought back to the day I took a pregnancy test during finals week. I'd wished so hard for that test stick to produce one pink line. All I'd wanted was to see one pink line, get back to my studies, and get on with my life. But I did not get my wish that night.

A wave of pride and contentment came over me as I reminisced about my twist of fate. I smiled at my mom knowingly. "Her name is Grace."

CHAPTER TWENTY-SIX
Grace

Once my hopes of reuniting with my bio-*not-so-logical* father on an all-expense-paid trip to California were shattered along with Nana Lynne's left hip, my dad stepped in to save the day.

"What's so great about the West Coast anyway?" he asked me one morning as I was eating a bowl of cereal, and then he handed me three tickets to New York.

I grabbed the three pages of printer paper from his grip and wiped milk off my chin with the back of my hand. "What's this?"

"It's three tickets to New York." He took the stool next to me and leaned on his forearm. "One for me, one for you, and one for Chloe. Unless of course you'd rather Patch come along." He smirked. "We won't make it for spring break obviously, but we'll go the first week after school gets out in June."

The tickets glistened in my hands like they were covered in Swarovski crystals. I hugged my dad, put my self-pity on a shelf, and called Chloe.

She screamed into the phone and accepted my invitation to tour the Big Apple without even checking with her mom first.

"There isn't anything she could possibly have planned for me that could trump this, so count me in!" she exclaimed.

I ran downstairs to tell my dad that Chloe would be my plus one and to thank him again.

"It's my pleasure. I'm happy that I can do this for you," he said, sitting at his desk in front of the computer. "Gracie, I know how upset you were about the trip to Los Angeles being canceled, and you've been walking around here with a really crappy attitude because of it."

I looked away, ashamed because he was right. One day I had accused Patch of stealing my phone and screamed at him for fifteen minutes, only to have my mom call and say it had fallen out of my pocket and into the back of her car. She then yelled at me for taking my anger out on Patch, for which I felt badly, but never apologized.

"The reason I did this for you is because you deserve it, not because anyone around here feels sorry for you." He paused to make sure I understood him. "It's because you got great grades, you made captain of the volleyball team, and Mom and I are immensely proud of the things you've accomplished and the young woman you've become."

"I know. Thanks, Dad."

"I hope so, because if you want to waste your time feeling sorry for yourself when you're alone, that's fine. But you're not permitted to take things out on the rest of this family, okay?"

"Okay." I twirled my hair.

"Your mom and I know what you're going through is tough, and if there was something I could do to change things…well, I wouldn't," he said. "You are a beautiful, smart, fortunate girl, and I don't want to see you acting out and being defensive about the hand you've been dealt. You're too good of a person, and I expect more from you than that." He stopped to make eye contact. "You're way too sweet to harbor all these grievances."

He used to say I walked around with a chocolate chip on my shoulder.

And from that day forward, I was able to put my insecurities about my height, my genetic mysteries, and my jealousy toward Patch behind me. Not the "behind me" where I toss everything in a tall kitchen garbage bag and walk away from the curb. But, like, in my back pocket "behind me" rather than front and center where those things tended to distract me from what really mattered. All thanks to my dad.

Our summer trip to New York was nothing short of memorable and amazing. We stayed at the Le Parker Meridien on West Fifty-Sixth Street, and Chloe and I truly felt like two of the hippest girls in town. The hotel room was ultra modern, like nothing I'd seen before, decorated in a charcoal-gray color scheme with accents of bright orange in the form of towels and accessories. The sink was a sleek slab of polished concrete, and the toilet flusher took me five minutes to locate. Outside our window were more windows. We looked straight into offices and coffee shops and apartment buildings so close we could almost touch them. The television in our room was positioned in the center of a half wall, and spun on an axis so that you could watch it from the bed or the couch. Dad slept on the bed, and Chloe and I shared the pullout. After we unpacked, we headed out to some proper tourist locations, but not before grabbing a cheeseburger wrapped in paper from the Burger Joint in the lobby. I can still smell that glorious greasy creation to this day.

My dad, Chloe, and I spent three days touring delis, museums, shops, landmarks, and theaters, and he surprised us with tickets to *Wicked* our last night in town.

I was so grateful for that trip and the experience he'd given me. I thanked him as well as any sixteen-year-old could thank someone for anything, but I hope he realized how much it meant to me.

CHAPTER TWENTY-SEVEN
Sydney

The C-section bought me five days of hospital stay, where all I had to do was push a button to call the nurse and she'd come in and change Grace's diaper. My dad came that first afternoon, after I'd woken up from a nap, and brought a dozen pink roses with him.

"She's a looker, Syd, just like her mom."

"Thanks, Dad. Sorry about turning you into a grandpa at the ripe old age of fifty-two."

"It's my pleasure."

I handed Grace over to him and he held her tightly wrapped in her blanket and cotton hospital cap. My father hardly had any gray hair and didn't look like anybody's grandfather, so it was easy for me to picture my own infant self in his arms twenty-two years before.

"How's she behaving so far?" he asked.

"Hasn't sassed me once."

"Just you wait."

My mom walked in with a tray of brownies and an enormous fruit bouquet. "More deliveries for little Gracie!"

I grabbed a brownie as she held the tray in front of me. "I mean, this is just rude. Don't people realize that I'm now in weight-loss mode? Who had the decent sense to send the fruit?"

My mom gave me a funny smile. "It's from Mr. and Mrs. Reynolds," she said. "And I also wanted to tell you that I spoke with

Caroline last night. She called the house to see how you and Grace were doing. Wasn't that lovely of her?" Mom asked my father and me. "She wanted me to give you a kiss, and let you know that she sends her prayers and well wishes. I must say, Sydney, she was very kind in her concern for you."

I looked at the fruit and felt shame. Ethan's mom was a wonderful, smart, sophisticated woman who knew the importance of die-cut fruit, and probably breathed a huge sigh of relief when she found out I wasn't carrying Ethan's baby. "That was very nice of her," I said to my mom.

Mom sat on the edge of my bed as my father walked into the hallway with Grace still cradled in his arms. "We're going for a stroll," he said over his shoulder and adjusted her cap.

Mom turned to me with a serious expression. "Honey, she also told me that Ethan is coming in to see you."

"Why?!"

"Because he cares about you and wants to meet your daughter I assume," she said as if I should've known.

"Oh, I'm sure Mrs. Reynolds is thrilled about that."

"She didn't seem to be bothered, if that's what you mean."

I wriggled myself up higher against the pillows. "I'm not ready to see him. He's going to look at me weird and I just don't know if I can handle it."

"Look at you weird? What does that mean?"

"I mean, he's going to take pity on me, or wish things were back to how they used to be, or, I don't know…wish I didn't have a baby. He's the last person I want to visit us right now," I told my mom, but I was lying. I did want to see him. In fact I'd thought of him so much over those few days in the hospital, I almost cried when I called home for my messages and heard his voice.

Congrats, Sydney. Hope you're feeling well. You are going to be the most amazing mother a girl could ask for. I can't wait to meet her.

I called my machine over and over before calling him back. I'd tried him on his office phone the next day but reached his voice mail.

Hi, Ethan. I got your message last night. Still in the hospital. We're both doing well. Thanks so much for checking in.

It was short and simple, but what I'd wanted to say was:

I wish this was our daughter, and I wish you were here with me gazing at her puffy lips and tiny hands for hours on end. I wish it were you pacing the floor with this little pink bundle and fielding phone calls from adoring friends and relatives. I wish you were sleeping in the room with me on the horrid, cramped daybed they have reserved for new dads…ideally ones who are less than five feet tall. And I wish that I didn't have to go this alone, and I miss you so much it gives me a stomachache when someone mentions your name. And I love you.

Mom leaned over and grabbed a daisy-shaped pineapple slice. "He's not going to pity you. Don't act like you don't know how much he still cares about you. It would be very cruel for you to ask him not to come. You've kept him at bay long enough and I won't stand for it," she demanded.

"You're sounding like a grandmother."

"I am a grandmother."

"He can come," I relented.

"You should call him. Kendra said he tried to reach you all day yesterday and even called her at home," she informed me.

"I left him a message at the office, but I will try again."

"Why don't you try again now?"

"Why don't you chase down my daughter from her easily distracted grandfather and maybe I can have a moment to myself?" I made a fake smile.

My mom lifted the phone off the side table, placed it on the mattress next to me, gave me a kiss on the head, and left the room.

Ethan answered on the second ring. "Hello."

"Hi, E." My voice cracked, and I pulled the thin, knit blanket over my still bloated belly.

"Hey, Mama," he said. "So how does it feel to be a parent?"

"At the moment, not too bad. I can finally breathe. That little monkey had been crushing my lungs for the past few weeks in a bad way," I told him.

"You can punish her, you know."

"I was going to, but she's pretty darn cute."

We had a few seconds of silence before Ethan spoke again. "Well, I hope it's okay with you, but I'm coming in sometime in the next two weeks, and I'd like permission to see you and meet Grace."

I closed my eyes and smiled. "Permission granted. How did you know her name?"

"My mom talked to your mom yesterday."

"Ah, yes, and she sent the most gorgeous fruit bouquet, each in their own geometric shape," I told him and we chuckled, like two people do when discussing one's mother. "How are things with you?" I asked, but I had only one agenda with my questioning.

"Things are pretty good."

"How are things with Robin?" I couldn't resist; it just came out. I'd been thinking about her almost as much as I'd been thinking about Ethan, and I was desperate to hear that she'd fallen off a moving train, or moved to Hong Kong.

He laughed quietly through his nose. "She's fine."

My mood took a left hook to the jaw. I swallowed hard.

"You just worry about yourself and Gracie, all right?" he said.

"All right," I said and closed my eyes. "Guess we'll see you soon then. I'll try and save some star-shaped kiwis for you."

"Sounds great. I can't wait to meet Grace and see you. Is there anything I can bring?"

"No, thank you. I can't wait to see you either."

"Okay, girly, talk to you later. Call me if you feel like chatting about breast-feeding, okay?" he said with a laugh.

I mustered a smile. "Good-bye."

"Bye, Syd."

Grace's new pediatrician entered the room later that afternoon for her first official checkup.

"Hi, Dr. Weinstein." I greeted him.

"Congratulations," he said routinely, and then went straight to the plastic bin she lived in for those first few days in the hospital. "I always tell my new moms not to get used to these house calls," he joked.

Dr. Weinstein examined Grace for about fifteen minutes, and then approached my bed. "She looks like a healthy young girl, that one. Any questions?"

I had about twelve hundred questions, but he seemed in a hurry and had his bag zipped and coat buttoned before finishing his sentence.

I tried to come up with something pertinent to ask, and my mother was looking at me like, "make it a good one," but I wasn't prepared for him. "Does she need to sleep with her hat on?"

He looked at me like I was a complete moron. "What hat?"

"Her hospital cap."

He glanced at my mother, then back at me. "Do you sleep with a hat on?"

I shook my head no.

"Good day, ladies," he said and walked out.

When my parents drove Grace and me home from the hospital, my dad topped off at about fifteen miles per hour. We'd had the crib and changing table from Taylor's mom delivered about two weeks prior so everything would be ready for Grace's homecoming. My mom slept over the first night and, after I burst into tears as she was about to leave the following afternoon, she offered to stay four more nights. Kendra apologized for not being able to stay over, but it was too hard for her with work and I think she was secretly pleased with how well my mother and I were getting along.

My own motherly instincts definitely began to kick in, but I was still a rookie in every sense of the word, and even a little scared of my own daughter. I watched my mother scoop her up and carry her around like a pro, yet every time I went to take Grace from her crib or bouncer, I did so with trepidation.

"You'll get the hang of it. Don't worry; she's not going to break," my mom would tell me.

"What if I scrape her face with my fingernail, or dislocate her shoulder by pulling her out too fast?"

"She'll be just fine, Sydney. You need to relax so she doesn't sense your tension," Mom advised me as if I were training a puppy. "I wish we could get her outside for some fresh air, but it's so darn cold."

"Honestly, I'm fine being holed up here for the next year or so. I don't want anything to happen to her."

When almost a week had passed, my mom packed her bags and headed home with the promise that she would be back to visit in two days. She wanted me to have some alone time with my daughter. That, and my dad was having a mental breakdown having to fend for himself.

Grace and I spent our time napping, cuddling, and napping.

Two days after my mom's departure, Ethan called to let me know that he'd be in town over the weekend and he planned on spending as much time with me as possible. Since I'd been in the same outfit for nearly ten days (sweatpants, heather-gray T-shirt, and no bra), news of his arrival jolted me into the shower and sent me into a mad panic looking for my makeup bag, which I hadn't seen since before Grace was born.

"It's me," Ethan yelled into the buzzer from the lobby of my building that Friday evening.

"Second floor, apartment C," I shouted back.

Waiting for him to reach my door seemed like forever. I paced my apartment twice, checked on Grace, who was sleeping, poured myself a glass of wine, and then finally heard him knocking.

When I opened the door he was standing there with a giant stuffed puppy, a bouquet of flowers, and a box of Double Stuf Oreos. I threw myself at him, his body still cold from being outside, and held on for dear life. He wrapped his fully occupied hands and arms around me and kissed the top of my head. He smelled like home.

"Wow, it's so good to see you!" I pulled back and looked up at him. "Please, come in," I said and nervously played with my hair.

Ethan walked around my apartment nodding and smiling. "Nice digs, Syd. Not too bad," he said, then turned to me. "These are for you, and this is for Grace. Can I see her?"

"She's asleep, but we can sneak in there and take a peek. And, please, be as quiet as you've ever been in your entire life. Trust me; you do not want to know the consequences of waking her before she's ready."

He crossed his heart and zipped his lips.

We tiptoed into my bedroom and spied on my little, sleeping angel. Her tiny mouth was open, but her eyes were shut and her body tightly swaddled.

"She's…"

"Shhhh." I threatened him with my finger, and we gazed in silence for another minute or so before sneaking back to the couch.

"She's beautiful, Syd."

"You're obligated to say that, but thank you. I agree entirely," I said and curled my legs up onto the cushion.

"So how does it feel?"

I smiled and pondered his question. "It's very surreal, just the mere fact that a human being came out of my stomach, let alone that this human being is now entirely dependent on me." I shook my head in honest disbelief. "I'm head over heels in love with that girl. It's really amazing," I said.

"It is pretty wild, and you seem like a natural. I always thought you'd be a terrific mom."

"Thanks." I felt proud, and then a little sad.

There was a time when I'd write *Sydney Reynolds* on a piece of paper, practicing my signature as Ethan's wife. I had assumed we'd have kids one day, maybe two or three, and that we'd have a huge, elaborate wedding beforehand. But I went and changed the course of our future in one fell swoop. One drunken evening filled with passion, carelessness, and Jägermeister. Yet, with Grace so sweet and flawless in the next room, it was hard to regret the choices I'd made that night, and the consequences that everyone, including myself, were initially so fearful of.

"It must be weird for you to see me with a baby," I said to him.

He nodded. "It's pretty…surreal, like you said. But I'm very proud of you for doing this on your own, and for making a very brave decision."

"I'm not exactly doing it on my own quite yet. In fact, if my parents weren't supporting me for these first few months, I honestly don't know what condition I'd be in. It wouldn't be pretty."

"Well, you do have their help, thankfully, and I'm sure Grace would have yours if she needed it. What's your plan as far as work goes?" he asked me.

"I have three months off, unpaid, and then I'm going to put her in day care. I have two places in mind. One is near my apartment and the other one is closer to work."

Ethan and I talked for another hour before Grace woke up. He followed me around as I excavated her from the crib, changed her diaper, gave her a bottle, burped her, and eventually put her back to rest.

"Not much of a party girl," he observed.

"Nope, things are pretty routine around here. Eat, burp, poop, and sleep. Try to contain your jealousy."

"It shouldn't be too hard."

Ethan stayed until she woke again around midnight, and I could barely keep one eye open to continue chatting with him. I was sad to let him go, but I knew he had to leave. We hugged goodbye and held each other so long by my door that I nearly fell asleep in his arms.

"Good night, Syd."

"Good night, E. Call me tomorrow, okay?"

"You bet."

Ethan spent the rest of his visit to Chicago inserting himself into Grace's routine and making sure I was taken care of as well. He brought me food, rented movies, and rubbed my head as I snored away on his lap. He never mentioned Robin, and I never asked about her again. When it came time for him to go back to Boston, I felt like a senior in high school again, watching him pull out of my driveway for the first time.

"Shhhh, don't cry, Syd. You know I can't stand it when you cry," he said from my doorway, about to leave.

"I'm sorry. I'm just so emotional lately," I said. "There's this 'Be Like Mike' commercial with Michael Jordan that I see every night, and all these kids are so happy, and he's like…Mike, you know, and all inspirational, and I burst into tears every time it comes on."

Ethan looked at me like I wasn't making any sense, and laughed.

"Anyway," I continued undeterred, "It's been great having you around. I wish you could stay." I widened my eyes and mouth in an effort to tame my tears. "And, Ethan," I said, shifting gears, "I also want to say, in person, how sorry I am."

He just smiled at me, knowing exactly what I was apologizing for.

I straightened my shoulders and continued. "Despite the beautiful little girl that is sleeping in my room, I want you to know how much I truly regret cheating on you, lying to you, and most of all… taking you for granted. You deserved none of it, and it kills me to think of ever hurting you like that."

Ethan nodded, pulled his sleeve over his hand, and used it to wipe my face. "It's okay, Syd. Thank you," he said and kissed the top of my head. "You have a lot going on here, and someone who needs you to be strong for her. I'm a phone call away, and will come back and visit my two favorite gals as soon as I can, okay?"

"Okay," I said and nodded.

Ethan went back to Boston, and I went back to being Grace's mother. But the time I'd spent with him that first weekend meant so much to me because I felt that we'd reconnected. Maybe not on a romantic level, but there was a bond between us that would never go away, and I still loved him. I never stopped loving him, and never stopped hoping that he would fall back in love with me as well.

Three months and one week after Grace was born, I returned to work. Kendra came with me at seven thirty in the morning the Monday I dropped Grace off at Happy Faces day care near my apartment, and we both held on to each other as one of the caretakers walked away with my daughter in her arms. Kendra and I stared through the glass observation window for about twenty minutes, drying our eyes and telling each other that she'd be fine.

I brought three framed pictures and a brag book filled with snapshots of Grace in every possible position to work that first day back. Midge had actually bought a gift for Grace from everyone in the client services department and had it waiting on my desk when I arrived.

Keri was the first to greet me with a hug. "It's great to have you back, and you look fantastic. I can't believe how quickly you've lost the weight."

"Thanks, I'm feeling much more like myself lately. Minus a social life that is."

Keri had tried to visit me during my maternity leave, but something always came up. "Well, I'm glad you're back. Midge has been pretty much the same, and Trevor has become a huge bore. Was it hard to leave her this morning?" she asked.

"It was soooo hard," I told her. "You should have seen my sister and me standing there blubbering like we were sending her off to war."

"Awww," she said and rubbed my back. "Will Panda Express for lunch ease the pain?"

"I think it might."

CHAPTER TWENTY-EIGHT

It only took me three weeks before I was able to drop Grace at Happy Faces without shedding a single tear, and needless to say, Grace was oblivious to any of it. Two days a week, my mom came downtown, picked Grace up early from day care around three thirty, and brought her back to my apartment for me. Those were my favorite days because, when I'd get home a little after six o'clock, there'd be dinner on the table, and a happy, fed, changed, sleepy baby in her jammies waiting to greet me. I used to tell my mom that she made the best husband. The other days were draining to say the least:

5:30 a.m.: alarm goes off

5:45 a.m.: last snooze button on alarm goes off

5:55 a.m.: shower, assuming baby is still asleep

6:00 a.m.: wrap hair in towel; get baby from crib; change diaper; shush screaming, famished baby; and race to kitchen

6:10 a.m.: pop bottle in microwave for twenty seconds, continue to shush screaming, famished baby

6:17 a.m.: begin to burp baby, check clock

6:18 a.m.: pat baby's back furiously, wipe sweat off own brow

6:20 a.m.: place baby in bouncy chair, throw clothes on self, and attempt to style kinky, half-dried hair

6:40 a.m.: turn coffee pot on—shit, meant to do that at 6:10

6:42 a.m.: apply makeup, check clock

6:50 a.m.: pour cup of coffee with cream and Sweet'n Low

6:55 a.m.: dress baby and pack her bag for the day—should have been done night before—wipe sweat from under eyes, smear makeup

7:15 a.m.: running late, dammit; grab baby bag and work bag; locate my shoes; dump untouched coffee in sink; grab baby; and head out the door

7:30 a.m.: drop baby at day care and run to bus stop

6:00 p.m.: pick up baby from day care, stop at Subway for dinner

6:30 p.m.: enter apartment, drop everything on the floor (except for baby), run to bathroom and pee while holding baby

6:45 p.m.: pop baby's bottle in microwave for 20 seconds and feed baby

7:00 p.m.: burp baby, play with baby

7:20 p.m.: give baby bath, put her in jammies

7:45 p.m.: put baby in crib

8:00 p.m.: take off coat, eat sandwich in front of TV

12:00 a.m.: wake up on couch, turn off TV, and crawl in bed

5:30 a.m.: alarm goes off again

By the time Grace was six months old, she actually looked forward to going to Happy Faces. She'd perk up as soon as I'd walk in the door and hand her off to her favorite caretaker, Miss Courtney. Courtney was my age and had studied child development at DePaul University in the city. She was going for her master's degree and hoped to be a child psychologist one day. She loved Grace, or at least she made me feel like she did, and that was all I really cared about.

"Stop me if I'm prying," Courtney said to me one evening at pickup. "Are you married?"

"I'm not." I shook my head and satisfied her curiosity.

"I hope you don't mind me asking. It's just that you seem about my age, and well, I'm always so interested in the kids' home situations."

She probably knew the answer to her question before she asked me because all she would've had to do was check Grace's file, but it didn't bother me. I much preferred it when people would question me directly about my situation, rather than just assume and make judgments without the facts to back them up.

"I don't mind at all. I appreciate that you're interested in her, and me. Her father and I don't have any contact. He was a friend from college, and let's just say he chose to look the other way."

She tilted her head. "I'm sorry to hear that."

"Please don't be sorry; it's fine." I took Grace from her. "She's as happy as a clam and has a huge fan club already," I said and kissed Grace on her puffy, pink cheek.

"I'm sure she does; she's such a sweetheart," Courtney said, and I truly felt her affinity for my daughter.

"Would you ever like to babysit for her? Are you allowed to do that?" I asked.

"We aren't allowed to, unfortunately, but my younger sister is a freshman at Northwestern, and she's always looking to make extra money. She loves kids almost as much as I do. I would be happy to ask her for you," Courtney offered.

"My budget is a little tight and I've relied solely on my parents to watch her on the *very* few occasions I've had weekend plans, but I'd love to have a backup. Please give her my phone number if she's interested."

I really didn't have the money to be hiring babysitters, but I figured the less I had to rely on my mom, the better, and I had put a couple hundred dollars away for social emergencies.

"Will do, thanks," she said, then grabbed a clipboard off the wall and headed back to the office.

Courtney's sister, LeAnn, called me the next day and came to meet Grace and me the following weekend. She was as cute and lovable as her sister, and I couldn't help but feel grateful that there were people like them that existed in the world. LeAnn, too, was studying child development and was getting her bachelor's in education so she could teach middle-school kids in the Chicago public school system one day. I, on the other hand, spent most of my days trying to sort out the superficial problems of weary hotel guests, like why the curtains in their rooms don't close all the way, or why the television rotated more to the left than the right.

Ethan was coming home in late July for his parents' anniversary, and he'd sent me an invitation to their party. I had Taylor find out if Robin would be there, and she heard from Andrew that she wasn't coming in with Ethan to the party.

"Andrew says they're not dating anymore," Taylor informed me one afternoon while I was at work.

"Is that right?" I said in my most professional tone, doing my best to pretend I wasn't on a personal call.

"That's what he told me. Have you talked to Ethan lately?"

"I'm so sorry, Miss. We apologize for any inconvenience."

"I hate when you're at work." She snorted in annoyance. "He found out she cheated on him with an old boyfriend of hers. He heard a message that some guy left on her machine or something," Taylor told me.

"I see," I said and dropped my head down. Poor Ethan. It killed me to be one of two girls that cheated on him.

I vowed to be at that anniversary party. And if he was truly single again, I was going to sit him down, tell him how I felt, and do everything I could to make him understand how amazing he was.

My mom was going to be out of town the night of the party, so I asked LeAnn if she could watch Grace for me that evening. Ethan hadn't been home since his last visit back in early February, but we'd kept in touch. The Reynolds were having one of their elaborate catered events and combining the anniversary celebration with their annual summer block party. I was thrilled that he'd asked me to go and really excited to see him, but at the same time, I was nervous about seeing his mother. Mrs. Reynolds had always intimidated me, and although she'd never been anything but polite on the surface, I couldn't help feel that she never really cared for me. Ethan told me on more than one occasion that I was being ridiculous, and that she always had nice things to say about me, but sometimes you just know when you're being judged…and getting a low score.

Either way, I was going and I would arrive on time, with a chilled bottle of chardonnay and Taylor Gold with me for support.

"I'm in town for one night. Why on earth would we want to go to that bore fest?" Taylor asked me.

"Obviously because Ethan will be there."

"Why don't you just tell him to meet us out in the city afterward? I have no interest in talking to my parents and their friends about my job and listening to how different things were for them back in the Dark Ages."

"I haven't seen him in months, and you know what this means to me. Please Taylor, his mother will be much less scary with you there."

"Fine, but by the time my father has his fifth bourbon, I'm out of there," she let me know. "Besides, you and lover boy aren't going to want me around anyway."

"Very cute."

"I mean it. I'm sure Ethan wants you to himself, and he knows if I'm there he's going to have to use a crowbar to separate us."

"It's not like that with him anymore. Trust me, I wish it were."

"Sydney, if you go by yourself, you'll have a much better chance of getting the alone time with him that you want," she said trying to convince me.

"I know where you're coming from, but we don't have that relationship right now, and he isn't going to spend the evening by my side like the old days. That's why I need you there to keep me company for the times when he'll be off chatting with all the other women that Mrs. Reynolds is probably having bussed in to court him."

"Court him? Oh Lord, you do need to get out more."

"So you'll go with me?"

"Yes."

"Great, what can I borrow?!"

The morning of the event, I picked Taylor up at O'Hare and drove to her parents' house in Winnetka, where she set me up with a great outfit: a black Donna Karan tank top with tiny black rhinestones on one shoulder, a black pleated miniskirt, and a pink Coach purse. The outfit alone could've paid my rent for two months. After I had my outfit, I headed back to the city and went to Marshall Field's, where I purchased a pair of sandals that were a knockoff of a Joan & David pair that Taylor owned. I could never understand why people would spend so much money on one pair of shoes.

When I got back to my apartment, I frantically tended to all of Grace's needs so that I could then focus on my own. Once she was fed and freshly diapered, I laid her down on a blanket and placed three of her favorite stuffed animals next to her. She wasn't quite crawling yet, just rolling from side to side, so she was still easily manageable in one spot. As I was drying my hair, the phone rang, and it was LeAnn.

"What's up, LeAnn?" I asked after we exchanged greetings.

"Sydney," she said gagging. "I am so sorry. I woke up this morning with a little cough and thought I could sleep it off, but after my nap I woke up with a fever."

I turned into a statue of a woman holding a hair dryer in one hand, phone in the other, mouth agape.

"Sydney?"

I placed the dryer slowly back on the sink counter and sat on the toilet. "I'm here."

"I'm so sorry. I called Courtney to see if she could cover for me, just this once, but she has plans." Cough, gag, cough. "I feel terrible. I know how much you were looking forward to going out. I just don't think you want me near Grace like this."

I shook my head. "No, of course. Don't worry about it. Just take care of yourself," I said, and we ended the call as my heart sank into my imitation designer sandals.

I walked into the next room and looked at Grace. She was rocking back and forth like a ship on the high seas and smiling at her furry deckhands. I sat down cross-legged next to her and called Ethan.

"Hey, you," he said.

"My sitter just canceled."

"Oh, no. Well, just bring Grace with you," he said without hesitation.

A burst of frustrated laughter shot out of my mouth. "I don't think so."

"Seriously, everyone would love to meet her."

"I can't bring her with me," I said with a sigh. Mostly because I hardly ever took her anywhere unless it was absolutely necessary.

She required so much crap that I always felt like a skycap whenever we were out together. The diaper bag, the car seat, the bottles, the pacifiers, the changing mat, the wipes, and all the toys in their primary-colored glory—none of which would complement my outfit.

"I'm not going to argue with you. I'm in town for two days, and I'm expecting to see you at my parents' party tonight, with Grace," he said with a very un-Ethan-like firmness.

"Ethan, don't be that way. You have no idea what it's like with her. First of all, she demands all my attention, and secondly, I won't be able to relax and enjoy myself with her there."

"You're being ridiculous. She's a baby, and you're acting like she's some demanding celebrity. I'll see you both tonight," he said and hung up.

He'd never hung up on me.

I immediately dialed Taylor.

"Yo," she answered.

"Tay, my sitter just canceled. I'm so upset! I just called Ethan and he said to bring Grace, and I told him that's impossible and how she can't just tag along like another girlfriend, and he said 'I better see you tonight' and HUNG UP!"

"Okay, Hormone Heidi, calm yourself *way* down," she said. "Take a deep breath, and let's figure out your options. First, you could absolutely bring her along; there will be plenty of people there who would be dying to take her off your hands, my mother being one of them. Or you can go for a couple hours and leave her with your dad."

I looked at Grace smiling and swaying next to me. "I'll bring her," I moaned. "I cannot believe this."

"Don't make such a big deal about it. You know she's going to be the life of the party."

I packed my car with every possible thing that Grace might need over the course of the evening: play pad, food, formula, pacifiers, wipes, bibs, pajamas, animals, her favorite blanket, and enough diapers to soak up three gallons of milk. The party started at five o'clock, and I didn't think I would be there much past her seven o'clock bedtime because I'd never put her to sleep anywhere but in a crib at night.

Taylor got in the backseat of my car and sat with Grace. She cooed and giggled with her during the ten-minute ride from the Golds' home to the Reynolds' home. The valet helped me out with the diaper bag and car seat while Taylor danced ahead with Grace in her arms, leaving me to my skycap duties.

"You are the sweetest little muffin!" Taylor was cheering, and then turned to me. "Let me take the suitcase. You should walk in with her. She might just be the best accessory a girl could have," she said and handed me my daughter as we stepped into the foyer.

Taylor placed the bag and car seat carrier next to a hall table by the stairs, and then winked at me. "You look great, girl. Let's do it."

The two of us walked out onto the back patio to a sea of people, almost all of whom instantly showered Grace with oohs and aahs. Ethan rushed over as soon as he saw a group of empty nesters begin to circle Grace and me like a swarm of zombies.

As predicted, Mrs. Gold was first in line. "Hand her over this instant!" she ordered and clapped loudly. "Oh, Sydney, she's the most beautiful little thing! Yes, you are. Oh, yes, you are," she said to Grace.

"Thank you," I said and gave Taylor's mom a kiss as she slowly pulled Grace from my arms. I never spent much time with babies before having one of my own, but everyone always told me how remarkable it was that Grace was willing and happy to be held by anyone. She never resisted or tightened her body or reached back for me once.

When I turned to give Ethan a hug, Mrs. Reynolds was standing by his side, gazing lovingly at my daughter. I looked over at Grace, who was in Mrs. Gold's arms, and she was staring back at Ethan's mom with the biggest, cheesiest grin on her face.

"Every guest in my home must see me first, Eddy, so hand her over," Mrs. Reynolds said to Taylor's mom, her arms outstretched.

"Oh, no, you don't, Caroline. I've only just got my claws into her."

"Don't make me escort you out of my party," Mrs. Reynolds joked.

"Oh, for goodness' sake," Mrs. Gold said and took a huge whiff of Grace's neck. "I could just take a bite out of her; she smells so delicious."

She passed Grace along to Ethan's mom, who had yet to say anything to me, and Mrs. Reynolds cradled Grace in her arms while whispering quietly to her so no one else could hear. Taylor discreetly pinched my side and the two of us exchanged glances with Ethan, who was also staring at Grace in his mother's arms.

"Sydney," her low, throaty voice startled me. "Can I have a word with you?"

Ethan spoke first. "No, Mom, you can't. She just got here."

Taylor and her mom watched closely.

"It's fine," I said. "I would love to catch up."

I walked with Mrs. Reynolds into the formal living room and she never took her eyes off of Grace. She was letting Grace grab her fingers, suck on her diamond pendant, and play with the fabric-covered buttons on her blouse. She could've cared less that in fewer than three minutes she went from being impeccably dressed to dripping in drool.

"She's a delight. What a good baby you are," she said to both of us.

"Thank you. She's been very easy so far."

"And she looks just like you."

"Yes, I hear that a lot," I said, and it was true. I would've loved Grace more than anything in the world regardless of what she looked like, but the fact that she truly resembled me more than Kevin was a welcome relief.

"Thank you for bringing her today."

"Well," I let out a small, guilty laugh. "It wasn't my first choice."

"I told Ethan a month ago to ask if you would bring the baby, and he said you'd rather not."

Ethan had never asked me to bring Grace to the party. "Oh, yes, well, it's just that she goes to bed so early, but my sitter canceled this afternoon and didn't leave me with much of a choice."

"I see."

Mrs. Reynolds was holding Grace and indulging her in whatever she wanted at that moment. I felt very comforted by her like never before, and realized I was smiling like a giddy cartoon character when she looked at me.

"I'm very proud of you, Sydney. You've proven yourself to be a strong, independent young lady, and a wonderful mother. You should be very pleased with yourself."

I strained to speak. "Thank you."

"Have you heard from her father?" She casually downshifted to the tough questions.

I began to readjust on the couch, uncrossing, then recrossing my legs. "No, I haven't. I really don't have any contact with him," I said and cleared my throat.

"I see," she said. "It must be very hard on you."

"It hasn't been too bad, and honestly, I never counted on him for anything from the beginning, so it's fine. I'd be at much more of a loss without my parents' help." I smiled, trying to lighten the topic.

"Your mother must be delighted."

"Tickled pink, that one."

Grace began to fuss, and I realized it was time for her to eat. "I think she's hungry."

"Well, then, no party guest of mine should want for anything, especially food. Where is her dinner?" she asked.

Ethan walked in just as his mom questioned me. "Your time is up," he said.

"Go on then. Sydney is about to get Grace's food, and you two can go have fun."

I looked at Ethan with concern.

"Mom, you need to unhand the child," he informed her.

"She's hungry, and I was going to feed her. Sydney, darling, where is her food?"

"It's in the diaper bag, next to the stairs," I said and instinctively reached for Grace.

"I will take care of her, if that's all right with you," Mrs. Reynolds said and took a step backward. "You two go and relax. I will come find you when we're done."

"Okay," I said flatly. She was not one to argue with, and Ethan was looking at me like an eager puppy, like, "Great, let's go!"

He took my hand and led me outside, but my eyes stayed on Grace and his mother until we rounded the corner and they were out of sight.

"Maybe I should just tell her how much to feed her?" I said to him, but looked toward the house.

"She'll be fine. She had babies of her own once," he said reassuringly.

We walked past a bemused Taylor, sitting almost on Andrew's lap and dangling one of her long legs over the cement wall, and Ethan led me to a wrought-iron bench tucked away in the woods behind his parents' home.

I took a seat and patted the wood slats next to me.

Ethan reached in his pocket before sitting down. "Now don't get all excited and weepy; this isn't for you," he said and handed me a little velvet box.

"Then why are you giving it to me?"

"It's for Grace."

I gently took the box from his hand and opened it. Inside was a tiny, delicate gold chain, with a small red gemstone hanging from it.

"It's garnet, her birthstone," he said. I'd had no idea what her birthstone was.

I shook my head. "You are unbelievable. Thank you," I said quietly.

"I know she's too young to wear it now, but one day you can tell her about me, and who it's from. I really wanted to do something special for her."

"It's beautiful, Ethan," I said and closed the box. "You never cease to amaze me." We sat and talked for almost an hour, until I couldn't stand not knowing what Grace was up to for one more minute. I checked my watch and saw that it was a quarter past seven.

"I better fetch Grace before she turns on everyone and ruins her impeccable reputation."

Ethan and I went back to the house and located Mrs. Reynolds in the kitchen as she was telling the catering staff where to put the desserts on the buffet table and which serving pieces were to be paired with which sauces.

"What'd you do with the kid, Mom?" Ethan asked.

"She's in my bedroom, asleep."

"Asleep?" I gasped.

"Why, yes," she said. "I changed her after she ate, then Taylor helped locate her pajamas and her carrier, and we rocked her to sleep. You're welcome to go up there."

Ethan and I tiptoed up the giant staircase and through the double doors into his parents' bedroom. Taylor and her mom were sitting on a loveseat in the corner of the room, deep in conversation, and Grace was sound asleep exactly like Mrs. Reynolds had said.

"Guess you can stay a bit longer." Taylor smiled at me, and Ethan led me back outside to the bench in the woods, where we sat until midnight without a care in the world.

CHAPTER TWENTY-NINE

After Ethan returned to Boston, we fell into a routine of lengthy phone conversations and a few short weekend visits. We'd discussed his failed relationship with Robin, but I never did get the chance to declare my true feelings to him. I was hesitant. We were rebuilding our friendship, and I was worried that I might scare him away, or make things uncomfortable for him. I did tell him that I wished he lived closer, and he confessed that he was looking into a job transfer that would bring him back to Chicago one day. We never really discussed our relationship beyond that, but there was an underlying hope on my end that we'd be able to rekindle our affection as more than just close friends.

When Christmas rolled around, he was able to get a week off work, and since we hadn't had any real quality time together since his parents' party in July, he promised to make the most of his time with Grace and me. He was once again my best friend, and truly the only person I looked forward to talking to each day. He'd listen to all of my complaints about Midge, all my worries about money, and every little concern I had for my daughter, of which there were plenty. My job was going well, but it was becoming more and more obvious that if I wanted to grow within the company, I was going to have to put in more hours, and that meant less time with Grace. The older she got, the harder it was to leave her. She took her first steps at day care, and after Courtney called to let me know, I spent my lunch hour crying on the phone to Kendra about it.

Three days before Christmas Eve, I asked for the afternoon off to get some shopping done. The excuse I gave Midge was that Grace had a doctor's appointment. I picked her up from Happy Faces that afternoon around one o'clock, bundled us up, and headed to the Christmas windows on State Street. I pushed Grace up and down the shoveled sidewalks, crunching kernels of road salt with the stroller and admiring the city's holiday splendor. We stood in a long line to meet Santa Claus at an outdoor winter market in the Loop, and she went right to him, sat on his lap, tugged on his beard, and gazed at him in awe.

Kendra was going to come over to my apartment around six o'clock that night to have dinner with me and wrap the few gifts we'd jointly bought for our parents, and it was almost six o'clock by the time we left Santa. I waved down a cab, shoved the stroller in the trunk, and we hurried home after our little girls' day out. Since Grace's birth, I'd never been on time for anything.

Grace was beginning to fuss by the time we got home, and once we were through the door, she began to scream for her food. She was the sweetest, most amiable little girl, but delay her meal by even one minute, and she would turn on you. Which only made things worse because once she was screaming and freaking out, I lost all ability to focus on the task at hand and acted as though I'd never fed her before. The jars were harder to open when she was screaming, her bottles were more difficult to fill when she was screaming, and I dropped almost everything I tried to hold in my hands when Grace was having a tantrum. In the midst of her cursing me out and me trying to find a spoon, I heard my phone ringing. I darted out of the kitchen and away from her, which only elevated the ear-splitting volume of her cries, and reached for the receiver next to the couch.

"Hello?" I answered breathlessly.

"Is this Sydney Shephard?"

"Speaking."

There was a pause, filled only with Grace's shrieks in the background. "Sydney, this is Kevin Hansen's mother, and I'd like to speak with you about my granddaughter."

CHAPTER THIRTY
Grace

You can't very well look your mistake in the eye and say, "Don't make the same mistake I did." So growing up, my mother always had to find new and less offensive ways to warn me about safe sex once I reached high school.

"Do you want to have the talk?" she'd ask me.

"Nope, I'm good."

"Listen, Grace. Obviously I hope you're not having sex yet at your age, but I'm not naive. Just please don't forget that there are many, many reasons to protect yourself besides getting pregnant, such as STDs."

"But getting pregnant would be worse, right?" I liked to torture her, purely for my own enjoyment.

"You're not funny."

"I'm kidding. It's just that look on your face is priceless." I gave my mom a squeeze and lifted her off her feet. Something else I enjoyed doing for sheer maniacal reasons. Once I crossed five foot ten, she was doomed to be my rag doll.

I had my first real boyfriend in high school when I was almost seventeen. His name was Nick, and his family was Italian. My dad always said that Italian boys are only after one thing.

"What's that, Dad?" I'd inquire.

"The same thing every other boy is after," he'd say.

"Then why does him being Italian matter?"

"It just does."

Nick and I had been dating for a few months when he asked me to the senior prom. I was thrilled to have a date, and also thrilled to spend the night out with Nick. My mom agreed to let me go along with four other couples after the dance to Nick's family's vacation home in Michigan. It was about an hour drive from downtown, but the boys had all split the cost of a limousine, so no one would be driving.

Nick came to pick me up that night around six thirty. He had the obligatory corsage, which I told him I would not wear, and he was wearing a rented tuxedo with Converse high-tops. I greeted him at the door; his forehead was moist and shiny.

"You're sweating," I said.

"Am I?" he asked and wiped his brow with his cuff. "Where are your parents?"

"Inside, camera poised," I said and watched the moisture turn to actual beads of water. "Would you relax?"

"Let's just get this over with and get out of here."

"My plan exactly."

We went into the den, where my parents horribly acted like they were just reading and watching TV, and hadn't heard the bell.

"We're leaving," I announced.

"Not so fast, smart-ass." My mom stood and grabbed her digital camera off the white laminate side table. "You look very handsome, Nick."

"Thank you, ma'am."

"If you write your mom's e-mail down, I'd be happy to send these pictures to her," my mom offered.

"Thank you, ma'am."

My dad looked at me with a raised brow.

"Make it quick, Mom. We have friends waiting on us," I said in my best teenage vibrato.

Before Nick arrived, my mom had asked me if she could get a picture of us in front of the fireplace and in front of the house. But once we all saw how nervous he was, she relented and agreed to the front of the house only. Nick wiped his forehead no less than twelve times and then followed the two of us outside. My dad trailed behind with a silly grin and his hands in his pockets, while Patch came bounding up from the basement with a video game controller in his hand and a smart-ass look on his face.

"Over there by the rose bushes, if you don't mind," Mom pointed.

"Of course, ma'am."

I slapped my forehead. He was acting so strange.

We turned and faced my parents, Dad grinning and relaxed, Mom with the camera covering her face.

"We're done," I said after about four takes. My mom gave me an annoyed look, and I grabbed Nick's damp hand.

"You two have fun tonight, and no alcohol," Mom said. Sure, she wasn't naive.

"Yes, ma'am, we will."

My mom handed her camera to Dad and gave Nick a hug. "Please, call me Sydney."

CHAPTER THIRTY-ONE
Sydney

Sydney, are you there?" Kevin's mom asked me over the phone. Shockingly enough, I heard Kendra's knock at the door over Grace's hollering and ran to let her in. I shoved a jar of baby food in Kendra's hands, along with a rubber-tipped spoon, and disappeared to the bedroom.

"Yes, I'm still here. How did you get my number?"

"I got it from my son," she said to my surprise. "I apologize if I've alarmed you, but Kevin's father and I just learned that he has a child. With you."

I sat on the floor at the foot of my bed. "Yes, he does. Her name is Grace," I told her, head spinning. Why was this woman calling me? What could she possibly want? My apartment was quieter once Her Majesty was eating; however, that phone call did nothing to calm my nerves.

"Oh, *Grace*," Mrs. Hansen cooed. "What a beautiful name."

"Thank you," I said and began to perspire. "What can I do for you?"

"The reason for my call is that I'm wondering if you would allow me and my daughters to come and meet Grace—and you. As you can imagine, this blessed news came as quite a shock to our family, and it has been a very painful and confusing two weeks over here."

Her phone call was equally jarring. "Are you in Chicago?" I asked.

"No, dear, we live in Los Angeles."

Grace was nearly a year old, and I hadn't received so much as a postcard from Kevin. I'd called him three months before she was born to let him know that I was having a girl but never got any reply. Then, after almost two years pass since he first learned of my pregnancy, he decides to admit everything to his mother.

"Mrs. Hansen…"

"Please, call me Lynne."

"Lynne, I have no problem with you coming to visit us, and it would be my pleasure to introduce you to Grace. But I don't know whether you realize that Kevin has had no contact with me since the day I told him I was pregnant. So I'm a little surprised and curious as to how this phone call has come about."

She sighed. "Let me just say that Kevin's father and I are not proud of his choices in this matter, and Kevin has been frank with us about his lack of involvement. That being said, I'm not here to speak for him or make excuses for him; I am solely interested in meeting my granddaughter."

He was frank with them? I highly doubt they know the extent of his cruelty, but I wasn't going to further tarnish his image to the kind woman on the phone with me.

She continued before I could speak. "So, if it's all right with you, Kevin's three sisters and I would like to come to Chicago and see the both of you. I realize you are a new mother, but a mother nonetheless, and hopefully you can understand how much it would mean to me to be able to meet Grace in person."

Most days, I did my best not to think about Kevin Hansen, but I'd have been lying if I'd said I never thought about the questions Grace might have one day concerning her father and his family. Questions about relatives whom I'd never met or knew anything about. I figured the day would arrive when she'd come to me with those difficult inquiries and eager hopes of finding her roots. I mean, it wasn't like she was adopted and I had no way of locating her biological parents. I knew exactly who her father was—only he wanted nothing to do with her. Wouldn't that be much harder to explain? But there I was, faced with a woman who was obviously as eager and hopeful as Grace would be one day to meet her distant relative.

"It would be my pleasure," I said.

"Oh, thank you, my dear," she sniffed. "We would like to come out as soon as possible. Would just after the New Year be all right?"

"I can't see why not. I will double-check my calendar and get back to you if there is a problem, but I'm sure that'll be fine."

"Wonderful. We simply cannot wait to meet both of you."

"I look forward to it."

"Good-bye."

"Good-bye, Lynne," I said and hung up the phone.

Kendra slowly opened the door to my bedroom with a much happier version of the ravenous devil-child in her arms.

"What's with the greeting at the door?"

"Oh, yeah, sorry about that…it was just KEVIN'S MOM on the phone."

"No shit!" she said, and we stared at each other, mouths wide. "What the hell?"

I tossed the phone on the bed and took Grace from her. "She wants to come here with his *three* sisters and meet Grace. Apparently his family was just informed that he has a child."

"You're joking."

"You know I'm not."

"So…what did you say?"

"I said that I'd be happy to meet them and introduce them to Grace," I said and balanced my daughter on my hip.

"When are they planning on coming?" she asked.

"After the holidays, first week of January."

"Did you tell her what a shit her son has been?"

"I think she has some idea. She said she was ashamed of his behavior, but that she wasn't going to make excuses for him."

"Well, someone should."

Kendra and I walked back out to the couch, and I placed Grace in the center of her play mat with seven different toys, each one brighter than the next.

"I have to call Jenna. She's going to die when I tell her that Kevin's mom just called me."

"You should call Mom first and get her take on this. It seems a little creepy to me," Kendra said.

"I know Kevin's been a complete ass, but he comes from a decent family, and prior to him shunning me, we were good friends," I said, reminiscing. "He really was one of my favorite people at one time."

"Well, I wouldn't look at this reunion as any sort of way to get his attention. He's shown his true colors, and I just want you to be careful."

"Thank you, but I have no grand illusions of him coming back into my life in any way, shape, or form."

"Sydney, there must be a part of you that wishes, at least for Grace's sake, that he would step up and acknowledge her. And just because he's come clean with his family doesn't mean he's going to do right by you. That's all I'm saying," she said, and she was right.

There were many nights I sat alone feeling sorry for Grace, that she would grow up without a father and one day learn why. How could she not take his rejection personally? There was a part of me that always assumed he'd come to his senses and feel the need, if not the obligation, to foster a relationship with her.

"I know, you're right," I agreed. "Maybe we should call Mom and see if she has a book on this."

CHAPTER THIRTY-TWO

Ethan came into town the morning of December 23rd, but I didn't get to see him until late afternoon on Christmas day. We both had family obligations to attend to but were able to meet up at my apartment around five o'clock that afternoon.

"I come bearing gifts," he said and kissed my cheek before entering.

"We love gifts!"

He handed me two boxes, one about the size of a shoebox and the other about half the size of the first one. "No jewels this time, just a little something," he said to prepare me.

I opened the little box first, which was addressed to Grace. Inside was the cutest, smallest pair of pink fuzzy slippers I'd ever seen. "They're adorable!"

"You like?"

"Ethan, they are so cute. We love them," I said, and then unwrapped a matching pair for myself in the larger box.

I'm not sure why, but I was hesitant to tell Ethan about Kevin's family coming the following week. I guess I figured that any time Kevin's name was mentioned, all he would picture was the two of us having sex. It was my own twisted theory, of course, and Ethan had never said anything that would've made me feel that way, but I hated the thought of mentioning Kevin's name around him.

"Do you want to stay the night?" I asked. "I can't promise you won't be woken up by the sweet sounds of a baby demanding something of me around 2:00 a.m., but we'd love to have you."

"Sure," he said with a shrug.

Ethan spent the night on the couch, stayed through the next day, and then one more night before heading back out of town. We had a few flirtatious, tender moments but never kissed, and I never mentioned anything about Kevin's mom.

Since I worked in a hotel, which was open 365 days a year, Midge couldn't afford to have her entire staff off on New Year's Day. So Trevor, Keri, and I were told to choose between New Year's Day, January 2nd, and January 3rd as our day off. Trevor basically teared up while begging us for New Year's Day, and once I knew of Mrs. Hansen's plans, I settled for January 3rd as mine—the day Grace would meet her new grandmother.

My mom had been a little wary when I first told her the news that Kevin's mom wanted to come visit us, but then she thought about it and felt a great deal of admiration for what Mrs. Hansen had done. Mom said she could appreciate where Kevin's mom was coming from, and complimented her integrity and desire to do the right thing. She went on to say that if she found out she had a grandchild somewhere on this earth, she, too, would do everything in her power to unite herself with that baby, and that I should go out of my way to make Mrs. Hansen and her daughters comfortable in my home. She also informed me that serving them anything less than a crudités platter, port-wine cheese balls, and iced tea would be an embarrassment.

"Be sure the dishes are put away, and that you also have a pitcher of ice water on the counter with at least six clean drinking glasses," she instructed.

"Yes, Mom."

"Don't be patronizing, Sydney. I think you should consider yourself very fortunate that his mother has reached out to you in this way."

The morning Kevin's family was due to arrive, Grace was sitting on the floor chewing the ear of her white chenille dog, the one that had a blanket for a torso, while I attempted to wipe the stickiness off a variety of surfaces around the apartment. I was not really nervous, just hoping that they would be kind—and brief.

The doorbell rang fifteen minutes before I was expecting them, so I scooped Grace up into my arms and opened the door.

Standing there were Kevin's mom, Lynne, and his three sisters: Gabrielle, Sharon, and Katherine. Their eyes went immediately to Grace, then to me.

"Hi." I broke the ice. "I'm Sydney, obviously. Please come in."

They filed into my tiny apartment with bags of wrapped gifts and groceries.

"Well, this here is little Gracie," I said in a high-pitched child-like voice that charmed my daughter, as I hoped.

Kevin's mother moved in slowly and carefully. "May I?" she asked.

"Of course."

As Lynne Hansen took her granddaughter from me and into her arms, she burst into tears and wept for nearly three hours straight.

Sharon, who was a year younger than me, asked if she and her sisters could show me what they'd brought. I said yes and offered them some ice water before sitting down by the couch. I didn't really have any extra money to spend on hors d'oeuvres like my mother had demanded, so Keri suggested I put out a bowl of M&M's next to the water glasses and call it a day.

"You guys didn't have to bring us anything, but thank you," I said, overwhelmed by their generosity.

"This has been very difficult, yet very exciting for our family," Sharon said. "We just wanted to do something nice for you, and Grace."

She didn't have to say that, but it was genuinely nice to hear.

Katherine continued. "We don't want to dwell on Kevin, but we all want you to know that we feel blessed to have this opportunity, and cannot thank you enough for allowing our mother to spend this time with Grace." Katherine was the oldest of the three, and recently engaged.

I smiled at them and felt equally fortunate. "It's my pleasure. I'm happy to meet all of you." I paused and watched Grace touch Lynne's tearstained faced as she was being swung around in her grandmother's arms. "And I'm glad for Grace...to have so much love around her."

"She's absolutely beautiful, Sydney," Katherine said.

"Thank you. She's a really good baby."

Sharon pointed at the gifts. "Let's get to the goods!"

I tore through the gifts they brought like a five-year-old girl at her birthday party.

A pink denim jacket, pink cowboy hat, pink sneakers, black patent Mary Janes, two pink teddy bears, a stuffed puppy with lavender ears, a wooden stool with GRACE carved into it, three bibs with witty remarks, two onesies, and a handmade picture frame with a photo of the four women who were sitting in my apartment at that moment.

By the time we'd finished the gifts, the M&M's, and three albums filled with photos of Grace's first year, it was almost four thirty in the afternoon and Grace had nodded off in the arms of Lynne Hansen.

"You've rendered Grace and me speechless," I said. "Thank you so much. I'm overwhelmed."

Lynne handed my sleeping beauty over to her daughter Katherine. "Sydney, honey, may I have a moment with you?"

"Of course."

I followed her into the bedroom as Grace's aunts were left fighting over who would hold her next.

"Please," she said, and tapped the bed next to her. "As you can see, this is quite emotional for me." She reached in her pocket for a fresh Kleenex. "I was shocked to hear that Kevin had a child, and I was equally shocked to hear that he has not seen her or provided any support for you."

Mrs. Hansen paused to wipe her nose before continuing. "But he is a grown man now, and he must make and live with his decisions." She nodded and looked me in the eyes. "He is fully aware of how his father and I feel about everything. Now, that being said, this gorgeous, perfect little angel is a true gift, and I want to thank you for having her…and for welcoming us into your home like this." Her voice was gentle and quiet. "If you will let me, I would like very much for us to stay in touch and be involved in her life as much as you feel comfortable with."

"Mrs. Hansen…"

"Please call me Lynne, Nana Lynne."

I wrapped my arms around her and we embraced. She was not an old woman, and she smelled glorious. A combination of lavender and cinnamon. It was one of the most comforting moments I'd had in months. I was glad to have her in our lives.

We said good-bye and I promised to send pictures and updates as often as possible. Once they were safely out of the building, I sat on my couch and stared at the puppy with the lavender ears, contented. For the first time during this whole ordeal I felt my support system growing. And although I highly doubted I'd be calling Nana Lynne or her daughters to fly in and help me out, it was good to know that they'd always be out there.

CHAPTER THIRTY-THREE

To celebrate Grace's first birthday, my mother held a very girly dinner party in her honor. She filled her dining room with pink balloons, the kitchen island with pink desserts, and the bar with pink champagne. And besides my father, no boys were allowed. The guests included about five of my mom's close friends, Kendra, me, Keri, and Taylor, who happened to be in town for work that weekend. After we opened gifts and took about forty pictures of Grace's introduction to buttercream frosting, I put her to sleep at my parents' house for the night and headed back to the city with Taylor and Keri where we reconvened over a bottle of wine at my apartment. It was quite a treat for me.

"That's awesome that your parents will keep her for the night," Keri said.

"I know!" I agreed with enthusiasm. "My mom ordered a crib about a month ago, and it arrived just in time for Grace's birthday."

Taylor filled our glasses and gave me a funny look. "Have you talked to Ethan lately?"

"We exchange voice mails more than we talk lately, but I think we connected last Monday or so. Why?"

"Well," she paused, looking uncomfortable. "I heard that he was back with that girl, Robin, at his cousin's wedding last night." She dropped a bomb and studied my face.

"Heard from who?" I asked her, concerned.

"Andrew."

I knew that Ethan and Andrew were both attending Ethan's cousin's wedding in Nantucket that weekend, but I certainly didn't know anything about what Taylor was insinuating. "What exactly did Andrew tell you?"

She shifted her body, pointed her toes, and leaned back against the base of my couch. I could sense her discomfort in relaying the information to me. "Andrew said that Robin was at the wedding, she was hanging on Ethan all night, and that they left together."

My stomach turned, and I squinted my eyes. "When did you talk to Andrew?"

"He called me this morning, not specifically about that, but then he mentioned what happened with Ethan."

Keri watched the whole conversation go down and had a very worried look on her face. Since she and I spent eight, sometimes ten, hours a day together, she knew pretty close to everything about me. Especially my insecurities about Ethan. "How can you be sure what happened from a third-party account, from whomever this Andrew person is?" she asked Taylor.

"Andrew is one of his best friends," Taylor quickly responded in a tone that indicated there was no way he would have reported false information. Then she turned to me. "Syd, the only reason I'm telling you is because I thought you'd want to hear it from me, and not through the rumor mill." She touched my knee. "Andrew also said that Robin and Ethan have been talking for weeks and planned on hooking up at the wedding the whole time."

I suddenly wanted to be alone and wished both of them would leave so I could call Ethan and get to the bottom of this stupid news that Taylor chose to gift me on Grace's birthday. Instead I grabbed a lemon bar from the tray of cookies Keri brought, and took the nonchalant approach.

"Ethan and I are friends; he's free to do whatever or whomever he wants," I said unconvincingly.

"No, he isn't," Taylor blurted. "He knows full well that you two are more than friends."

"We're really not, Tay. I mean, I would love for us to be. But he hasn't made any promises," I told her, still trying to talk myself into believing what I was saying.

Taylor threw her hands up. "Well then, all is well," she said sarcastically.

"Why are you trying to get me riled up about it?"

"I'm not, but I was really upset for you when Andrew told me that, and I feel like Ethan is leading you on. Isn't he trying to get transferred here for you?"

"Yes, but not for me."

"What the hell for then? So he can hang out with you and get close to Grace, and then leave you for some cheese head?" Her eyes were looking for an answer.

"I have no idea. This is obviously the first I've heard of any of this, so I guess you should call Ethan and ask him."

Keri shot Taylor a dirty look.

Taylor took a deep breath and smiled. "I'm sorry, Syd. I really was annoyed for you, and whether it's based in truth or not, you know I wouldn't hesitate to tell you something like that." She looked over at Keri, trying to justify shifting us all into downer mode. "Let's not let it ruin what a great day this is, okay?"

"It's fine. Of course I would want to know something like that, and I will call Ethan tomorrow and see if he mentions anything."

After the girls left, one of my few opportunities to sleep through the night was squashed by what Taylor had told me. I squirmed and twisted all night thinking about the one thing that hardly ever crossed my mind during those months: the thought of Ethan with another woman. Selfish as it might've seemed, my hope for our future together was so strong that it never occurred to me that he might've been pacifying me as he bided his time, waiting for someone else. He was way too kind to ignore me, especially once I had Grace in my life. He knew how I'd struggled, and he would never have let himself fall out of our lives entirely. The thought of losing him made me nauseous.

My mom dropped Grace off around noon the next day and rushed into the apartment. "Honey, she was a delight, an absolute angel from the gates of heaven, but I promised to meet Mrs. Cunningham at Marshall Field's today, and I'm about an hour late," she said while handing the baby to me. "Did you get some rest?"

"Yes, thank you," I lied to make her feel useful.

"Oh, good. Glad we could help."

It was time for Grace to eat, so I set her down, placed an empty bowl on the tray of her high chair for her to entertain herself with, and began to prepare her food. I was still so worked up about Ethan and Robin that I could hardly form a rational thought, let alone decipher the directions for instant oatmeal, which I'd easily made fifty times prior to that moment. Grace was squealing and pointing frantically at a banana that was sitting out of her reach on the counter, but I didn't have the energy to get it for her. Taylor's report from Andrew had consumed me, and nothing could distract me from it. I left the kitchen in search of the phone.

Grace cried out from her high chair, begging to be set free, but I had no interest in her needs at that moment. Ethan didn't owe me anything, and he certainly wasn't going to play this pathetic game of house with me forever, but I never imagined I would react so violently to the thought of him getting back together with Robin. The left side of my stomach was cramping so hard that I had to lie on the couch in order to keep the pain at a minimum. Grace began to scream when I didn't return, and was none too happy to be alone with no food in her bowl. I assumed the fetal position on my couch, and began to cry as soon as she turned up the volume and started to wail.

The only image in my head was that of Ethan and this woman. I'd never seen her, but I believed her to be tall, thin, stylish, and absent of any children or adolescent drama in her life. She probably had a great job, a killer apartment…and surely she came from money. I could see his face, and his eyes looking into hers as they rekindled their love at his cousin's wedding.

Grace flung her bowl and it hit the floor with a serious CRACK! I guessed that was exactly what she had intended because I instinctively ran into the kitchen and released her from the three-point harness she'd been struggling with for twenty minutes.

"I'm sorry, baby. Mommy's here," I said through my tears. Somehow her twelve-month-old brain was able to sense my distress and she clammed up immediately. I handed her a bowl of dried Cheerios and she didn't make a peep for the next thirty minutes while I came out of my freak session.

Ethan had said he would call me that weekend after the wedding, but by Sunday I still hadn't heard from him. He was probably with Robin, wind blowing through their hair as they laughed in slow motion over a continental breakfast. I decided to call him at home and pretend I never talked to Taylor. His machine picked up.

"Hey, it's me. Just seeing if you survived the wedding. Call me later."

It was seven o'clock when I left the message, and eleven o'clock when I went to bed.

CHAPTER THIRTY-FOUR

Monday morning I dropped Grace at day care and headed to work, with no word from Ethan. I had no intention of calling him again, and I hated going to work with something else weighing on my mind because it was nearly impossible to talk to people and pretend I gave a damn about their itchy towels.

I was eating lunch at my desk when he finally called me.

"This is Sydney. How can I help you?" I answered, even though Midge told us never to answer the phone while we were eating.

"How's it going?" Ethan asked. "You at lunch?"

"Yeah, what's up?" I was short with him.

"Nothing much. How was your weekend?"

"Uneventful," I said curtly.

"Oh, I thought you had Grace's party. How'd that go?"

"Fine." I was a little surprised at the amount of sass in my voice, but I simply couldn't help myself. Every girl I knew would, when upset, pout and act like nothing in the world was bothering her, even though her tone and demeanor clearly indicated otherwise. And every guy I knew would read all the signs like a driving test. They knew immediately to goad and prod and to find out what was wrong despite the fact that they were being told everything's peachy. Passive-aggressive behavior had taken over my end of the conversation.

"You okay? You sound annoyed. Is it me or Midge?" he asked.

"Neither."

"Do you want to call me later?"

"Sure."

"Bye, Syd."

"Bye."

I hung up the phone and felt worse after my ridiculous, child-ish behavior. I'd been waiting to hear from him for two days, and then I acted like an asshole when he finally called.

After I picked her up from day care, Grace and I headed to Target to get some much-needed wipes, diapers, and laundry deter-gent. And although that's all I needed, I tossed a pair of shoes, a bottle of Malibu Rum, a Nirvana CD, and two striped throw pil-lows into my cart.

"I'm sorry, Miss, but your card isn't going through." The cashier looked at me, and then glanced at the three people in line behind me. "Would you like to use another one?" she questioned, then handed the credit card back to me.

"That's weird. Can you try again?" I asked.

She took the card back from me and swiped it again with mild force. "Still declined. Do you have another one?"

As soon as she repeated the question, I realized the automatic withdrawal had been taken out of my checking account for Grace's day care. I quickly rummaged through my purse for some cash, and came up with enough for just the diapers. Grace had been happily chewing on the Nirvana CD case, and screamed her head off when I took it from her and handed it over to the cashier. I completed the transaction with my eyes to the floor.

After getting home, feeding Grace, bathing Grace, dressing Grace, and reading to Grace, I placed her in her crib and crept out of the room. I was dying for a drink.

I grabbed the phone, fell onto the couch, and called Ethan.

"Sorry about earlier," I said as soon as he answered.

"Rough day?"

"Not really. Rough weekend." I dove right in.

"I could tell you were crabby. What happened?"

I debated whether to confront the issue with him or not, and decided I simply had to get it off my chest. There was no way I was going to make it through another day without talking to him about what Andrew had told Taylor. "Taylor told me about you and Robin," I said.

"What?" He sounded angry. "What about me and Robin?"

"That you two were together, at the wedding."

"What the fuck are you talking about, Syd?"

I tossed my head back and ran my free hand through my hair. I had really hoped we could avoid the whole paddle tennis game before getting to the meat of the conversation. "Taylor told me that you were with Robin…your cousin's friend from Wisconsin…who you used to date," I said mockingly. "And that the two of you left together."

"What? Is she back on the blow? Taylor doesn't know shit about what she's talking about, and she should mind her own fucking business."

"Enough with the profanities. I get that you're mad she said something to me."

"I'm not mad she *fucking* said something; I'm mad she's a two-faced, lying bitch."

I didn't respond.

He spoke tersely. "Syd, nothing happened between me and Robin. Yes, she was at the wedding; no, nothing happened…end of story."

I sat motionless, regretting the direction his mood was going in. "You don't owe me any explanation," I mumbled.

"Obviously I do!"

The conversation wasn't going as planned, and I hated the tone of his voice. Besides Grace being in pain, nothing upset me more than when Ethan was angry with me. It was then that the floodgates opened.

I wept as quietly as I could, but the pain of him drifting away was too difficult to bear. "No, you don't, Ethan. I am so sorry. Your friendship means everything to me, and I have no right to lay that bullshit on you. You don't deserve it…especially from me."

Ethan let out a long, frustrated sigh. "Sydney, I don't know why you're crying…but I hope it's because you're in love with me half as much as I'm in love with you," he responded in a much gentler tone and let the words sink in before continuing. "You are too smart to think that I would hook up with Robin or anyone else at my cousin's wedding, or any other night for that matter. I have loved you since the very first day we met, and if I had my way, we would never be apart. I'm sorry it's been so long since I've reminded you of that." He paused. "Okay, Syd? So please don't cry."

It had been too long since I'd heard those words from him, and even though our friendship had grown stronger over the past year, I missed him so much. I was desperate for him to hold me and touch me like he used to. Like we didn't have a care in the world except for what time to meet at the beach. He hated it when I cried, so I was trying to catch my breath.

"I love you, too, Ethan, so much."

"Okay, good."

"Please come visit."

"I'm going to do better than that," he said. "My transfer went through, and I'll be moving back to Chicago at the end of next month."

He was still in love with me and he was coming home. It was like winning the lottery twice in one day.

"That's amazing!" I cheered. "If I weren't already crying, I would certainly be now."

"Wonderful."

"That is the best news I've had in a long time." I stood and filled a wine glass with ice water.

"I thought you'd be glad to hear that, and you and I are going to make a fresh start, okay? I'm committed to rebuilding what we had, and being there for you and Grace. I love you, Syd, and it feels good to be able to say it out loud again."

Ethan was back and settled into his new apartment in Chicago within six weeks of delivering the good news. His parents had a welcome-home party for him, and he held my hand almost the entire evening. He traveled two days a week for his job, but on the days when he was in town we were inseparable. And for the days he worked from home, I'd signed a two-page waiver so he could get Grace from day care, and they'd be in my apartment waiting for me after work. Grace adored Ethan almost as much as I did.

One Friday evening, I grabbed the mail from the lobby of the building and boarded the elevator with sandwiches from Mr. Beef for Ethan and me. I flipped through the small stack of bills and junk mail and saw an envelope hand-addressed to me from the law offices of Field & McBride. I put it on top of the pile and reached for my keys once I was at my floor.

"Hi, makeshift family!" I yelled from the entryway.

"Welcome home, Mama," Ethan yelled back, and Grace came running to me like a puppy.

I set everything down on the armchair next to the couch and scooped Grace up into my arms. "Scary legal mail in today's delivery," I said.

"What do you mean?" Ethan asked and looked at me.

I scooted Grace up onto my left thigh. "Not sure. There's a letter here for me from the law offices of Field & McBride."

"What does it say?" he asked.

"I haven't opened it yet."

Ethan stood and took Grace from me so I could open the letter. The paper for both the envelope and the letter were ivory and had a soft, scaly texture to them. As I read the letter, my face went pale.

"What is it, Syd?"

"Oh my God," I gasped, and dropped the paper on the floor.

Ethan was deliberately calm and placed Grace in front of her toys about two feet away from us. My throat was tightening and I couldn't breathe properly. He led me to the couch and retrieved the letter. He read aloud:

Dear Sydney Shephard,

My client, Kevin Hansen, has filed a petition to establish paternity, and to seek joint custody of his daughter, Ms. Grace Kendra Shephard. This letter serves as a request for you to submit a DNA test on behalf of Ms. Grace Shephard by April 15th of this year. Please have the test submitted to the DNA testing center at the Cook County courthouse. If you should have any questions regarding this matter, please contact me at the number below.

Sincerely,

Tom Field

Partner

Field & McBride

Ethan looked up slowly from the paper and jumped right into damage control. He knelt on the floor in front of me. "Sydney, don't you worry. We'll take care of this bastard. I don't know how he thinks he has any right to a relationship with Grace, let alone joint custody, but we are not going to let any of this happen."

I was comatose. The blood had drained from my head and left me feeling faint, my limbs frozen. My tongue felt like a raw filet mignon, sitting cold and heavy in my mouth, preventing air from getting to my lungs. I stared blankly into Ethan's eyes.

"Syd, don't do this to yourself. It's going to be okay." He tried to reach me, but I was gone inside my head.

What in the hell was Kevin doing? After all I'd been through, after every time I extended an olive branch to him with no response, this was how he chose to handle himself. Why now, why at all? He must've known I had no money for attorneys. Why?!

I tried to focus on Ethan. He held my hand and looked at me, trying to determine whether I was going to pass out or freak out.

"How could he?" I asked quietly, like a woman on the verge of a breakdown. I begged Ethan for an answer with my expression.

"Let's not dwell on why and instead deal with making him go away, for good."

"He said repeatedly that he wanted nothing to do with her." I kept talking, without absorbing anything Ethan was saying. "He has no right to do this to me or to Grace. Does he honestly think he's entitled to joint custody?!" I hollered and drew Grace's attention away from her alphabet wagon.

Ethan read the letter again, shaking his head. "I hate to say it, but first thing you're going to need to do is get yourself a lawyer."

I sat motionless and then reached for the phone.

"Who are you calling?" Ethan asked.

"I'm calling Kevin's mother," I said, like he should've known.

"Kevin's mother?" he questioned, and snatched the phone from me.

"Yes." I extended my hand, attempting to get the phone back.

"You know his mother's number?"

I wasn't in the mood to be challenged or to fill him in on my relationship with Kevin's mom, but it looked as though that was the only way I was going to get my phone back. "She called me a while back and came here to meet Grace," I said. "She came with his three sisters for a visit and said she wanted to be involved in Grace's life to whatever extent I was comfortable."

He looked confused and deceived. "Why didn't you tell me that?"

"I didn't want to hurt your feelings."

"How the hell would that hurt my feelings?" He shook his head in dismay and stood. "Sydney, I know this isn't the time to get into this, but if you and I are going to have a relationship, you are going to have to be honest with me about everything."

"I know. I'm sorry."

He handed me the phone.

"She's a very nice woman, and she was crying and apologizing for Kevin's behavior," I told Ethan. "Not making excuses for him, but you could see that she truly cared about Grace and was ashamed of how her son had abandoned his responsibilities where Grace and I were concerned." I waved the legal notice at him. "I have to believe that she must have some insight into what is going on here."

"Then you should call her." He nodded and sat back down. "I mean it. The most important thing right now is to find out as much as you can," he said. "Maybe you should just call Kevin."

I rolled my thumb over the number pad on my cordless phone as I held it in my hand. "He's never taken my call before. I'm guessing this time wouldn't be any different."

"When have you called him before?"

"Not very often. I've actually just left him messages a couple times over the last two years. Once to let him know I was having a girl, and once when she was born."

Ethan looked sorry for me. "And no response, ever?"

"Nope," I confirmed.

"I don't know, Syd. Maybe you should talk to a lawyer before calling anyone."

We nodded in agreement and called our parents instead. Ethan had to leave the room because my mother was screaming profanities so loudly he could hear them through the phone. My father eventually got on the line and tried to convince me that Kevin didn't have a leg to stand on, and that his lawyer should be embarrassed to have even agreed to take the case.

"Everything is going to be fine, sweetheart. I promise," my dad reassured me. "Are you okay?"

"I'm okay. Ethan is here, and he's going to call his dad right now," I told him. Ethan's dad was a tax attorney and one of the biggest in the city. Not exactly family law, but he had a tight circle of colleagues and golf buddies that included the best legal minds in every field. I felt confident that he could refer me to someone, yet not confident that I could afford that person.

Ethan hung up the phone and sat next to me on the couch, but Grace began to scream just as he was about to speak.

"Well, well, well," I said to her nervously. "Look at all the drama you are causing tonight." I scooped her up off the floor. "I better get her down."

After I put Grace to bed, Ethan told me his dad was going to make some calls and that he should have someone for me to talk to in the morning.

"Thank you," I said to him.

"Don't thank me. I am in this with you. I'm not going to let any of this come to fruition, okay?"

"Okay," I agreed, and was beginning to believe him. After talking to my father and seeing the confidence on Ethan's face, I felt good about winning this legal battle with Kevin. It was the personal fight that I was more insecure about. I still, for the life of me, could not fathom how he could do this to us. He'd shown nothing but complete disregard for both Grace and me. How could he expect me to take him seriously on this? I agreed to talk to a lawyer before calling Kevin's mom, but it was hard; I wanted answers.

My mom drove down to my apartment in the morning to sit with Grace while Ethan and I went to see the lawyer his father recommended. It was a Saturday, but I learned that most lawyers work eight days a week. We took the elevators to the fourteenth floor of the John Hancock building, and Ethan opened a large glass door that had "Rosenberg, Levin, & Slater LLP" etched across the front. I was surprised to see Ethan's mother sitting in the reception area when we arrived.

"Mrs. Reynolds?"

"Hello, Sydney," she said as she stood. "Hello, dear," she said to Ethan, and he gave her a kiss on the cheek.

"What are you doing here, Mom?"

"Your father told me about the letter that was sent to Sydney, and I was appalled. I have no intention of letting this go any further, and I want to make sure that Greg Rosenberg knows exactly how I feel."

Greg Rosenberg was a senior partner at the firm and married to Mrs. Reynolds's best childhood girlfriend, Marcy. She and Marcy grew up together, went to the same college, and married fraternity brothers from the University of Pennsylvania.

"I don't know what to say," I said, and felt very small. "Thank you so much. You didn't have to give up your Saturday to deal with this mess."

"Don't be ridiculous. I have never heard of such an entitled and heartless person as this Kevin Hansen—"

"Mother, please," Ethan interrupted.

She shot him a look. "Sydney, I am here to support you and do everything in my power to make this go away." She looked at Ethan again and then back at me. "If you are uncomfortable with me being here, I understand, and I will leave."

Standing before me was a woman who I'd been intimidated by since high school. Yet despite everything, she never made me feel uncomfortable on purpose. It was always me who had invested so much in getting her approval, when I should have invested more time in just getting to know her. Her support meant more to me than I could express at that moment.

"I would be honored to have you sit in on the meeting with us. I don't know what to say. Thank you."

"Don't mention it." She readjusted her tote bag on the crook of her arm and unbuttoned the top button on her double-breasted wool blazer. "If there's one thing more important than having friends in high places, it's knowing when to call on them."

The three of us were ushered into Greg Rosenberg's office and were asked to take a seat on the leather couch in the center of the room.

"Good morning," he said as he strolled in five minutes after us and tossed a briefcase on his desk. "Caroline, you're looking way too good for a Saturday morning."

Mrs. Reynolds smiled. "Don't flirt unless you're holding a glass of chardonnay for me," she answered sharply.

"I never flirt at the office," he announced, and winked at Ethan and me as he extended his hand. "Greg Rosenberg, of the Mayflower Rosenbergs."

Mrs. Reynolds rolled her eyes.

"Sydney Shephard. Nice to meet you. Thank you for seeing me this morning."

"No trouble at all. I'd be here anyway, and this way I get to see an *old* friend."

"Careful," Mrs. Reynolds warned him.

He rummaged though his briefcase while the girl from the front desk brought in a tray of water bottles and coffee mugs. "I read the letter that was sent to you from the fine folks at Field & McBride. I actually studied with Tom Field at the University of Chicago," he began. "Anyway, I have some questions for you, but I was hoping you could first fill me in. You know, catch me up to speed on your relationship with," he paused to glance at the letter, "Mr. Kevin Hansen."

His tone was businesslike, but I was feeling less than professional at that moment. The thought of recounting my relationship with Kevin in front of Ethan was enough stress to bear, but the thought of telling the painful details in front of his mother was making me regret having her in the meeting with us.

"Do you want my mom and me to leave?" Ethan asked, sensing my discomfort.

"No, it's fine. I'm glad to have you both here," I said as convincingly as I could and sat on my hands. "Kevin and I were good friends in college, never dated, but went to a couple fraternity and sorority dances with each other. On one such occasion, we spent the night together, and a few weeks later I discovered I was pregnant." I finished my sentence with my head hanging so low, it was nearly resting on Greg Rosenberg's Berber carpet.

"I know this is hard, but please get me to where we are today," he said and pointed to the letter resting on the coffee table.

I took a deep breath and forged ahead. "Once I decided to keep the baby—her name is Grace—I knew I had to tell him about it. It was the night before we were both set to leave Purdue, and I asked him to come over to my apartment. He showed up acting very distant and uninterested in why I'd invited him over, and when I told him that I was carrying his baby, well…he told me that he wanted nothing to do with either of us." I paused and noticed Mrs. Reynolds shaking her head, and Ethan sitting very still. "So that was pretty much it, as far as I thought. I knew going in that I was on my own, and really the only reason I told him was because I thought it was the right thing to do at the time. I have reached out to him twice since then. Once when I found out I was having a girl, and once after she was born. I never received a call back from him either time. Then when Grace was a year old, I got a call from Kevin's mother, asking if she and her daughters could come and meet Grace and me." Mrs. Reynolds cocked her head to the side and widened her eyes when she heard me say that. "I told her that she could come, and we met at my apartment—she and Kevin's three sisters. They were very kind, brought gifts, stayed for a few hours, apologized for Kevin's behavior, and even thanked me for keeping the baby."

"How did they find you?" Greg asked.

"I assume Kevin gave her my name, and possibly my phone number. I had left it on one of my two messages. Maybe he wrote it down at some point."

Greg was taking notes. "Did his mother mention anything about Kevin? Whether he had gotten married or anything like that?"

"No, we really didn't talk about him at all, and I didn't ask. I tried to respect her visit and made it about Grace, not me."

He lifted his fax copy of my letter off the table. "So this obviously comes as a surprise to you?"

"Very much so," I said.

"Honestly, Greg, what sort of legal leg does this boy have to stand on?" Mrs. Reynolds asked.

"Well, not much really. I mean, is he legally entitled to see the baby? Yes. Is he entitled to establish paternity? Yes. Can he and his lawyer reasonably assume that he'd get joint custody? I can't imagine.

But the question is, why go about it this way? You said you were friends, and he knows you've extended courtesy calls to him in the past, so why take this approach?"

His question lingered in the air while we all shook our heads in dismay.

"Have you tried contacting him?" he asked me.

"No."

Ethan spoke up. "She wanted to call his mother."

I looked at my lawyer for a reaction.

"Why?" Greg asked me curiously.

"Because I thought she'd have some explanation, or some information about this whole thing. When we met, I really felt that she truly wanted what was best for Grace."

"She cares more for her son, I'm sure," Mrs. Reynolds added.

Greg nodded. "Then you should call her."

"Really?"

"Yes, you're probably right. I would be surprised if she couldn't provide some insight for you. It might not help me in any way, but you have every right to talk with her if you'd like."

"I'd like to call her."

"Let me know what she says."

"I will."

Greg Rosenberg stretched his arms over his head. "Well, I will contact Kevin's lawyers on Monday, and we will draft our own letter stating your desire to maintain sole custody of Grace. I will warn you, however, you may still have to cooperate in his request to establish paternity by submitting Grace to a blood test. But it's pretty routine, and something you should do anyway if you ever want to seek any sort of child support from him."

"I don't."

"Well, it's a simple blood test, and typically in the best interest of everyone involved to have it on record."

Ethan put his arm around me for a quick squeeze.

Mrs. Reynolds had a confident smile on her face, one I wished I could replicate myself. "Thank you, Greg," she said and reached for her purse. "I have no doubt you will take care of everything."

"Thank you for your vote of confidence, Caroline."

"Sydney, how do you feel?" she asked me.

"I feel…grateful to have you all here, and sorry to have to drag everyone down with me."

"You're in good hands, Syd. There's nothing to worry about," Greg said.

"Thank you."

We all stood, shook hands, and gathered our respective belongings. As Ethan and I headed for the door to Greg's office, I saw Mrs. Reynolds whispering something to him. Ethan noticed me staring at them.

"I'm sure she's planning on footing the bill," he said softly in my ear.

"What!"

He pulled me into the hallway. "I'm sure she's offering to pay his fees, Sydney, and don't you dare tell her not to."

"I can't have her do that. Are you crazy? This is not her burden…at all!"

"She and Greg are good friends, and either he'll trade his services for a round of golf and drinks at the club, or she'll pay the nominal fee."

Being in her debt was not a place I was comfortable with, but the truth was, I had no money to hire anyone, let alone someone of Greg Rosenberg's caliber. "What should I say?"

"Don't say anything. I'm sure she doesn't want to discuss it with you," he told me.

Caroline Reynolds left Greg's office and met up with us near the reception desk. "I think that went well, and he told me in confidence that he believes Kevin doesn't have a chance at securing anything other than a paternity test."

"Thank you so much, Mrs. Reynolds. I would never be able to fight this without your help."

"Don't mention it." She smiled. "You can thank me by bringing Grace for a visit."

"I would love to."

"Thanks, Mom." Ethan embraced her.

When we got back to my apartment, I filled my mom in on everything. She was very pleased to hear that Mrs. Reynolds had accompanied us to the appointment and said she would call her later that afternoon.

"Mom," I said, "I'm going to call Kevin's mother; the lawyer said I could."

My mom looked skeptical but would never have argued with me in front of Ethan. "I think if you're comfortable with asking her about it, then you should call," she said diplomatically.

"I'm not really comfortable with any of this, but there's a part of me that wants to talk to her and see if she knows what he's done." I paused. "And there's another part of me that wants her to know about it, in the event he chose not to tell her."

My mom understood. I took the phone into my bathroom and dialed Mrs. Hansen's number.

"Hello," she answered.

"Hi, Lynne. It's Sydney Shephard."

"Why hello, Sydney. What a lovely surprise. Is everything all right with Grace?"

"Grace is doing really well, thank you." I swallowed. "Uh, I received a letter from Kevin yesterday, well, from his lawyers actually."

"His lawyers?" she asked, taken aback.

"Yes, he's seeking joint custody of Grace," I told her and waited about eight seconds before she spoke.

"Sydney, I had no idea," she said slowly.

"Do you know why he might be doing this to us now, after all this time?"

I heard her make a regretful noise on the other end, and I felt mildly sorry for involving her, but selfishly happy about the phone call Kevin would soon get from her.

"Kevin was recently engaged, and his fiancée is unable to bear children." Her words left me stunned. "She must be behind this, Sydney. She is a wonderful girl, but I cannot imagine Kevin going about this on his own volition."

A bomb went off in my brain and I began shaking with rage. "She can't have a baby, so she wants mine?!" I blurted out.

"I am only guessing. Have you tried calling him?"

"No, I haven't." I was enraged and my voice reflected it.

"Perhaps he's had a change of heart and would like to do the right thing by Grace?" she said hopefully and then paused, but I could not speak. "I'm sorry you're upset, dear. I will speak to him for you, and if there is anything I can do to help I will."

Do right by Grace? Was she on crack? My voice exploded into the phone. "You can make him drop this case!" I shouted, not remotely concerned with whom I was talking to. I could have cared less that Kevin's kind, generous mother was doing her best to keep her composure and assure me that everything would work out. I was livid.

"Sydney, you have my word—" she began, but I cut her off.

"You tell him that I have hired the best, most expensive lawyer in the city of Chicago to handle this, and that he better drop this lawsuit or neither of you will ever see Grace again!"

My mother burst into the room and snatched the phone from my hand. "Hello, hello, this is Sydney's mother, Judy Shephard. I am so sorry…"

My entire body was shaking, and my heart was pounding so fast that it felt like I'd just finished running a marathon. Ethan stood in the doorway and aggressively waved me out of the bathroom. I tried to stand, but my legs were like gummy worms. He lifted my arm and led me to the couch.

"What the hell happened?" he asked.

"His wife is trying to take Grace from me!"

"He's married?"

"He's engaged, she can't have kids, and this barren bitch is trying to take Grace instead!"

"Stop yelling. First of all, look at yourself. You need to get a major grip," he said through gritted teeth.

"Ethan, do you have any idea what I am saying?" My eyes were like flames; there was no moisture in them whatsoever, and blinking was nearly impossible. The frenzy had literally consumed me. "Kevin still has no interest in any sort of relationship with Grace! But his fiancée probably sees some sort of consolation prize in the fact that he already has a daughter for the taking," I said and began to pace.

My mother came out of my bathroom in her own fury. "I realize you are upset, but that gives you no right to yell at this poor woman," she said in a familiar tone from my childhood. "You are acting like a complete brat when you should be acting like a woman and a mother. I expect you to call Kevin's mother back and apologize for yourself." She pointed to the phone and then put her hands on her hips. "I made an attempt to do it for you, but it's not sufficient as far as I'm concerned. She was very forgiving and understanding, but she deserves your respect, and you should be ashamed of your behavior just now. Learn how to handle yourself when you are tested, Sydney. Be smart about this!" She threw her hands up.

My mother's words snapped me out of my fog and into one of immediate regret. I looked at her face, filled with her own frustration and disappointment in me. I began to sob uncontrollably, my limbs still shaking. Mom apologized to Ethan for having to be part of the drama, then walked over to me and gave me a good solid hug.

"Everything is going to be fine; no one is going to take Grace away from you. But you have to be strong for her."

I couldn't speak, I was so scared, and the fact that some strange woman was the impetus behind the whole thing made it worse.

"Let it all out, Sydney, and then you are going to have to put on a brave face and get through this the right way," my mom said and pulled away to look me in the eyes. "Okay?"

I nodded.

She and Ethan looked at each other. "I have to go, and I trust that Ethan will keep you in line while I'm not here," she joked.

"My pleasure, Mrs. Shephard," he said.

"Thank you, Ethan. As for you," she said looking back at me, "I expect you to get on with your life, be grateful for everyone who loves you, let your lawyer do his job, and take care of your daughter." She raised a finger. "And you call that woman back and apologize."

"What did Mrs. Hansen say?" I asked.

"She said that she would call Kevin and try to get some answers."

"Thanks, Mom," I said.

In that moment I was ashamed of myself, just as she said I should be.

CHAPTER THIRTY-FIVE

Almost two weeks after my first meeting with Greg Rosenberg, he called me on a Friday afternoon. The results of the paternity test were back, and, to no one's surprise, Kevin was the father.

"Should we send him a baby gift?" I asked Ethan.

"Absolutely."

"Greg said that all of the paperwork has been filed on our end, and that he's just waiting to hear back from Kevin's lawyer. He told me that we sent a motion to have the whole thing dropped based on the fact that Kevin has made no contact, and that he verbally told me he wanted nothing to do with Grace before she was born."

"When does he expect to hear back?"

"He said it could take a while, that he doesn't have a time limit," I said and walked to the kitchen.

"Everything's going to work out, Syd."

"I hope so."

Ethan grabbed Grace's diaper bag because we were driving up north to drop her at my parents' house, and he and I were going to a party at the Golds'. Taylor was in town for work to attend a *My Cousin Vinny* movie premiere and was assigned the task of carrying a sweater for Marisa Tomei in case she needed it. She didn't.

My mom opened the front door as we pulled into the driveway.

"Excited to babysit?" I asked her.

"Come inside. I need to talk to you," she said and waved us in the house. Ethan took Grace into the den where my father was sitting, and I followed my mom into the kitchen.

"What's up?"

She sat on one of the stools at the island and pulled another one out for me. "I spoke with Kevin's mom about fifteen minutes ago," she told me.

"You called her?"

"No, I had given her my number when I spoke with her at your apartment," she said, and lowered her chin but kept her eyes on me. "She told me she never heard from you."

I did feel bad that I yelled at Kevin's mother, but I was still bitter about being legally attacked by her son and hadn't felt the immediate need to make amends. "Is that why she called you? To tell on me?"

Mom leveled her chin. "No, something much better." She smiled. "Kevin is dropping the lawsuit."

"What?!"

"She told me that she spoke with him alone, and then together with his fiancée, and that they aren't going to pursue joint custody of Grace."

I was stunned to be hearing this news from my mother. I had hoped and expected it to come in a phone message from Greg Rosenberg, Esq.

"My lawyer hasn't said anything. In fact, he just confirmed Kevin's paternity today, about two hours ago."

Mom took a sip of her lemon water. "Well, I'm sure he'll be hearing something soon enough. I just spoke with her, and she promised me."

"Oh Lord, I've got you two mother hens on the phone making promises, when the legal team of Field & McBride is still going for my jugular."

"I think you have every right to believe what she told me, Sydney." She straightened her posture defensively. "Why don't you call her yourself? You owe her a call anyway," Mom said, brows raised.

"Give me the phone."

My mom handed me the phone and scrawled Mrs. Hansen's number on a yellow Post-it note. "I'll be in the den," she said and walked out.

I studied the number for a moment before dialing the phone.

"Hello," she answered.

"Hi, Lynne. It's Sydney."

"Hello, dear. I'm sure you've talked with your mom by now, and she told you the news."

I paced the floor. "Yes, she did, and I was obviously thrilled to hear that, but I'm a little concerned since I haven't had any sort of confirmation from my lawyer."

She cleared her throat. "I can understand your concern, but I assure you that Kevin has no intention of dragging this out any further. Apparently, it was not something he was very interested in doing in the first place."

No shock to me, I thought.

"Well, he should have thought of that before I was forced to hire a lawyer and endure this mental torture," I said calmly, but I could not help myself. Hearing her voice made me want to lash out. It made me wish that it was Kevin on the line, and that I could let him have it, like he deserved. I realized then how much pent-up anger and bitterness I was carrying around.

"I know, dear. I'm sorry you had to be put through that scare."

I took a deep breath. "I know you are, and I owe you an apology as well. I had no right to take my anger toward Kevin out on you. You've been nothing but kind to me, and I hope you know how much I appreciate your eagerness to be in Grace's life."

"Thank you. That is nice of you to say, and despite Kevin's behavior, he is my son and I love him," she told me. "And if he ever does decide to become a part of Grace's life, he will have my full support. You will understand one day."

I was nodding, even though she couldn't see me. "Thank you for your hand in all of this. Something tells me I have you to thank specifically for talking Kevin and his fiancée out of this lawsuit."

"Well, I think they just came to the realization that their plan wasn't very well thought out prior to them taking legal action. And they certainly would've had to move away from California if they wanted joint custody, now wouldn't they?"

"So it was the Chicago winters that deterred them?"

She chuckled. "A little bit of mother, and a little bit of mother nature."

"Thanks, Lynne."

"We'll talk soon."

"Okay, bye," I said, and immediately dialed Greg Rosenberg. There was no answer, so I left a lengthy message on his voice mail.

"Hi, Greg. It's Sydney Shephard. I just spoke with Kevin's mother, Lynne Hansen, and she has told me that Kevin plans on dropping his petition for joint custody, that he doesn't think he'd win, and that he doesn't think it's worth pursuing any longer. Is there any possible way you could confirm this with his lawyer so my family and I can celebrate and enjoy the weekend? Thank you so much!"

Ethan walked up with a huge grin on his face. "I heard the great news," he said and kissed the top of my head.

"I know. I just wish I'd heard it from the lawyers, you know what I mean?"

"Yes, but it sounds like everything is fine. Did you call his mom?"

"I did, and she said he's backing off."

Ethan sat down on the stool next to me. "I think we should celebrate."

Everyone was so optimistic and certain, why couldn't I be? "Okay," I said. "I think you're right."

He leaned on the island with his forearm. "Let's stop by Taylor's and then go grab dinner, just the two of us."

I nodded.

"Don't you dare start crying on me, Sydney Shephard."

I fell forward into his chest. Nothing made me feel better than being buried in those arms of his. I closed my eyes and hoped that our legal mess was behind us. Grace would never know what her father had put my family through, and the pain he'd inflicted on me for no reason at all. I hated Kevin by then and had no intention of ever mentioning his name in our household. I could only pray that, one day, Grace would understand.

CHAPTER THIRTY-SIX
Grace

It was August 2009, and I was about to start college at my mother's alma mater. She was giddy about the opportunities to visit her old stomping grounds and watering holes, and I was eager for my freedom. Not that I disliked anything about my home or family, but simply because I couldn't wait to be on my own, with no one to look after me.

I wondered if my California relatives had told my father that I was going to Purdue. I wished I could ask them. I thought about him often that summer before my freshman year of college, and I grew more and more determined to see him. There I was, attending the same school where he and my mother were friends for so many years. He would certainly find that interesting, wouldn't he? I'd matured enough to know that I wanted to find him. I wanted to have a visual image of him, a history of his adult years, and an understanding of who he had become. I just hadn't matured enough to pick up the phone and call him.

My mom had information that belonged to me. She knew my real father, his personality, his intellect, his facial structure, and as I got older, I felt entitled to that knowledge. Over the years I'd formulated my own opinion of him, based solely on what I thought someone who produced half of me would be like. Handsome, smart, strong. He probably ran a company or worked somewhere that required him to wear a suit and tie every day. Or maybe he was more of a casual executive, in khaki pants and rolled up sleeves.

It always bothered me that my mom never sat me down and discussed him. Didn't she think I would want to know more about him? I mean, even if she hated him, which I would also love to know, wouldn't it occur to her that I should be allowed to formulate my own opinion? Maybe I would hate him, too, and we could sit around and bad-mouth him together. But instead, she left it up to me to paint a picture of him in my head, so I painted a favorable one, of course. This only made her look crazy because how could she dislike this strong, handsome businessman?

"What's my father like?" I ambushed her in the laundry room one day as we were packing my bags for school. It'd been a while since I'd broached the subject, but she knew who I meant.

"Grace, why are you asking me that?"

"Because I want to know, obviously." I jumped up and sat on the dryer.

She was folding Patch's favorite Bears jersey. "He's tall." She smiled and glanced at the top of my head.

Her answer was intended to shut me up, but it only pissed me off. "Why can't I know more about him?"

"There's not much to tell."

"Either he's a serial killer and lives in a straightjacket, or he's so entirely fabulous and broke your heart so badly that you can't bear to say his name without a box of Kleenex around." It was a little harsh, but she deserved it.

She looked up at me with a hint of moisture in her eyes that caught me off guard. "You have an amazing dad who loves you, and you should be ashamed of how you're acting," she said quietly.

I felt only a shred of remorse. "Mom, if you would just put yourself in my shoes and tell me the things I want to know, I wouldn't be acting this way."

"It's always my fault," she whined.

I hopped off and pushed past her into the garage, then stormed outside. I walked over to Chloe's house and we sat around and spent the afternoon trying to decide whether my father was George Clooney or Ben Affleck.

"Ben Affleck is taller," Chloe remarked.

"George is cuter though. However, I think he's much older than my mom."

"Yeah, I guess you're right. Your father is definitely Ben Affleck," she concluded. "Won't he be thrilled to meet you one day?"

We laughed. "Who are we kidding?" I said. "My mom could never get Ben Affleck."

CHAPTER THIRTY-SEVEN

The day I met my father, I was twenty-two years old, the same age my mom was when she gave birth to me. I'd just graduated college, and a month prior to meeting him, she'd given me his phone number and said I should be the one to call him. I didn't know at the time that she'd already e-mailed him that I would be doing so. She still never trusted him to do the right thing by me, and was always going out of her way to make sure I never felt slighted.

I was anxious to make the call but kept my expectations low, as my mother reminded me to do a thousand times. Kevin was at his office when I reached him for the very first time, and I heard him excuse himself in the background.

"Hi, Grace." His voice was deep.

"Hi, Kevin."

"How are you?" he asked, like a grandfather would ask a distant grandchild.

"I'm good," I said, then paused. "I was wondering if you would consider meeting me one day next month."

"I'd be happy to."

"I'm sure you know, your mom is flying me out there as a college graduation gift, and I told her that I would like to try and see you while I'm there."

After my high school spring break trip to L.A. was canceled due to Nana Lynne's hip surgery, she promised to regift the vacation when I'd finished college. I never thought much of it, but she must've had this master plan in her head for many years. She never once suggested that I contact her son, but she knew at that age I'd be mature enough to make the decision on my own, and I did.

"Yes, she did mention that to me," he said, and I could tell by the tone of his voice that my phone call was no surprise.

"Well, I guess it'd be best to catch up in person. Will Kate be joining us?" Kate was Kevin's wife, and the mother of my two make-shift sisters, Lauren and Julia, both adopted. Lauren was eighteen and headed off to the University of Texas, and Julia was seventeen and finishing her senior year of high school.

"She won't be able to join us; it'll be just me and you. Would you like to have dinner?" he asked.

"Sure, I love dinner."

"All right, then. I'll make us a reservation somewhere nice."

"No need to go all out on my account," I said, and he didn't respond. "Just kidding. Anywhere is fine with me."

"I will see you in a few weeks then. You can call me on this number when you get in. It's my cell phone."

"Sounds good. See you soon." I clicked my phone off and ended a brief conversation with the one person I'd wanted to talk to my entire life.

A month later, I was on American Airlines flight 465 to Los Angeles. We landed at LAX and I was instructed by Nana Lynne to take a taxi to her house in Santa Monica. I passed two In-N-Out Burger locations, and recalled my dad telling me not to leave the state without trying their Double-Double. Patch had been dying to visit the West Coast, but had never had the chance. Nor was he invited on this trip. I rubbed it in pretty good, too, because I'd never outgrown my desire to make Patch wish he were the illegitimate child.

I arrived at my Nana Lynne's house around noon that day and was surprised to see my three aunts standing behind her at the front door.

"Surprise, my beautiful Grace!"

"Hi, Nana." I hugged her and inhaled her comforting scent. I'd only ever seen her in person three times prior to that day. But despite her distance, she'd gone out of her way to make me feel like family over the years and to keep a presence in my life. Not to mention she sent fifty bucks every birthday, Easter, and Christmas. Valentine's Day only warranted twenty-five. My aunts, on the other hand, I had no recollection of meeting, but my mom said they came to visit me when I was one or two. Apparently they showered me with gifts in hopes of creating a smoke screen around their brother's shame.

We spent the day going through old photo albums and catching up, and I showed them pictures of Patch and some friends on my phone.

"I'm going to call my father now," I announced around six o'clock, after which many glances were exchanged.

"I'll get you my phone," Nana said and hurried into the kitchen.

"I meant Kevin," I said to his sisters.

"We know," his sister Katherine said with a smile.

Kevin's sisters were adults and all had families of their own. In fact, Nana Lynne was a nana to eleven grandchildren, including me. Make that ten and a half, I guess.

She called for me to join her in the kitchen.

"I thought you might want some privacy, dear," she said, and handed me her cordless phone.

"Thank you," I said and sat down on one of the eight leather-bound chairs that surrounded her enormous breakfast table. It was a rich mahogany, mission-style table with a wrought-iron chandelier hanging over the center.

No one ever gave people like me much credit. I could see it in their faces—the pity. They felt sorry for me because I had to leave the room and call my father, who'd abandoned me and left me to be raised by wolves. And nothing irked me more than enduring people's pity. I was constantly being reminded that my life was different, and worthy of additional compassion. Why was it so hard for people to see what a great life I'd been given, and how lucky I was to have my parents? Sure I had my moments over the years where I felt sorry for myself, but the one person who made the biggest impression on me was the person everyone assumed I'd feel the least connected to, and that was my dad. Not Kevin Hansen, but my dad who raised me. He never let me forget how lucky I was to have his love. Not in a boastful way, but in a way that made me appreciate my life regardless of how many hurdles I had to jump to get what I wanted. And everyone's assumption that I hoped for some sort of future relationship with Kevin couldn't have been further from the truth. There was nothing I wanted from him but the opportunity to meet him face-to-face and to remove that hurdle from my adult life.

My second conversation with Kevin was almost as brief as the first, and he agreed to meet me at an In-N-Out Burger close to his mother's house. He'd made a reservation somewhere nicer, near the beach, but I told him that my dad said these were the best burgers in town, and that's where I wanted to go.

I arrived about twenty minutes late because the traffic everyone had warned me about turned out to be a reality. I recognized him immediately from the recent photos of him that were scattered around my nana's house, and he stood up as soon as I walked in. I smiled immediately when I realized that he was about six feet five inches tall.

He extended his hand, and I hugged him instead. Nothing dramatic, just a quick, friendly gesture. He sat, and I threw my purse into the booth and scooted onto the bench opposite him.

"You look like your mom," he said, staring at me with a tiny smirk of his own.

"I get that a lot."

He nodded and couldn't take his eyes off of me.

"You're not going to cry are you?" I asked.

He laughed. "I wasn't planning on it."

"Good, because I've never seen a grown man cry before."

I was starving, and the glorious smell of fried food and fresh grease was giving me hunger pains, but I didn't know how to properly break the ice and take the awkward focus off of me and onto the menu.

"I'm glad we have this opportunity, Grace, to meet and get together like this."

"Are you?" I asked, surprised by my own question. I didn't mean for it to come out as confrontational; I was truly interested.

"Yes, I am," he said, unoffended.

"I didn't mean it like that. It's just that I've always wondered why you never wanted to meet me before this," I said. "You made me initiate contact with you. Why?"

He sighed. "I wish I had the perfect answer for you. I really do. And there are many things I wish I'd done differently. I assumed you, and your mom, would've rather had me leave you both alone after the way I'd behaved so many years ago."

"I understand." I nodded at the stranger across from me. I felt no connection with him, even as the conversation got personal.

He continued. "I apologize to you for not making an effort, and I owe your mom more apologies than I can count."

"I can pass that on if you'd like." I offered.

He folded his oversize hands on the table and continued. "I'm not proud of how I acted toward her all those years ago, but I'll be honest with you, I was not ready for a child and I was angry at her for trying to decide my future without my consent."

I sat and listened.

"We both made the same mistake, no offense, yet I had no say in the outcome. She'd made up her mind, and I wasn't about to stay and let her tell me how I was supposed to live the rest of my life."

"It's okay, really. I'm not looking for an explanation—"

"Please, let me finish," he said, stopping me. "But now, looking back, and after having raised two daughters, I have an entirely different perspective on the man I was back then, and I am ashamed of how I treated your mother. I really am."

"I will add that to the apologies." I made a check mark in the air.

"Well, I'm glad you can make light of it, but it's important for me to let you know that I am sorry for how I handled things." He pursed his lips. "Your mom has obviously done a fantastic job of raising you, and it's my honor to be here with you today. Thank you."

I smiled at him. "You're welcome. I really didn't mean for this to get so heavy," I said. "It's kind of weird, sitting here with you, and meeting the source of my size 11 shoes. I mean, everyone thinks that I have all these expectations of you, and I really don't. It's really been more of a burning curiosity than anything. You've been such a vague, inaccessible figure my whole life, and all I ever really wanted was to simply make the connection." I held my grin. "And now I have," I said. And I really had no intention of making him squirm or apologize. All I ever wanted was to meet him, and see him, and unite with him on any level.

"So, how about that Double-Double?" He slapped the table.

"I thought you'd never ask!"

Patch picked me up from the airport when I landed back in Chicago and drove me home to Glenview, where we lived. It was a Sunday night and my parents were out to dinner at a friend's house for their weekly supper club. I loved that no one made a fuss over my encounter with Kevin. I'd already called my mom the night I met up with him for dinner, filled her in on everything, and patiently answered her horde of questions. She was silent when I told her all the remorseful things he'd said, and I could almost hear her grinning.

My dad came in my room around midnight when they got home from their dinner party to see how my flight was.

"Was Patch there on time?"

"Yeah. He's a little rusty on the expressways though."

"We're working on that," he said. "So, how's big Kev?"

We smirked at each other. "Oh, you mean my father?"

"Yeah."

I was sitting on my bed with my laptop resting on my outstretched legs. "He may be six foot five, but you're a much bigger person, Dad," I said and gave him a wink.

"Smart girl." He smiled, flashing his chipped front tooth.

"I love you, Dad."

"Love you, too, Gracie."

CHAPTER THIRTY-EIGHT
Sydney

I t was Christmas Eve, and Grace was almost two years old. Midge left the InterContinental to work for a property in Scottsdale, near her ailing mother, and Keri and I were promoted to co-supervisors. Trevor had left months before to work for Playboy, in the promotions department of their Chicago headquarters, so Keri and I had a staff of three new college grads. It was tempting to put them through the same misery that we endured when we started, but neither she nor I could pull it off.

The holidays were always much more fun with Grace around. Everyone in the family lived vicariously though her and her over-whelming excitement for all things swathed in wrapping paper. My mom bought her a doll that came with a miniature tea set, doll-size table and chairs, and two outfits with matching shoes. She individually wrapped every piece in the set—each cup, each shoe, each saucer, et cetera—and Grace had the time of her life tearing through the pile. After dinner with Kendra and my parents, I took Grace over to the Reynolds' house to have dessert with Ethan and his family. His mother opened the door and led me to another ridiculous pile of gifts for my daughter, but all Grace really wanted anytime we went over there was my high school nemesis, Sparky.

"Barky! Barky!" Grace would yell as we entered Ethan's childhood home.

Mrs. Reynolds reached out her arms, asking Grace permission to carry her, but Grace shook her head no. "All right then, hold my hand, and we'll go look for Sparky."

They didn't have to go very far because a second later he exploded into the living room, his nails clicking along the hardwood floor as he ran.

"Barky!" Her eyes lit up.

"There he is!" Mrs. Reynolds squealed with her.

Ethan appeared at the entry to the room and waved for me to quietly escape with him.

"I'll be right back, okay?" I said to Grace and Mrs. Reynolds, but they were long gone.

Ethan took my hand and I followed him downstairs to the basement, where he'd made his own buffet of sweets for me, along with a coffee and Baileys.

"Does your mother know you've pilfered her dessert buffet?"

"She's busy with Barky," he said.

I took a sip from the warm mug in front of me. "You have my word that I will never buy a dog for Grace, no matter how hard she begs or how many tears stream down those pudgy cheeks of hers."

"Sure you won't."

"I won't. I'm just not a dog person."

He leaned back into the chenille couch. "Well, maybe I'll buy her one then?"

"You wouldn't dare."

He scooted closer to me and had a stern look on his face that made me shudder.

"What's the matter?" I asked, and placed the mug back on the table.

There was an awkward pause.

"I want to adopt Grace." His eyes were glistening.

The words were both comforting and confusing, even though they were quite clearly spoken. "What do you mean? Why do you want to adopt her?"

"I want her to have a father, one that she deserves, and I love her," he said without removing his eyes from my face.

"I don't know what to say." I choked up. "She loves you, too…I love you."

"Say, yes, then." Ethan reached under the couch in front of me and pulled out a small, velvet black box. A signature of his. "I did a little research though…and you'll have to marry me first," he said with a smile.

The End

ACKNOWLEDGMENTS

First and foremost, I would like to thank my friend Meg for sharing her very personal story with me and in turn inspiring this one.

Without the support and encouragement of the following three people, very little would get accomplished in my life, least of all writing novels: My mother, for joining me in the laborious task of reading and rereading all my manuscripts and still thinking they're great each time. My husband, Jeff, for his unwavering confidence in me. My son, Ryan, for being so proud of his mom, and for Googling my name at school to show his friends he's not lying. Also, he's the most awesome person I've ever met.

Additionally I would like to thank the following people for taking this book from its self-published roots and allowing it to reach a wider global audience: Liz Egan—editor. Thank you for sending me the best e-mail ever and taking a chance on an eager, yet relatively unknown, talent. I live to make you as proud of me as my son is. Deborah Schneider—my agent. You immediately trusted my work, and you get things done at lightning speed. I'm truly grateful for both of those qualities in you. Jessica Park—author and all-around cool chick. Cheers to you for holding my hand when you completely didn't have to, for chatting on the phone with me, and for being ridiculously generous with your industry connections and insight.

Lastly, thank you to all my amazing family and friends, for (despite their initial shock each time I finish a manuscript) truly expressing their pride and making me feel accomplished.

ABOUT THE AUTHOR

A graduate of Purdue University, Dina Silver has worked as a copy-writer in the advertising industry for the past fifteen years. After seeing the bulk of her professional prose on brochures and direct-mail pieces, she is delighted to have made the transition to novel-ist. Her debut, *One Pink Line*, was chosen as a 2012 Top Title by IndieReader and was also a finalist in their 2012 Discovery Awards. Silver lives in Chicago with her husband and son.